Be Not Afraid

Be Not Afraid

A Novel

Robert L. Wise

THOMAS NELSON PUBLISHERS
Nashville

Published in Nashville, Tennessee, by Thomas Nelson, Inc., in association with the literary agency of Alive Communications, 7650 Goddard St., Suite 200, Colorado Springs, CO 80920.

Library of Congress Cataloging-in-Publication Data

Wise, Robert L.
Be not afraid: a novel / Robert L. Wise.
p. cm.
ISBN 0-7852-6977-0 (pbk.)
1. World War, 1939–1945—Veterans—Fiction. 2. Aged women
Fiction. 3. Oklahoma—Fiction. I. Title.
PS3573.I797 B4 2001
813'.54—dc21 00-061273

Printed in the United States of America
2 3 4 5 6 QWD 05 04 03 02 01

For Gene, Eloise,
and Elaine

Acknowledgments ~

The author deeply appreciates the contributions of Gene and Eloise May of Oklahoma City, Oklahoma, in describing the events in the Battle of the Bulge and Gene's time in German prison camps. These scenes were detailed in his notes left posthumously. In addition, Pendleton Woods, also of Oklahoma City, counseled and gave advice from his experiences as a prisoner of war in this same battle.

Friends always make the difference.

Prologue ~

Dr. George Lewis closed the hospital door and walked quietly over to the patient's bed, where an elderly man lay stretched out beneath white sheets. The man's eyes shrank into his pale face, with dark circles underneath. His color looked dull and gray, and he appeared worn and drawn. He turned restlessly, his thin arms pulling the covers up around his neck.

Lewis opened the man's file and quickly read through the test results. He kept shaking his head and thumbed back to the first page of the patient's chart to check the latest vital signs taken by the nurse earlier that day. "Hmm," he mumbled to himself. "Not good."

The patient suddenly jumped and opened his eyes. "Where am I?" he blurted loudly.

"You're here in the hospital."

"A hospital?" The man looked around frantically. "Oh, no!"

"We haven't met before, Bob, but your regular doctor asked me to help him with your case. I'm here to make sure that you get the best care."

The patient pushed himself up on his elbows and stared at Lewis. "Feels like a train hit me."

"That's one way to describe what happened. Your condition is like someone crawling out from under a massive head-on collision of two freight trains."

Bob Walker took a deep breath. "What I need is a good cigarette."

"Now, Bob," Dr. Lewis chided. "You know better than to be smoking in here. We have our rules."

"We'll see, Doc." He winked at Lewis. "It's a nasty habit, but I plead addiction. Got to have my fix every now and then."

Dr. Lewis shook his head. "Bob," he said soberly, "you've got a more significant problem than you realize. You've had a serious heart attack that has exposed the possibility of additional problems. We're going to need to do surgery."

"Surgery!" Bob huffed indignantly. "You've got to be kidding."

"You're feeling poorly today because of the heart attack. That's why issues like smoking, dieting, exercise, and other matters are going to be very important. You're not in good shape."

For a moment Bob only looked at the doctor. He ran his hands nervously through his thinning hair. "Doc, I don't know you, but I'm sure you're here to do me good. Unfortunately, life's been a bit rough lately. I'll have to think about anything that you want to do to me."

"I'm part of a team that has no other purpose than to help you recover." Dr. Lewis forced a smile. "You've got a strong military background and are entitled to the best treatment that we can offer. The government pays for everything. Our only reason for working with you is to give you the best care possible."

Bob nodded his head. "Yeah, I knew I was having a heart attack last night. I could feel the throbbing in my chest and the aching running down my arm. Sorta tried to overlook the problem, but I guess I passed out during the card game."

"That's correct. Some of your friends called an ambulance that brought you in." Dr. Lewis cleared his throat. "Let me be frank. If they hadn't acted as quickly as they did, you probably wouldn't have lived. That's why we feel the need to operate immediately."

"Sure." Bob laid back on the pillow and stared at the ceiling.

"We believe it's important," the doctor reiterated.

"Okay, Doc. Whatever you've got to do, have at it."

Dr. Lewis shut the file instantly. "We'll begin setting up the procedure as quickly as possible. I believe you've made the right decision." He turned and hurried out of the room.

~

For a long time after the doctor left, Bob stared up at the ceiling, thinking about his wife's death. Nine months ago her problem had started the same way. One night out of nowhere she awakened him, moaning and screaming. In minutes everything was over. Gone. Finished. All the hopes and dreams they once had vanished like a puff of smoke in the evening breeze.

Adjusting to losing Donna had been extremely painful. Facing the fact of her death and accepting the emptiness nearly killed him. Bob thought about eating every evening meal alone now, the lonely evenings, the silent nights. His wife's passing had proven to be almost more than he could bear. Even thinking about her sent a dark cloud of depression swooping down low, hovering over his bed. Too much to remember any more. He needed to fasten his mind somewhere else, to anything else.

Bob turned and looked out the window. Someone he hadn't thought about in a while abruptly came to mind. There had been another woman. A very special woman. A woman he had loved. Years ago. He used to think about her but had tried to push her out of his mind, although it hadn't been easy. So many times she'd floated back into his mind from out of nowhere. This thought was apparently another one of those unexpected visits.

"I wonder what she's doing *right now,*" he said to himself. "Where is she? What's become of her life? I hope she's all right." He shook his head and looked out the window for a long time, thinking about her. Finally he said out loud again, "What would she say if she knew what I'm about to face . . . completely alone?"

One

Oklahoma, January 2000

A cold, threatening winter wind whistled through the bus-stop village of Burlington. The tired, wind-blown town, located about thirty miles southwest of Oklahoma City, already looked like a retirement village. As the wind picked up, the trees shook as if in foreboding of a coming storm, warning everyone to get inside and make sure all windows were locked. The air hung heavy and dark.

Burlington still looked like a town of the early 1900s. Horses grazed in pastures inside the city limits, and most of the citizens wore cowboy boots. At the top of the two-story office building on Main Street, the date 1902 remained engraved in the brick. The increasing wind hurled dirt in the air and shook the tall, thin windows that climbed up the side of the red brick structure, just as it did when buckboards rolled down the dirt street nearly a hundred years ago.

The howling wind gave the small town an eerie quality,

as if warning of something coming down the street. People hurried home, trying to get inside.

Time in Burlington seemed to slide from one decade to the next, with little happening except for a new wheat pasture springing up. But this afternoon felt different and ominous. No one said much, because generally the people of Burlington went about their business quietly, leaving the rest of the world to find its own way.

Most of the time.

~

Christmas was only seventeen days past when seventy-eight-year-old Mary Oliver realized the time had come to put her house in order. Located on the same area that had once been the feedlot, her home showed wear. Monday, January 11, was a good day to begin to reorder the residence. George had died more than two years earlier, and in that time she'd done precious little to their deteriorating home. Built in 1955, the rambling ranch-style house had been expensive forty-four years ago, but now the cedar siding looked dated and needed another coat of stain. Eaves needed to be tacked back in place before a hard rain knocked them completely down, and the roof needed to be reshingled. Even a decade earlier, irises had bloomed in thick clumps in front of the house, but now they were little more than green blades shooting up from an unruly flower bed that badly needed weeding.

Unfortunately, Mary Oliver's physical condition wasn't

any better than the condition of her house. She felt tired much of the time, but she thought she had enough spunk left to get the place looking like it once had—before George walked off into the valley of death. Mary had not felt a zest for anything since George's funeral.

"Andrea," Mary pleaded with her daughter over the telephone, "I truly need your help. I know there's no good reason for you *not* to come down here and help me, don't you know."

"Mom, I have so many responsibilities here in Denver that just won't wait. Honestly!" Andrea's voice started to waver. "A few days are all that I can spare."

"Few?" Mary's tone rose. "That's the best you can do for your tired, beat-up old mother? Andrea Cole, I need *several weeks.*"

"Weeks! Mother, you are shameless."

"Shameless?" Mary smiled but made her voice sound weak because she was winning. "Yes, I am! And I need you to plan to come down here and help your poor old mother work on this house."

"*Please*, Mother!"

Mary counted on the fact that Andrea's two daughters, Alicia and Carol, were grown and gone from home, making a difference in her availability. At age fifty-three and about thirty pounds overweight, Andrea could use a little more exercise. Taking care of some of the odds and ends would be good for her. She had time on her hands and owed her mother a visit anyway. Only a little more coaxing and Andrea would agree to come for the whole stint.

"Oh, I guess so." Andrea finally threw in the towel.

"Well, good!" Mary said resolutely as the sides of her mouth raised. "The Lord will bless you."

Mary hung up the phone and grinned. She had won this battle.

"Maybe I should put new furniture in the living room," she mused. Mary felt the edge of the worn couch that was probably twenty-five years old. "Long overdue." She walked around the large area and leaned against the picture window that looked out over the front lawn. The yard needed work. "Absolutely." She sighed.

"Why not paper this room again?" Mary rubbed her chin. "The place looks too drab." She took a couple of steps and shook her head. "Too dark." Shadows lingered around the furniture. "Could recarpet my bedroom." She peered down the hall. "Definitely paint the bathroom. Heavens! The garage hasn't been cleaned out in more than a decade, don't you know."

She continued talking to herself, walking around the room. "Probably got some good ideas in these *Good Housekeeping* magazines." As she reached for the periodical on the coffee table, a sharp pain struck like a bolt of lightning. An excruciating tightness hit the center of her chest. Heaviness settled over her, and Mary knew she had to sit down.

"My arm," Mary groaned. "My left arm feels numb." Throbbing started crawling up her neck.

Mary's breathing became more difficult, and she slumped into the living room chair nearest the window. Like a spear, pain shot through her body.

"Help me!" Mary cried across the empty living room.

"Help!" She slumped back in the soft chair, fighting to catch her breath.

Mary lay as quietly as possible with her legs extended out across the rug, her hands on her chest. When the living room swirled and tilted, she closed her eyes tightly. She tried to take deep breaths, but the effort hurt. Mary was dizzy and felt like she was slipping away into darkness. The torment was driving her in and out of consciousness.

"Dear God, help me," she groaned. "It hurts! Oh, the pain! I'm going to die." A fog settled around her, and the room faded into whiteness before disappearing into blackness.

Some semblance of awareness returned, but when Mary tried to open her eyes again, a cloudy layer of light seemed to hover above her. She felt as if her body were being forced into a deep cavern, and she fought to escape . . . but couldn't. Her legs and arms wouldn't move easily. The light floated above her . . . somewhere. She couldn't seem to open her eyes.

I'm dead, Mary thought. *Everything is so dim, so quiet, and I don't seem to be in heaven. What did I ever do that was so bad? So evil? I went to church. Where am I? Where did I go wrong?*

Darkness, like the surging tide, rolled in again and covered her body. Mary sank into a bottomless pool, her legs dangling into nowhere. She wanted to scream but couldn't. The surface of returning life seemed near, and then something pushed against her face. Her nose hurt; strange sensations nudged until she slipped again into the blackness. Consciousness disappeared, and time vanished.

After the seemingly endless blackness, light returned. Voices were out there . . . somewhere . . . possibly above her. People seemed to be near. Maybe she'd arrived in heaven after all.

"I believe she's about to wake up," a woman said.

"The signs look good," another voice answered. "We're getting there."

Got to get my eyes open, Mary thought. *Must do it . . . now.*

"There's definite movement," the first woman said. "I agree. Looks like our girl's waking up."

Mary slowly realized she was in a bed in a small room . . . looking up . . . staring at the ceiling above her. "Where am I?" she muttered and realized the light was coming from a wall behind her.

"You're in the hospital in Oklahoma City," the nurse said. "Saint Anthony's. We brought you here in an ambulance from Burlington."

"From Burlington?" Mary tried to understand. "Burlington, Oklahoma?"

"Yes. Your postman saw you through the window, slouched in your living room chair. He knocked on the picture window but saw that you were unconscious. The man probably saved your life."

Mary blinked several times, still trying to grasp what she heard. *"Saved my life?"*

"Yes, dear," the nurse explained. "You've had a very serious heart attack."

Two ~

FEBRUARY 2000

A month later Andrea Cole looked out the picture window of her mother's Burlington house, watching the cold February rain wash away streaks of red mud from the side of Mary's fifteen-year-old Oldsmobile. Black clouds made the sky look like a snowstorm might start at any moment. The January deluge of ice and snow still covered much of the lawn, and through the thick glass of the front window she could feel the biting outside temperature. The early February winds blew big splashes of rain against the window, making it hard for her to see. Occasionally a car sped down the street, spraying icy rainwater up over the curb. Andrea shivered and turned back to the living room.

Early morning sunlight made her dark brown eyes sparkle but still cast shadows under her eyes. A heavyset woman with a pretty face, Andrea had been in Oklahoma for the past month since her mother's heart attack. With her blondish graying hair pulled back, she looked more like a concerned nurse.

For a week, Andrea had thought her mother might die. Then Mary had abruptly turned the corner, but recovery hadn't been easy. For three weeks Andrea had lived in a motel near the hospital, but by the first of February, the doctors allowed her mother to come home.

"What do you think about the weather, dear?" Andrea's mother asked from the doorway across the room. "Doesn't look good to me." She put her hand to her heart and took a deep breath. "Awfully cold."

"Probably our trip to the mall had best wait another day," Andrea mused thoughtfully. "I came down here simply to help you rest and assist in catching up. What works best for you is my command." She forced a smile.

Andrea Oliver Cole had left home well before her parents settled into the four-bedroom house in Burlington twenty years ago. Virtually no one ever stayed in the fourth bedroom more than a night. Age had chewed the paint and eaten the corners of the house. Things needed to be done, but Andrea didn't intend to do many of them. She certainly wasn't a carpenter or workman.

In past years, Andrea's family often spent a couple of days at Christmas and Thanksgiving with her parents. They'd also visit now and then on the Fourth of July, when Oklahoma steamed in the summer heat, but actually they came as few times as possible. Her children didn't like the constant arguing between Andrea's parents.

Mary Oliver slowly sat down in a large brocade chair

closest to the fireplace and rubbed her forehead. "Let me see," Mary mumbled. "I think maybe we have some other options this morning." She pulled on her chin and stared at the fire.

Andrea studied her mother's face. The regal Scottish profile Andrea remembered from her childhood remained, but her mom's cheeks sagged more these days, looking tired and strained. Mary habitually fretted, but since her husband's death the ravages of age set in and made matters worse. Although her hair still had a good healthy red sheen, lines had deepened around her eyes and walking with a cane had become a necessity.

"You know, our biggest job is cleaning out that awful garage," Mary declared. "Blasted thing! Only heaven knows what your father was forever throwing out there in that dismal place. He piled up the junk right and left. Terrible! We must get that junk out to the curb so the trashmen will haul it off." Mary rubbed her chin again. "They collect the garbage tomorrow. Maybe that's what we should do. What do you think of cleaning up that mess this morning?"

"Sounds fine to me, Mother," Andrea replied. "If you want the garage straightened, I'll be glad to spend the morning putting things in order."

Mary pursed her lips and stared into the fire. "It'll probably take more than a morning, but I think that would be a good way to spend today. Working out there would make a big start. There's a stove in the corner to heat the place a bit." She slowly got up. "I'll need to put on a sweater." Mary started back to her bedroom. "It'll only take a second, don't you know."

Andrea watched her mother trudge down the hall. Mary had always been a vital, active person, but her usual brisk step had slowed after George's funeral and then disappeared following her heart attack. George Oliver's death had started Mary's downhill slide.

Mary simply hadn't expected George to die. She had griped at her husband incessantly about his terrible eating habits, but even after his lingering illness he hadn't listened. He never had. Mary had been surprised when he closed his eyes for the last time, and Andrea had been devastated. Her father had been difficult and had made her mother's life hard. He wasn't an easy guy to like, really. Nothing that she did connected with him. In her teenage years Andrea had tried to avoid the man as much as possible. Yet she was surprised at how upsetting his death was. She thought again about how he once looked and glanced above the fireplace.

Her father's portrait had hung over the mantel for more than ten years. George had been a vice president at Kim-Co Manufacturing, a chemical supply plant, and the company had given him the painting when he had retired after forty-three years. Good old George had liked the sales game and loved being the center of attention whenever possible. Andrea remembered the clashes between her parents when he had paid too much attention to some other woman, which had been often.

Andrea shook her head. No one except her mother had

ever thought of George as having actually strayed. Maybe he had; maybe he hadn't. At best, Andrea had never heard such a rumor, but her father had done too much window-shopping and had fancied himself to be a charmer. Everyone knew George's supply of enchantment came in short amounts, and he had usually ended up only making women uncomfortable.

"I found the key to the safety latch on the back door," Mary said from the hallway. "You can let yourself back in. Whenever you're ready we can take a look."

"Sure." Andrea knew her mother was ready to go into the garage. "You know, we don't have to lock the door." She smiled. "Probably about now would be a good time to begin the job."

"If you insist." Mary started toward the kitchen without a second look at her daughter. "I'll light the wall stove." She determinedly plowed ahead toward the back door. "We'll be nice and warm."

Andrea snickered. In a matter of minutes they had gone from a question to her mom's decision on how to spend the rest of the day. Mother had her way again, as she usually did.

Mary kept talking over her shoulder. "I haven't been out there in years. Didn't go into the garage much when your father was alive because it was his place. Just didn't feel right out there. After the funeral I probably didn't open the back door for a year. Hurt too much to look out back. I simply kept the door locked, and that kept everything safe." She stopped at the kitchen cabinet and picked up a book of matches. "It'll sorta be nice to use the place to put the car away again on these cold nights."

"It can get terribly cold in these winter months." Andrea thought of her mother's fifteen-year-old Oldsmobile. "I think your car could use a little sheltered resting place during bad weather."

"Would make it easier to start, don't you know."

"Don't worry, Mom. I can get this mess cleaned up and done today. By nightfall you'll have your garage back again."

Mary unlocked the back door and turned on the garage light. "See what I mean? Just look at the junk out there."

Andrea stepped into the dim garage. She blinked several times. Old pieces of wood were piled up around the room, and broken stumps of saw boards lay on the floor. Half-completed projects and boxes of trash stood in the corners. Old Christmas decorations had been left to gather dust. An array of junk was piled against the back wall. Only hammers and screwdrivers had been carefully replaced; everything else was hit-and-miss, heavy on the miss.

"We've got quite a job to do out here." Mary bent over to light the small stove. "Things are bad in this garage." She put her hand over her heart. "He didn't even sweep the floor."

Andrea gave the garage a long look. "You go back into the house and drink that second cup of coffee by yourself. I'll just get started."

"But you'll need me to—"

"To tell me what not to throw out," Andrea cut her off.

"No, that's exactly what I don't need. I know your pack rat tendencies. I won't have a bit of trouble knowing what to do."

"But—"

"Mother?" Andrea raised an eyebrow.

Mary shrugged. "I know you're going to need some help." She looked at Andrea out of the corner of her eye. "Perhaps, some advice—"

"I'll call you, Mother, if I need you," Andrea said firmly.

Mary trudged back to the door. "You will call me?"

"I will call you."

Mary frowned, shook her head, and went inside with her hand on her heart. Andrea picked up a broom.

Three ~

Because the garage ceiling had never been painted, withering brown streaks ran the length of the room. Age and drifts of dust splotched the faded walls. Cold wind kept slipping in around the corners of the door, threatening the warmth, but the wall heater beat it back. Andrea worked fast and cleared a space on the trashy floor. She next tackled the back wall where boxes were stacked. Andrea soon sorted through the top layer and filled several plastic garbage bags with trash.

At the bottom of the stack was a particularly discolored old crate that looked like it had been untouched for decades. Andrea pulled the ancient Kerr's canning box out from the wall, loosened the string, and looked inside. Her mother's high-school and college yearbooks were on top, lying neatly by a host of programs, corsages, a diary, and mementos from dances, parties, and special school events.

She began slowly turning the pages of the high-school annuals from the late 1930s and the early 1940s and watched her mother develop from a girl into a young woman. Complimentary adages were written on the flyleaves and pages of the annuals. Andrea read the cute, clever quips.

Andrea knew that her mother's name had been Mary McCoy and that she had been a looker. No apologies there. Her pictures were stylish and attractive. In each photo Mary carried herself with dignity and a touch of class. Andrea smiled and felt proud of her mother. She knew her great-grandparents had come to America from Scotland nearly a hundred years ago and moved south into Kansas. The family became wheat farmers and turned into regular prairie people, surviving the Depression days of the 1930s. Not an easy task, but Mary McCoy looked like a little gem.

For twenty minutes Andrea thumbed through the yellowed pages, tracing her mother's journey from high-school student to university coed and then teacher at Sterling College. Andrea thought about the differences between her mother's yearbooks and her children's. Her mother's acquaintances dressed as if they were going to a church service or to a special event. Goodness and dignity oozed out of the pictures. Not so with Andrea's children and their friends. Every day they looked like they were going to a dogfight.

In the middle of the box, Andrea found a packet of letters tied with a faded red ribbon. Picking them up, she noticed that many of her mother's letters had been returned, still unopened. Other letters were addressed to her from someone called Lieutenant Robert Walker. At the bottom of the pile Andrea saw an eight-by-ten picture of a serviceman.

The man in the brown Air Force uniform looked handsome, with dark eyes that appeared intelligent and perceptive. *He must be Lieutenant Walker,* Andrea thought. His forehead, nose, and lips had a sharp, noble cut, and the man's chin had a Cary Grant–like cleft. Walker looked tall and strong, the kind of soldier who took charge and could lead an attack up a hill.

Andrea had never seen the picture before. Whoever Lieutenant Robert Walker was, he certainly didn't play any part in her past. Andrea looked at his picture for thirty seconds before standing up with the photograph in her hand and hurrying inside.

"Mother, I found the most amazing things in that pile of boxes at the back of the garage." Andrea kicked the garage door shut behind her and dropped into the nearest kitchen chair. Andrea patted the top of the kitchen table. "Sit down and look at what I found."

Mary glanced at her watch. "Good heavens, it's nearly eleven o'clock. We've had a busy morning, haven't we?" She sat down and heaved a long sigh. "One has to distance oneself." She smiled at her daughter. "We'll have to start lunch in just a few minutes, don't you know."

Andrea spread the letters across the table. "Remember any of these things? Take a good look."

Mary leaned forward and squinted. "Looks like old letters. They don't ring a bell. Where'd you find them?"

Andrea reached into her pocket and thrust the soldier's picture before her mother's face. "And who is this, Mom?"

Mary's eyes widened. Her mouth dropped slightly. "Why . . . why . . . my goodness! That's Robert!"

"And who is Robert?" Andrea grinned.

Mary held the picture in both hands. After several moments she said hesitantly, "An old friend." She turned the picture over slowly, placing it on the table facedown.

"Old friend?" Andrea's voice rose an octave. "I've never even heard of this guy. He's right there in the center of your memories box. There must be a real story here."

"You wouldn't know about him. He was around before you were born." Mary put her hand over her heart and took a deep breath.

"Obviously. I was born after the big war." Andrea pointed toward the letter. "But you and he must have been awfully good friends." She picked up a handful of letters. "How many of these did you write?"

Mary reached out and gently touched the letters. "Robert's letters! I'd forgotten about them," Mary said as she picked up an envelope and pulled it close to her face. "My, my, my!" She picked up another one and took the letter out of the envelope. The paper was brown and stiff, having faded over time. "I can't believe what I'm seeing!"

She began reading aloud:

> My dearest Mary,
>
> I'm sitting by myself after a day of flying over the Low Countries. We had a rough encounter and lost a

number of airplanes. For the first time I saw the Germans up close. It was not a pretty sight . . .

She stopped speaking and started reading to herself. Andrea watched her mother's eyes move down the page, reading every word. Andrea suddenly realized she had never thought of her mother as being anything more than a homemaker, the wife of George Oliver. A nice, easygoing homebody who painted pictures and made pretty things. But the truth was, Andrea didn't know anything about her mother's past. Mary Oliver had a love life that Andrea hadn't even known existed. She had stumbled upon a pack of her mother's secrets.

Mary finally folded the letter and put it back in the envelope. Saying nothing, she stared at the table.

"Come on," Andrea urged. "I want to know who this guy is. Give me a few hints."

Mary blinked several times. "An old friend," she repeated to herself. "A very old friend."

"Well . . . ?" Andrea gestured for her to continue. "Tell me something about this *old* friend."

"He was a man I knew during the war . . . when I taught at Sterling College in Kansas."

"And . . . ?" Andrea kept beckoning with her fingertips. "Yes?"

"That was an awfully long time ago, Andrea. More than fifty years ago." Mary glanced up at the ceiling. "I guess . . . maybe . . . at least fifty-six years ago, don't you know."

"He obviously made quite an impression on you."

"Yes. Yes he did."

"Mother! I've never even heard of this guy. He was obviously an important part of your life at one time, and you haven't even mentioned the man. Come on. Tell me about him. Share his story."

"There's no story." Mary looked stern. "I need to get to washing the dishes." She scooted back to stand up.

Andrea grabbed her mother's hand. "Mom, do I need to put you in a time machine? You obviously have an incredible story that I've never heard, and I want to know about this Lieutenant Robert Walker."

Mary looked down at the floor for a moment. "Just an aviator that I knew during the war."

"An aviator? You mean this guy was a fighter pilot?"

"Yes." Mary sounded guarded. "He flew airplanes in Europe."

"And the two of you were close friends? You dated? You corresponded?"

"Yes."

"Come on, Mother. You've never been a one-syllable person. Tell me about Lieutenant Robert."

Mary rolled her eyes. "Your father was never comfortable about Robert. I avoided discussing the subject around you."

"My father didn't want you to talk about an old boyfriend?" Andrea laughed. "That's a hoot! Mother, you mean he was your boyfriend before Father came along?"

Mary nodded.

Andrea's mouth dropped. "Mary McCoy Oliver! After

all these years you are just *now* getting around to telling me about one of the most important love affairs of your life?"

"Andrea!" Her face flushed. "It wasn't a love affair! We didn't do that sort of thing in my day!"

"Come on, Mother. Give me the straight scoop on this man. He was a dashing soldier. I'm sure he must have been a real lover."

"Andrea! I told you that we didn't do things like that when I was a girl. We were proper. Decent. Good Christian people. Don't you be putting words in my mouth!"

"Okay, then tell me *anything* about the man."

"I don't know," Mary finally muttered. "It's been such a long, long time ago," She cleared her throat.

"Come on," Andrea pleaded.

"Everything happened decades ago," Mary began. "Robert and I met not long after the war began and . . . " Mary stopped and looked at the tabletop. She cleared her throat again. "Things became complicated." Mary seemed to be talking more to herself. "Our relationship got so involved . . . " She stopped.

Andrea watched her mother's troubled eyes. "Mother, I'm intrigued to know the details, but I don't want to push you to talk about anything painful. If you want to drop the matter, I will certainly understand."

Mary did not speak for nearly twenty seconds. "I have nothing to hide from you, Andrea. Your father always tried to make my relationship with Robert into something that it never was, and so I eventually pushed everything out of my mind. George was so jealous and fearful that Robert would come back that I just didn't think about Robert for years." She smiled sadly.

"I understand." Andrea relaxed and leaned back in her chair. Mary ran her hand through her graying red hair. "Robert was the first man I was seriously involved with." Her smile faded. "He was certainly handsome and very much a gentleman." She paused for a moment. "We did have a very *significant* relationship. I was in love with Robert when he went to Europe to fight in the war."

"Whatever happened to him?" Andrea squeezed her mother's hand.

Mary shook her head. "I don't know. Robert disappeared during the war. I never heard from him again."

four

Even though she looked straight into Andrea's eyes, Mary no longer saw her daughter. As if she were slipping into a time tunnel, Mary felt herself propelled back to that fateful 1944 December afternoon.

~

KANSAS, DECEMBER 1944

Little patches of snow dotted the grass in Sterling, Kansas, and the wind felt cold; the leaves had fallen from all the trees forty-five days earlier. That night Mary and Robert ate supper at the Hobbs's house where Mary lived, and Mrs. Hobbs developed a convenient need to run down to the church or wherever she could disappear to for as long as was necessary. Mary cooked two small steaks, painfully maneuvered out of the butcher shop because most of the local meat was going to the European front. Mrs. Hobbs threw in a jar of vegetables she'd canned the year before, and everything else fell together.

Mary and Robert ate supper and hurried off to the movie, walking down one of Sterling's side streets where they wouldn't be noticed by the locals. Teaching at the college kept Mary's life so public that she did everything possible to guard her privacy. Two cars loaded with college kids drove by and waved, which was a little embarrassing but typical of small towns. Three blocks later Robert and Mary paid a quarter apiece and walked into the local picture show. The movie proved to be an American shootout with the Japanese. In the 1942 *Flying Tigers,* John Wayne and his crew barely survived, but the infantry triumphed and everyone went home happy.

"What a glorious evening," Mary said. "You can still smell a bit of fall in the air, but winter's coming."

Robert slipped his hand into hers. "Yeah, a little brisk, but a great evening to walk down the street." He looked out across the grassy square in the center of town. "Want to go anywhere?"

"Wherever you'd like to go, Robert."

"Let's amble through the park over there." He pointed to the large area in the town square. "I'd like to see if any of the mums are still around."

"I bet you would." Mary smiled. "I can certainly see this fearless P-38 pilot bending over to smell the frozen flowers."

"Hey, I'm basically a nice guy."

Mary leaned next to his shoulder. "Yes, I'd say you're a very nice guy."

Robert pulled her hand, and they walked across the street. Several 1930s cars buzzed past. No one waved. A good sign of increasing anonymity.

"Let's sit over there." Robert pointed to a green wooden bench with a wrought-iron frame. "I'd like to talk some."

"Sure. Sounds good to me."

The couple sat down and watched a school-age boy chase his dog across the far end of the park. Several older ladies strolled on the opposite side of the park. Everything felt quiet, unusually warm for December, reserved, and, best of all, secluded.

Mary glanced at Robert. His dark eyes and strong mouth fit perfectly in a handsome triangular pattern. Good-looking black wavy hair and eyes seemed to match his brown military suit. He could have been one of the dashing men in the movie.

"How's the training going, Robert?" Mary asked. "You must be about to the end of learning to fly those P-38s." Mary kept looking at Robert's face, feeling there was part of Robert she'd never seen. Something about him eluded her.

"I need to tell you about what's been happening." Robert's voice changed, becoming serious. Firmness pushed the playful sound aside. "You see, I actually finished working with P-38s some time ago."

Mary blinked. He'd never given her a clue of doing anything more than learning to fly fighter planes.

"I'm actually flying much larger aircraft." Robert sounded

like he was reporting over the radio. "My training is now done, over."

"Done? You mean *finished*?"

Robert nodded his head. "Yeah," he said, "I'm afraid so." He looked away. "I can't be as forthright as I'd like." Robert rubbed his forehead. "Much of what I do is more secret than I've ever told you, Mary. I can't really discuss the details of what I've been trained to do."

"Robert!" Mary's mouth dropped. "I don't know what to say." She shook her head. "I don't understand."

"Unexpected dimensions of the war have changed how we fight," he said. "Unfortunately, I'm part of a changing military air system." He rubbed his mouth. "The best that I can tell you is that I've been trained to do secret work and use airplanes in a number of ways that are still classified."

"Oh, Robert!" she cried. "You must be in great danger!"

"I don't want you jumping to any conclusions. Just accept the fact that much of what I do is secret for the time being. Someday I'll be able to tell you more details."

Mary looked more closely into his eyes. "I'm not sure that I'm following you."

"Mary, I've finished my training, and the Air Force is ready to send me to Europe."

"To *Europe*?" she said in disbelief. "When?"

"Tomorrow."

Mary reeled back against the bench. "To-tomorrow?" she gasped.

Robert nodded soberly. "I just found out this afternoon," he said as he looked down at the sidewalk. "My commander took me by surprise. I was called in and told that tomorrow I'll be on my way to Europe. Our unit flies out at daybreak."

Mary stared and her mouth dropped. She opened her lips to speak, but no sound came out. Her eyes searched back and forth, probing every line in Robert's face. She could only squeeze his hand.

"I'm sorry," Robert mumbled. "I had no idea."

"Why didn't they give you some warning?" Mary's voice shook. "A hint of what was coming?"

"The operation is secret," Robert repeated. "I guess by keeping everything confidential, the Army is better able to protect our actions in Europe."

Mary began sobbing quietly. Robert put his arm around her shoulder and pulled her close, shielding her face from the public, but no one was on the square watching them anyway. They were virtually alone, and it was getting colder.

"I'm sorry," he said again.

"Forgive me." Mary pulled a handkerchief from her purse. "I'm overwhelmed. Just didn't have any idea this was coming. Not this soon."

Even though Mary always wore suits as an art professor at Sterling College so that no one mistook her for a student, she still looked young, more like one of the coeds. Her brown, tear-filled eyes glistened in the light of a distant streetlight. She felt warm and soft next to Robert's shoulder.

"I guess it's always like this," Mary said. "I suppose if you'd told me a month ago, I'd have pushed the thought aside and hoped you'd be here forever."

"I was afraid to tell you tonight," Robert confessed. "I started to say something at the house, and then I . . . I . . . couldn't." He shook his head. "I don't want to leave you, Mary."

Mary seized his face and kissed him. "I don't *want* you to leave," she said. She clung to him as she kissed him again.

"I'm sorry," Robert said once more. "So very sorry."

Mary held his shoulders tightly. "I'm suddenly so afraid."

"I know."

"Time is so short."

Robert shook his head. "Yeah," he groaned more than said.

"You know, Robert," she said quietly against the side of his face, "last Sunday, the minister's sermon touched me deeply. He was talking about how the Bible describes God protecting people. I thought about you all during the sermon."

Robert nodded his head gently.

She squeezed his hand. "We haven't talked about our faith much in this short time, but I know that you believe in God."

Robert sighed and shook his head. "My faith keeps me going when things get tough."

"The minister told the story of Jesus' disciples sailing across the Sea of Galilee to Capernaum. Remember?"

Robert nodded but said nothing.

"After they had rowed quite a ways across the lake, Jesus came walking out to them. They were frightened to see a man walking on the water, thinking that He was a ghost.

Then Jesus said something amazing to them: 'It is I; be not afraid.' Do you understand the point of this story?"

"No. I don't think so . . . at least not exactly."

"The pastor told us to never forget those words—*be not afraid*—because they remind us that our Lord is always with us. Jesus was reassuring His apostles. He also watches over us wherever we go. We don't have to be afraid, even when the future looks bleak."

The lieutenant nodded his head. "I hope so."

"Robert, as you go to war, remember that God will be watching over you."

"I pray so, Mary. I can't begin to tell you how much I pray so."

Mary whispered in his ear. "I'll pray that God keeps you safe. Don't be afraid. He will sustain you from falling on that battlefield."

Robert struggled to keep his composure. "Sure," he finally said.

"Don't worry, don't worry. We don't have to be afraid."

"I trust so," Robert eventually answered.

Andrea's face slowly began to come back into focus. She seemed to emerge from the mist-covered memories flooding Mary's mind. For several moments Mary felt as if she were in two places at the same time, with part of her lingering on the old green park bench fifty-six years ago.

"Are you okay, Mother?"

"Yes," Mary said slowly. "Yes, I'm okay."

"Something is wrong." Andrea touched her mother's hand. "You don't seem to be with me."

"I need to go to bed." Mary pushed back from the table and stood up. "Getting late, don't you know."

Andrea looked at her, inspecting her. "You're tired, Mother," she concluded.

"I'll see you in the morning." Mary swallowed hard and shuffled out of the kitchen.

~

For a long time Mary lay under the covers in her bedroom, rereading the first letter Robert had sent her. Surely Andrea had gone to bed by now. At least she wouldn't be outside the door, waiting for another story about her mother's past. For a moment Mary listened to the cold February wind howling outside. She pulled the thick comforter closer around her neck and started reading the letter again.

Robert described his pain and reservations in leaving her and Kansas behind. No longer did he see the war as a great adventure. His relationship with Mary had slipped under his skin, and now reservations about the war stuck out everywhere. Robert knew that he had an obligation and wanted to serve his country, but yet he was leaving Mary, and that hurt him greatly.

Each time Mary reread the letter, something new and unexpected touched her. She felt herself drifting back through the decades. The airport scene came alive in her mind. Mary could feel, smell, see Robert walking down the runway to catch the airplane on that winter morning. She felt like she could almost experience his departure as if she were there, by his side, flying off with him to England.

five

KANSAS, DECEMBER 1944

A cold winter wind blew across the flat Kansas runway and sent a chill up Lieutenant Robert Walker's spine. Time was short. He looked up at the C-47 waiting to take him to England and drew deeply on his cigarette. Other pilots hurried past him and boarded the airplane immediately. The huge propellers were already running, drowning out any conversations. Everything he had done for months should have prepared him for this moment, but it hadn't. The wind stung his face and made his eyes water. Robert knew that he needed to get on the airplane, yet he couldn't make his feet walk up the stairs.

Someone yelled from the door of the plane and gestured for him to come up quickly. Robert took one last drag from his cigarette and tossed it aside. He firmly gripped his duffel bag and trudged up the steps. Walker nodded to the crew member at the door and dropped down on the seat next to a window. The large entry door slammed shut, and the gooney bird was ready to go.

Moments later the airplane taxied down the runway. The engines roared to full throttle, and the C-47 raced forward, pushing Robert back in his seat. The transport lifted, and seconds later it made a winding turn into the sky. As the plane finished the traffic pattern, Robert saw the rooftops of the town of Sterling off in the distance. Somewhere down there in the maze of houses and streets, the woman he loved was probably asleep in bed, unaware that he was leaving.

The sun's rays barely broke the horizon; most of the terrain still lay in cozy darkness. Robert pushed his face against the window, hoping for a view of something, anything, but the plane quickly cut into the clouds, and the Kansas countryside disappeared under the dawn haze.

Someone handed him a blanket, and Robert realized that the C-47 might not be warm. He looked around the airplane and noticed that no one was talking. The droning roar of the engines made conversation difficult and offered a good excuse to settle into the solitude of silence. Each man appeared lost in his own thoughts, hope, dreads. Loneliness settled over the sparse interior of the roaring airplane. Like Robert, the rest of the soldiers were going to war and leaving their loves behind.

Robert thought about Mary McCoy. At first, she had been no more than a diversion, a source of entertainment, but everything changed when the appendectomy laid him out helplessly flat on his back. He remembered waking up that dark night and finding her standing above him in the shimmering light of the wall lamp.

~

"Are you all right?" Mary whispered.

"Where am I?" Robert blinked his eyes, trying to bring the blurry room into focus.

"You're in the hospital. You've had an operation."

"Oh yes." He felt the pain. "That's right."

"I'm here to help you." Mary sounded low and intense. "I'll stay as long as you need me."

Robert raised his head again, trying to see her face clearly. She seemed only a few feet away. "Thank you," he finally groaned. "I don't feel very well." He grabbed her hand.

"You're going to be much better tomorrow." Mary took his hand in hers. "Just rest tonight."

"You're Mary, right?"

"Yes. Mary McCoy."

Robert stared at the ceiling for a few moments. Everything looked white and far off. "I was supposed to have a date with you this evening"—he swallowed hard—"wasn't I?"

"You got delayed by the doctor."

"I'm sorry," Robert groaned.

"Don't worry. Everything is fine."

"It is?" He tried to sit up. The lingering effects of the ether pushed him back.

"Sure. I understand. Just takes a little time to get up on your feet."

Robert lay back on the bed. He could feel the warmth of Mary's hand, the assurance that she would care for him. Her presence began to fill the emptiness of life on the military base. Even though his side hurt, something good was happening. He squeezed Mary's hand before drifting off again.

~

"Got a cigarette?" a rough voice sounded in his ear.

Robert blinked and realized that another pilot had slid in next to him in the C-47. "Sure." He flipped the man a cigarette out of the top of his pack.

"Thanks. I owe you one." The man hurried back to the other side of the airplane, leaving Robert alone again. Several soldiers started lighting up, and a cloud of smoke drifted across the cabin.

The increasing roar of the airplane pushed another set of images into his mind. Robert wondered about his family and how they were doing in that small Oklahoma town he hadn't seen for six months. He hoped life in Fort Towson hadn't been changed by the war.

In many respects Robert was only a small-town boy jettisoned into a larger world that he hadn't intended to live in. He had grown up in the hilly, tree-filled country of eastern Oklahoma, where his family had lived for decades. The comfortable familiarity of small-town life had been pleasant and easy. School hadn't proved difficult for him, and he hadn't thought of much else until bombs had begun falling in Europe.

"Here's a pillow." The crew member on the C-47 leaned close to Robert's ear. "Gonna be a long trip today, ya know. After Maine, we stop in Iceland to refuel."

"Thanks." Robert took the pillow.

"Ya need to try and sleep sometime in the next few hours. We touch down twice before we get to England. Put the pillow somewhere. Anywhere." The soldier hurried on to the next man.

Robert pushed the pillow under the seat and looked out the window. Fort Towson was miles and miles away, with most of the town's population still asleep. Robert closed his eyes, and his mother's face drifted before him. He could almost smell breakfast cooking. Mom used to fry eggs and bacon, stir the orange juice, perk the coffee. She had the cook's touch that made everything taste good. Robert felt a painful yearning to be back around the familiar old kitchen table. Before the divorce her breakfasts had been the start of every day, but after she left, things changed. The Walkers were the only divorced family in practically the whole county. People just didn't do that sort of thing around Fort Towson.

"You'll need rations." Another one of the airplane's maintenance crew tossed a couple of cans at Robert. "Put them where you can grab one when you're hungry."

Robert caught the small parcels and cringed. The thought of military rations crushed memories of breakfast in Fort

Towson. Not much encouragement for a long trip. He settled back against the side of the airplane and looked out across the clouds, which were now turning into enormous cotton cushions that extended from horizon to horizon. The billowy clouds looked soft and inviting, as if he might walk out to the edge and sink into their softness, like settling into a goose-down mattress.

He looked at the tin can of rations. What a contrast! But that's the way things were. Life was filled with illusions and surprises.

And what would he find in England? Robert had attended the military lectures and knew what the instructors said. He had learned what was expected of him and had acquired the unusual credentials to fly both a P-38 and a B-17. Most important of all, he had received top-secret instructions and knew what to do when an airplane crashed. He had been trained to survive behind enemy lines and supposedly had been prepared for a new, intense blitz on the Nazis. What more could any airman want? He should be ready for the thick of battle.

But Lieutenant Robert Eugene Walker felt nauseous.

Six ~

EN ROUTE TO ENGLAND, DECEMBER 1944

The loud droning of the airplane engines wrapped the inside of the C-47 in a monotony that eventually pushed all the passengers toward doziness. The airplane had already stopped in Maine and Iceland to refuel. Lieutenant Robert Walker had been sound asleep for some time when an airman poked him in the ribs. Awaking with a start, Robert struggled to remember where he was. For a moment he couldn't identify that he was inside an airplane.

"Look down at dem!" The soldier crowded next to Robert and pointed out the window. "We're a comin' to the White Cliffs of Dover!"

Robert blinked, trying to clear his head. The cold airplane and the Army rations hadn't done much for his frame of mind. He glanced out the window and began to realize they were nearly in England.

"Always wanted to see dem White Cliffs," the airman

spoke loudly to Robert. "Quite a sight down there." He settled back in the seat with his hands behind his head.

Walker pressed his face against the cold window and watched the massive cliffs coming closer. He had never been out of the United States and sensed the thrill of putting his feet on foreign soil. In minutes they would actually be over England!

"Can you believe it?" the pilot sitting by him shouted in Robert's ear. "We're almost there!"

Walker nodded and looked back out the window again. Clouds dotted the terrain, but a huge mass of land was coming into view. As the C-47 drifted downward, he realized that snow covered much of the emerald ground. Winter had already set into England with a greater fierceness than he'd seen in Kansas. He realized that many other airplanes were flying in and out of the area they were approaching. What first appeared quiet and peaceful, quickly turned into a massive movement of aircraft. England was very much at war.

The C-47 turned into the landing pattern and began circling what appeared to be a makeshift airstrip. From the looks of what was below him, Robert decided the terrain must have been an acceptable strip of ground for landing airplanes of all sizes and had simply been turned into an airfield. It looked like at least forty or fifty bombers and small planes were parked around the area, and a significant number of buildings surrounded them.

Minutes later the C-47 hit the ground and bounced thirty feet. Robert wrenched against the seat, fearing for a moment they would crash into something. He put his hands over his face.

"Hey!" an airman behind him yelled. "The pilot's trying to kill us before the Nazis even get a good shot at us!"

"Easy there!" another airman cried out. "Or we'll go back to Kansas!"

Men clapped, hooted, and hollered while the transport plane rolled to the end of the landing strip and then turned around. The laughter didn't deceive Robert. Even though they clapped, the other pilots were obviously as nervous as he was. The airplane rumbled on until it came to a stop in front of a long row of Quonset huts.

"The ride's over, boys," one of the airplane's crew announced over the PA system. "Get your gear together. This is where we get out and the real fun begins."

A side door dropped and the passengers began hurrying down to the ground. Walker lined up with his duffel bag in hand and quickly edged into the queue. He was finally in England.

A cold northern wind hit Robert in the face, and he braced himself. The gale's bite cut deep. While the temperature probably wasn't much lower than it had been when he'd left Kansas, the feel was different. He'd have to adjust to the climate.

"Here's your housing assignment." A soldier pressed a sheet of paper into Robert's hands. The man's long green overcoat and helmet looked like the outfit had seen more than a few rounds of battle. "You're to be at the administrative building at ten hundred hours." The man saluted.

Robert returned the salute and hurried to the tail of the airplane where the crew was unloading their gear. He picked up his large canvas bag and trudged toward the barracks listed on the instruction sheet.

Blowing snow stung his face, and Walker recognized the need for the heavy leather coats that pilots wore when flying at high altitudes. England wasn't offering much of a welcome, but he knew the first few days wouldn't be easy. By midafternoon, the Kansas night would be settling into his bones long before the English sun set. It would not be easy to adjust to the six-hour time difference. He hurried on through the snow accumulating across the landing strip.

Walker found the Quonset hut in the middle of other barracks set aside for pilots' quarters. He shut the battered front door quickly and instantly felt the warmth of the long room. One quick look around the place told Robert that he was the only man in the building at that moment. The exposed two-by-fours and overhead beams made the building look a lot like his quarters in Kansas. Around the room sat thin metal beds with their webs of steel springs exposed.

Near the back, Walker found an empty bed with a foot locker. A wooden cabinet stood next to the bed. He immediately unpacked, and in the middle of his green canvas bag he found what he wanted far more than anything else: Mary McCoy's picture.

Her thick red hair had been pulled back and combed up on top of her head. Mary's face was turned sideways in an angle exposing the royal Scottish profile Robert loved, and her brown eyes sparkled with loveliness. Mary's suit probably meant that the college had used the picture in one of their publications. By now, Mary would have completed a day of teaching. He knew that she would have thought about him far more than once or twice that day. He put her picture in the top section of his locker and stared at it for a full minute.

The lieutenant suddenly realized that his watch was still on Kansas time, and he worried that he might be late. Six hours' difference meant that he'd best hurry to the meeting in the administration building. He closed the door to the cabinet, turned his overcoat collar up, and hurried back out into the cold winter day. Walker pulled his cap down to his ears and trotted toward the administration building.

Even before Lieutenant Walker stepped into the long wooden building located only feet away from the landing area, he sensed the place was packed with airmen. Sounds of talking and shuffling boots carried out into the crisp morning air. The floor creaked when he walked in, and the wood didn't sound too stable. He stopped at the door and looked around the big room. The open area was filled with men drinking coffee and talking to each other with an easy casualness that seemed to dominate the multitude of conversations. Some of the men looked like old-timers; others seemed to be as new as Robert felt. He walked over and picked up a cup of black coffee. Standing alone near the back, he carefully assessed what was happening. Men huddled around and by the tables, and no one seemed to the least concerned about fighting a war. The place looked more like a party.

At the front of the briefing room, an elevated stage had been built for a teaching or an assignment area. Spread across the front wall was a huge map of the Northern European coastal area. Pins and markers appeared to trace the evolution of the constantly changing battle lines.

Abruptly a front door opened and three men walked in. One of the officers immediately bounced up the stairs, and all talking in the room ceased. "Attention!" one of the officers shouted, and the pilots snapped to. The haphazard atmosphere disappeared instantly, and the happy-go-lucky mood evaporated. The war was back on.

"At ease, men! I'm General Alexander Smith, in charge of this operation. I want to welcome the new pilots who arrived in the last twenty-four hours. You have come at an important time. We're glad you're here. Please sit down." He motioned for everyone to be seated.

Pilots quickly settled into their places behind the wooden desks. No one spoke. Robert grabbed a chair at the back and sat down. Casualness evaporated like snow settling on a red-hot stove.

"Every one of you will be in the air within the next twenty-four to forty-eight hours at the latest. The assignments are going to be tough and dangerous." The general crossed his arms over his chest and looked at the men with a hard, intense stare. "We're entering a difficult time in this war, and airpower is going to be a crucial factor in what happens." He turned and pointed to an area on the map that extended across the Netherlands and Belgium. "Even at this moment, the Germans are attempting to break through our lines. The conflict area around the Ardennes Forest is a keg of dynamite, and the place could explode. We must do everything in our power to prevent a breakthrough. Are we clear?"

Robert looked across the room. No one moved. Whoever General Smith might be, the man didn't need to say anything to motivate this group. Walker knew that the pilots already realized the price being paid in Europe. Everything he'd learned through months of training was now on the line. He would be part of this battle.

"I wish that I could welcome you new men to a nice little vacation in England," Smith continued. "Sorry. I'm afraid we're going to taste hell before this thing is over. You'll find your assignments posted on the front wall to my left. Get 'em and pay careful attention." General Smith suddenly saluted. "Good luck, men!" He turned, walked down the steps, and left the room.

Seven ~

Oklahoma, February 2000

Throughout the night February's winter winds blew hard, causing the Oliver house to creak and groan. The old elm tree in the backyard that should have been pruned last spring rubbed against the roof and sounded like someone crawling through the attic. Mary tossed restlessly in her bed, struggling with fitful and disturbing dreams. Several times she awoke and glanced at the alarm clock before plunging back into troubled sleep. Her heart pounded hard, and its beat seemed irregular.

Sometime after seven o'clock A.M. the grayness vanished and the sun began to break through, sending golden beams through her window, and Mary awoke. She looked out the ice-covered window at the great ball of fire rising above the eastern horizon, sending ever-increasing rays of light over the top of the back fence and through the trees and bushes. Since her heart attack, Mary had been getting up later in the morning, and today she got out of bed even more slowly. The past had crawled into bed with her for a long visit.

Her thoughts were on Robert Walker. The truth was that she had lost touch with an important part of their story. For weeks after Robert had left Sterling, they had corresponded. Then suddenly she lost all contact. Her letters were returned unopened, and nothing more came from him. On this cold February morning she again felt the worry and doubt about what had happened to Robert.

Mary remembered George Oliver's tyrannical rages about her ever making contact with Robert. As if it were yesterday, Mary could see George pacing up and down in the small living room of their first home in Kansas, screaming about the tall pilot possibly showing up again. She had innocently mentioned Robert's name when describing a dance at Sterling College, and George had instantly exploded.

"I guess you're expecting this flyboy to come marching back any day now." George had sneered over the top of the newspaper. "Looking like a war hero."

"George, please!" Mary pleaded. "You're making absolutely nothing into something horrible."

"Horrible?" George's eyes narrowed. "What did the two of you do that was so *horrible?*"

"Us?" Mary bristled. "Absolutely nothing!"

"Don't you understand?" George seemed to swell in size as he shouted. "I'm trying to save my family from adultery."

"What?" Mary felt her eyes widen. "Adultery? I wasn't even married to anyone at the time!"

"You know what I mean." George's eyes narrowed as he looked at her. "I'll kill the honky-tonkin' birdman if he ever returns."

Mary caught her breath. Never had anyone threatened her with such frightening and terrible accusations. Her husband's words ate away at her dignity, leaving her feeling diminished and broken.

"I'm no fool." George's face pressed nearly two inches from her nose like an animal descending for the kill. "Don't toy with me," he growled.

Mary clenched her fist for a moment, wanting to hit him as hard as she could. With overwhelming effort she made herself stop and forced her fingers open. Her fingertips tingled. She wanted to slap his face. Instead she turned away, sobbing.

"Crying won't deter me," George screamed at the back of her head. "Understand? A few sniffs and snorts aren't going to stop my quest for the complete truth about this conniving sneak."

Mary shook her head. She wouldn't answer.

"If I ever hear anything more about this side-winding, yellow-bellied, vicious snake—" George threatened and then stopped to catch his breath, and Mary ran to the bathroom, locking the door behind her. She slid down the wall to the floor, her feet pressed against the side of the old bathtub. Even after he quit yelling, George's voice echoed from the other side of the door, a thundering roar, rolling endlessly around inside her mind.

Mary tried to make her pounding heart settle. Nothing had ever upset her so much. George had taken her basket of memories and turned them upside down in the sink, splattering what had been precious into a million broken pieces and making her feel disoriented and dizzy.

Eventually Mary's mind began to clear and her breathing became more regular. Her dilemma started to come into focus. Since George had sniffed out the depth of her relationship with Robert, their marriage had turned into a maelstrom of chaotic fighting, with George becoming increasingly more abusive and violent. If she had slapped him as she'd wanted to, he probably would have hit her back—very, very hard. She shuddered.

Mary had discovered a truth about her new husband that she'd never suspected. The mere mention of Robert's name set him off like a Roman candle. The issue was simple. If she ever uttered Robert Walker's name again, she and George would almost certainly end up in divorce court. If the lieutenant disappeared forever, the Olivers' relationship might survive.

Mary had to make a decision to do one of two things. She had to choose between her husband and a man who had vanished in a war across the ocean. The choice was inevitable. Mary was pregnant.

The scene from more than fifty years earlier faded from Mary's memory. Her husband's scowling face slipped away, and George no longer was shouting through the bathroom door as he had back there in Kansas. As the past disappeared, Mary sat up in her bed and realized she had virtually forgotten everything that now was foremost in her thinking.

She stared at the mirror. Her frazzled red hair stood up in every direction like a clown's wig. She was probably fifty pounds heavier than what the scales had registered when she was a young woman. Time had pulled at the ends of her face, causing her eyes to droop and her cheeks to sag. The passing years had certainly left their mark. Yet what had happened to her memory was far more significant. She hadn't fully realized the depth of what had been pushed out of her mind by that terrible fight decades ago. The door was shut tightly on her memories of Lieutenant Robert Walker, the entrance sealed by George Oliver. But on this bright winter morning, she could no longer ignore the facts. A host of emotions were bottled up in her soul. Mary had never before faced the truth, but the time had come.

~

"Good morning, Mother!" Andrea kissed her mother on the cheek when she came into the kitchen. "Looks like you slept well last night."

"Thank you, dear." Mary sat down at the breakfast table. "I wouldn't exactly say that I slept well." She smiled. "Actually I had a quite fitful night." She put her hand over her heart.

Andrea pushed two pieces of bread into the toaster and flipped on the coffeemaker. "Maybe our evening discussions might have been, shall we say, distracting?"

Mary looked out to the backyard where yesterday's rain had become today's ice. Even though the sun was up, a thin layer of sparkling ice covered the trees and turned the grass into a glittering white slickness.

"You seemed to have gone to bed under a cloud." Andrea smiled at her mother and set the jar of jam on the table. "I had the feeling that we'd touched a few raw nerves last night."

"Oh no, no. Nothing of that sort." Mary shook her head. Andrea studied her mother's face for a moment and turned back to the stove. "Would you like an egg? Maybe scrambled?"

"Sounds nice, Andrea. Yes, scrambled eggs sound good this morning."

Andrea took the eggs out of the refrigerator but kept watching her mother. She had learned as a child that her mother never admitted it when she was most upset. She set the eggs on the cabinet and took a large mixing bowl out of the upper cabinet. Andrea shot a quick glance at her mother, who was staring out the window. She didn't look good.

"Did you dream last night?" Andrea asked.

Mary blinked her eyes several times. "I did. Yes, as a matter of fact, I had strange dreams."

"Interesting." Andrea broke the eggs against the rim of the bowl. "I imagine you took a fascinating trip around the world in your sleep."

"The wind made a lot of noise. Hard to sleep with blowing wind," Mary replied.

Andrea poured the eggs into the skillet. "I'll have breakfast for you in a flash."

"Mercy! I'm just sitting here doing nothing." Mary started to get up. "I'm sure you need some help."

"No, Mom. Keep your seat. I'm basically done." She reached for a dish in the cabinet. "The eggs are on their way in a second."

"Actually," Mary said, "I kept thinking about Robert, and some pieces of the past broke loose. I simply hadn't thought about him in so long."

Andrea put the eggs on the table in front of her mother. "There you are, Mom. I'll pour you a fresh cup of coffee."

"I know it sounds strange, but I literally hadn't thought about Robert Walker in so many years that it's like accidentally getting on a train that takes you back into your past. The memories proved to be, well, somewhat startling."

Andrea sat down across from her mother. "I was thinking after you left last night that the children would be totally fascinated with your story. Why don't you write about what happened to you back in the forties?"

"Nobody would want to hear about my past," Mary scoffed. "Just old history. Nothing there to tell."

Andrea laughed. "You just got through saying that all these memories kept you awake last night. You think they're not worth reading about? I know that I would love to hear the story."

"Really?"

"Sure. My kids don't know anything about the world that you grew up in. I think that your story would be great—and educational."

Mary ate the eggs but didn't say anything. The plate was nearly clean when she spoke again. "You really think Alicia and Carol would be interested?"

"Absolutely."

"Well, that's an interesting thought. I'll think about it this morning."

"Great, Mom!" Andrea squeezed her hand. "If nothing else, the project would be good for you. Get you back into the swing of things."

"Thank you, dear." Mary looked out the window again.

Andrea watched her mother out of the corner of her eye. She kept straightening the kitchen as if indifferent to her mom's thoughts, but she knew her comments were working. The arrow had hit the target.

Eight ~

Mary said little as Andrea finished the dishes and put the kitchen back in order. Occasionally Mary glanced up, but she had confidence that her daughter could find the right place for the glasses, dishes, and silverware.

Mary turned her attention to the pile of letters Andrea had brought in from the garage. The heap looked like the mess the McCoys always found after returning home from a vacation. Umpteen pieces of mail lying in random accumulation from the postman's cramming the junk letters through the mail slot. Mary worked at getting the pile in chronological order according to the dates on the envelopes. Once she had the letters in satisfactory order, she picked up where she had left off the previous night.

The experience of the evening before was so fresh in her mind that she didn't take long to slide back into the pace and the beat of the narrative in Robert's letters. In fact, the past sounded strangely more familiar than events that had occurred a week or two before. Once again Mary slipped into the world that Robert Walker had descended into when the airplane landed in England. She could feel Robert's feet walking through the winter grass and the roaring of the airplanes in the distance.

~

AIR BASE, ENGLAND, DECEMBER 1944

The skies were still black when Robert Walker awoke in the Quonset hut in the middle of the pilots' barracks area. Gray fog hung over the field, and the air smelled damp, heavy, humid. The roar of airplane engines awakened him. Nothing felt normal or right. One day in England had done little to change his orientation. He still felt the time difference between Kansas and England. Sleep had been hard and the night fitful, but he knew that the crew's briefing would be finished quickly and that he'd be on his way well before the first light of day crossed the skies.

Walker struggled out of bed, slipped into his uniform, and hurried through the mess hall, eating at a frantic pace. By 5:30 he was in the administrative building seated behind the same wooden table, waiting for the officer of the day to arrive with the instructions for attack. The room appeared drab and makeshift, the walls barren and empty. Robert watched the other pilots silently file in with cups of coffee and sit down. No one said much, and before long the aroma of coffee hung in the air.

Walker looked around the large room and recognized that the assembly of pilots was much smaller than it had been the day before. The party was over, and this crew were fighters. No nice howdy-how-are-you with these men. Their stern coldness unsettled him.

Brigadier General Howerton came through the same door that General Smith had walked out of the day before. Like Smith, Howerton had a no-nonsense attitude and stood more than six feet tall. He'd obviously done this task many times before. When Howerton stomped in, the pilots stood more rigidly at attention than they had done yesterday.

"At ease, men." The brigadier general motioned for the airmen to sit down. "We must move fast today and will leave immediately after orders are given." Howerton turned toward the map behind him. "You will be flying a bombing mission in the forest area that surrounds the town of Arnhem, just north of the Rhine River and east of Rotterdam." The general pointed to the large map across the wall behind him, tracing a large area with a long pointer. "You men flying P-38s will support the bombing run being made by our B-17s. Intelligence tells us that the Germans are preparing to bring, or have already brought, panzer units back from the Russian front to hit in this general area." Howerton swung a large circle between Apeldoorn, Doetinchem, and Arnhem. "Some of you are going to strike this area hard and fast between the village of Bivels and the German town of Gemund. Intelligence suggests that we should have good opportunity to find major troop movement on these roads. I've asked my intelligence officer,

Major Jimison, to explain some of the details of what you can expect in this region—particularly if you get knocked out of the sky."

A young man, dressed in the same type of pants and coat as Howerton, began a general lecture about the people and their customs. His youth and the fact that he sounded like he was reading details out of a book Walker had read six months ago sent Robert's mind elsewhere.

Mary McCoy would be sound asleep, or she'd be getting ready for bed. He knew that she'd pray for him and his assignment that day. Her prayers would be fervent and sincere, asking God to keep him from peril. Nothing could be more important to his assignment than knowing that the woman he loved remembered him before God. Major Jimison's dull summary of the facts of Belgian life didn't camouflage the certainty that any flight across Belgium could be deadly for someone.

O Lord, Robert thought. *Please hear her prayers. I need You to be with me today.* He could feel the heat building in his neck and going down his back. *This attack won't be easy.*

Brigadier General Howerton picked up the lecture again. "You've got a general picture of what to expect if the Germans hit your airplanes. I don't need to tell you that we're facing extreme danger. Each of you must be aware of the simple fact that you will be in the very center of the conflict." Howerton looked around the room slowly. "Pay attention. Your life depends on it."

The room became completely silent. No one breathed or moved.

"Last fall our dear friend *der Führer* called that great light of German nobility and culture, General Gerd von Rundstedt, up to the *Wolfschanze* and made him the commander-in-chief of the Western front." Howerton's voice rang with sarcasm. "The word is that Hitler doesn't like good ole von Rundstedt much but is smart enough to recognize a touch of true genius when it comes along." The general crossed his arms over his chest as he lectured. "Since then, the Germans have been turning out new airplanes like nothing you've ever seen before. Single-engine pursuit craft rose from 1,260 planes in September to over 2,000 flying this month. Get the picture?" The general raised his right eyebrow and smirked.

General Howerton stared at his captive audience, letting the impact of his talk settle. Walker felt the threat of the increased German airpower settle into his bones.

"You men are their target," the general continued. "They expect to send you down in flames. Every Kraut has got his guns aimed at the sky. Today's not a scrimmage. We're fighting the real war. Got it?"

Robert wondered when someone would call him forward to inquire about military secrets brought from America. Maybe the assignment hadn't arrived yet. It might be a week or more before the information came. He had no choice but to say nothing until the military asked him.

Howerton stepped aside, and the operations officer began reading a list of flight assignments. Within two minutes Walker knew he'd be flying that day. It was a warm-up assignment, preparing him for other things. He was placed in a P-38 and given the task of flying as support and protection for a B-17 group, aiming at targets to the east of the center of Arnhem. The railway system and a terminal on the outskirts of the city were their primary targets, with a caveat to watch for a panzer division moving tanks into the area. As the new man, Walker had been assigned the far-wing position in the formation, with the additional task of breaking away to hit anything moving on the ground that needed closer attention.

Robert found his assigned group standing outside the administrative building. He saluted. The men only stared at him.

"Lieutenant Robert Walker," he said, identifying himself as he stood at attention

"Morning, Walker." A lanky man in the center of the group saluted back. "I'm running the show today. Jones," he said casually. "The name is Major Randy Jones." He pointed around him. "This is our unit."

The pilots nodded, saluted, and mumbled some greeting, but no one gave a name. Walker nodded casually to the group.

"We'll get better acquainted after the flight," Major Jones said. "Not much time for chitchat right now." He didn't smile.

Walker felt a distance between himself and the other men. No one knew him, and he didn't have any reputation with them. They were waiting to see how he flew, what he did, before anyone got close. Maybe he didn't know anything, couldn't fly. Maybe he wouldn't come back. It was wait-and-see time.

In the crew's preparation room, Walker snapped on a parachute. *Maybe he wouldn't come back.*

Happened all the time. Planes got blown out of the sky every day of the week. He might turn out to be nothing more than one of the new recruits who made some miscalculation, a fatal error, and *boom!* only to disappear in a cloud of smoke. Just another statistic.

The thought of failure gripped Robert's mind, and he swallowed hard. Back in Kansas he'd been told that he couldn't afford to let his mind wander or lose his perspective. Everything had to be locked down with his attention focused on the flight. If he let his thoughts wander around loose in his head, the anxiety could destroy him.

At that moment Mary's encouragement two nights ago flashed through his mind. *"It is I; be not afraid."* She had given the message to him, and if there was ever a time he needed to live the words of Christ, it was now. With a mighty heave, Robert pushed his fear aside. He would do well today! Grinding his fist in the palm of his hand, Lieutenant Walker walked determinedly toward the P-38 he was to pilot. Minutes later, his squadron was on its way to Europe.

Belgium

The squadron flew directly into the Strait of Dover and turned up the English Channel, flying northwest toward Ghent, Belgium. Not to be taken for granted, the Channel had improved significantly since the Normandy invasion, but the crew was warned that the *Luftwaffe* could appear suddenly out of nowhere. The P-38s had to be ready for immediate response at any moment.

Lieutenant Walker could see many ships and boats sailing the ever-expanding sea. The war seemed to be moving at a slow, leisurely pace. No signs of strife or attack. The ocean looked almost placid, and Robert liked the feel of the airplane. Instructions had said radio silence would be maintained until Jones broke the seal. No problems were expected going over, and the formation seemed easy to fly. His initial fear disappeared. Robert settled into his seat and thought about Mary. Time seemed to mean nothing as he glided along.

"Heads up!" Major Jones's voice crackled in Robert's earphones. "We're going east." The big B-17 veered to the right, and the formation turned. "We're on our way." The radio went dead.

Minutes later Robert could see the coastline of Belgium. The formation abruptly climbed in altitude. Somewhere below him lay Ostend, and the little town of Bruges went past. Minutes went by quickly. Nothing felt particularly different from flying over Kansas. The airplanes would find their target, drop the bombs, go back to England, and the day would be done. He was getting used to the job. Things weren't so hard after all.

"We're almost there," Jones's voice crackled in his ears. "Keep the radios on and say what you need to. Prepare for the strike."

Robert gripped the stick more tightly and felt his adrenaline surge. Suddenly the sky filled with *ack! ack!*

and mortar fire. Out of nowhere the Germans had picked up on them.

"Nazis!" some pilot screamed in the radio. "At one o'clock. Watch out!"

Walker glanced above him, and his mouth went dry. Five Nazi ME-109 fighters were descending upon them, and one of the attackers was aiming at him.

Nine ~

Lieutenant Walker stared at the five Nazi ME-109s turning in a wide swing out of the clouds above him. His mouth went dry, and his heart pumped faster. He gripped the stick in the center of the airplane with a steely, cold clutch, knowing that any second the enemy would be on top of him. He ground his teeth.

"Okay, boys," Major Randy Jones's voice crackled in his headset. "Here come the Krauts. Do your stuff. Go get 'em."

With reflexes of mechanical accuracy honed to a fine edge from weeks of training over American soil, Robert edged his airplane out of the formation and peeled to the left. Seconds later, the Nazi plane coming at him hurled past him, blasting away at the B-17 bombers. The abrupt explosion of gunfire shook Robert so badly that he did nothing but hang on to the stick that guided his airplane, his hands frozen in place and his heart pounding like a drum.

At the last moment Walker realized that a second fighter wasn't far ahead of him. Automatically he blasted away at the approaching Nazi warplane. The ME-109 suddenly veered straight up out of his path and disappeared far above him in the clouds.

Robert swallowed hard and tried to get his bearings. When he could see nothing in front of him but empty sky, Robert realized that the exchange had turned him around backward and that he was flying in reverse direction toward the English Channel. He wasn't flying with his comrades any longer.

Jerking back on the stick and instantly climbing upward, Robert rolled back in the opposite direction. The squadron was now in front of him, and the original five Nazi airplanes had become ten, swarming down on the Americans like mosquitoes at twilight. Robert watched nervously, trying to pick out which of the Nazi planes he'd shoot at when they came back around.

Suddenly from out of the clouds overhead, a Nazi plane dropped straight down, flying for Major Jones's B-17. Walker pushed the throttle forward and started to shoot, but the angles of the German fighter and the bomber were too close for him to fire without possibly hitting the American plane. His finger relaxed.

In the second that Walker hesitated, the Nazi cut across the bomber with unceasing fire. Robert saw holes sliced through the fuselage and the wing. The gunner in the plastic bubble slumped over as the German's bullets blew holes in the dome's cover.

"We're hit!" Jones's voice resonated in Robert's ear. "Got to evacuate. We're jumping." The radio went dead for a moment. Suddenly Jones came back on. "Keep your course, men, and give 'em hell when you hit the target. We'll try to make sure we're over Allied territory before we jump."

Even before the bomber broke from the squadron's formation, smoke streamed from underneath its wings. Watching from above, Robert could see that the B-17 was slowing. Two men leaped out the side door, parachuting toward the ground. Robert eased back on the throttle, slowing to cover the bomber's descent.

Flames broke through the skin of Jones's airplane near the tail. The flames were spreading fast, and the plane spiraled downward.

"Jones!" Walker yelled in his microphone. "Get out of there! The tail's on fire. Everything's coming apart. Get out *now!*" He waited a moment. "Can you hear me?" he shouted. No one answered.

The B-17 erupted in a huge ball of orange fire and black smoke. A big piece of metal barely missed Robert's canopy and hurtled past the fighter. Before he could respond, Robert flew into the cloud of smoke and fire. He found himself suddenly on the other side of the blackness, looking again at an empty sky.

Robert caught his breath and turned to keep from going farther away from the rest of the squadron again. Robert felt nauseous and swallowed hard. In just a split second Major Jones and anyone else left on that airplane had been destroyed. Regardless of the temperature outside the airplane, he was sweating and beginning to feel lightheaded.

The Germans outnumbered the Allies. The Nazi fighters now numbered fifteen and were coming from every possible angle. For a moment a wild thought raced through Robert's mind. *Get out of here! Go home before they get you! Run. Now. Do it.*

Robert hit the throttle again, flying directly at the ME-109s, which were still firing at the other bombers. But the Nazis were skillful and hard to hit. Robert kept posturing closer, trying to get in position to protect one of his own planes.

"Behind you," a voice popped in Walker's earphone. "A Kraut's dropping on you from the rear."

Robert thought the warning must be for someone else but tried to look behind him. Nothing on the left. He turned to the right. The roar of an approaching aircraft filled his ears, and then the thundering noise of machine gun fire echoed through his airplane. His plane shook as an ME-109 shot past not fifty feet away. His hand shook.

The Nazi plane sprayed the back of the B-17 in front of Robert but didn't disable the airplane. Robert veered sideways for a second look and realized the gunner in the bubble on the rear of the bomber had been hit. At that moment he also saw holes in the left wing of his own plane. Purely by God's grace, he had been spared from being blown out of the sky.

"We're at the target," another voice came on the radio. "Unload the bombs and get out of here."

In thirty seconds the American bombers started dropping their loads over the zone outside Arnhem before the Nazis had the opportunity to attack again. Once they were on the other side of their targets, the squadron turned back toward the sea and began their journey back to England.

Two minutes later the Nazi fighters returned, shooting at the fleet, but this time the Americans hit two ME-109s, exploding the airplanes in the sky. When his squadron regrouped, Robert realized that two other P-38s weren't with them. The American aircraft had simply disappeared.

"We're missing two planes!" Walker barked into his microphone. "Where are our men?"

"The Nazis hit 'em," someone answered. "On that last attack, they got our boys at the rear. I saw the airplanes blow up."

Robert took a deep breath and beat gently on his chest for a moment. Never had he been so close to death so many times. He kept watching in every direction, expecting to be hit again from somewhere, anywhere. He turned his head back as far as possible, trying to see behind him. He felt frightened and edgy but saw nothing.

In ten minutes the squadron wasn't far from the Belgian coast, and they'd soon be back over the sea, making a surprise attack less likely. The Nazis didn't come back. Walker found his proper place in the formation returning to England and started counting airplanes. They had lost three B-17s and five P-38s. His own lack of experience could easily have made it six.

The ride back to England seemed louder and filled with noises Walker didn't remember on the flight over. Probably wind blowing through the bullet holes in his airplane. No one said anything until they approached the English coast, and then the airplanes fell in line for the landing. Robert settled into the order, descended, and taxied across the grassy runway. Once the sound confirmed that his wheels were touching the ground, Robert relaxed for the first time since they had started across Belgium, yet he still felt the shaking inner convulsions of his first airborne baptism of fire.

The P-38 pulled to a stop next to the other planes, and Robert shut down the engines. For a moment he looked at the floor. "Thank You, God," he whispered. "Thank You for saving my life. Please be with those men who went down today. Keep them in the hollow of Your hand."

Bang! Someone pounded on the side of the airplane. *Bang!* "You all right in there?" a mechanic yelled.

Robert slid the canopy back and unbuckled his helmet. "Yeah, I'm not hurt."

"Man, they really shot you up!"

Robert looked out at a mechanic standing beside his airplane. "Shot holes up and down the side of this airplane! You're plum lucky to be alive."

The lieutenant stood up and leaned over the side of his P-38, taking a hard look at the holes the mechanic pointed toward. Up and down the airplane's body were at least six or eight gaping holes.

"Yeah," Robert said. "I sure am." He suddenly felt nauseous and grabbed his stomach. Robert threw his leg over the side of the cockpit and scrambled to get to the ground before he vomited onto the controls.

Ten ~

Allied Air Base, England

Walker trudged across the grass toward the base canteen. The dogfight over Belgium had left him feeling disoriented and shaken. Talking about it wouldn't help; he needed quiet and solitude to pull himself back together. He didn't speak to anyone but looked for a back corner in the Officers Club where he could sit and unwind. He didn't want to discuss the flight or what he'd seen. Things inside him needed to settle. Robert's sense of his own mortality crowded him and left him feeling frighteningly vulnerable. Sitting alone and getting his wits back would be ample for the moment.

The Officers Club was filled with more men than he expected to see at this time of day. Most of them talked and drank beer, and everyone seemed to be smoking. Robert suddenly realized that most of the airplanes had left around the same time that he had, at dawn. He had to adjust to a new schedule. A quick glance around the room told him that while the men talked with each other, others sat alone. Their faces looked grim and determined. No one bothered them. Robert picked up a bottle of beer and found a place near the back where he could look out the window.

Airplanes kept coming back from their missions, landing one after the other in long lines. The base mechanics rushed out each time to greet the airman. Robert could see that many airplanes bore the marks of battle, with holes in the wings or the fuselage. A number of the P-38s had holes in their wings and tail. The day had not been easy for many others. Periodically a plane came in with serious damage and was barely able to land. Recovery action on the runway was fierce and frantic. For thirty minutes he watched the flurry of excitement, thinking nothing, but only staring out the window.

Robert Walker had never been a fearful person. He was prudent and thoughtful, and he seldom did anything that was foolish or impulsive. But in the sky there wasn't much time to consider what the enemy might do when he came barreling down on you at a couple of hundred miles an hour. Pilots acted and reacted. Little more. Hopefully they did the right thing, but there were no guarantees. Robert knew that if he made one mistake he'd be dead.

He rubbed his forehead and took a long drink. The beer was cold and felt good. He had been trained well and knew what to do under most circumstances, but up there in the clouds something new and different could arise at any moment. He needed eyes in the back of his head. No one could give him that edge when the Nazis were diving down from every conceivable corner of the sky.

The freaky uncertainty of an airplane hitting him out of nowhere made Robert think of his mother. She used to come up behind him and whack him on the back of the head, scaring him to death. Martha Walker seemed to like to hit people and had tried it a few too many times with his father. Eventually their fights got so violent that Robert hid when they started in on each other. The thought of her slaps still frightened him and made Robert want to hide, just like the Nazi airplanes did.

Eventually the Walkers divorced and Martha moved to Los Angeles, where she remarried. Robert hadn't ever visited her and didn't really want to, either. He thought of her more as a street address than as a person. Mrs. Samuel Mills. That's about the best he could do. Not Mom or Mother. Just Mrs. Samuel Mills. And watch the back of your head when you were around her. She could strike from out of nowhere.

After thirty minutes of watching the B-17s and their crews return, Robert again thought of Mary. Another day was starting in Kansas. She'd be getting ready to teach at the college. Only three days had passed since they'd been together, but it felt like he had gone to a different planet in that short time. English accents, the towns, the terrain, the people, and the circumstances created an entirely different world. Everywhere he looked, Robert saw only men. Women didn't seem to be part of the battle scene. He felt lonely and isolated, and he longed for Mary.

Robert took out the paper form that he had to use for his

letters and started to write. When he was finished, the letter would go through a security check to make sure there was no leak. Then the letter would be photographed and the thick copy sent on. At first he wrote quickly.

> My dearest Mary,
>
> I'm sitting by myself after a day of flying over the Low Countries. We had a rough encounter and lost a number of airplanes. For the first time I saw the Germans up close. It was not a pretty sight.

He stopped and looked at the few lines. The words made him want to retreat again. An image of his mother returned.

Would the censors let the letter through? Robert read it one more time. Nothing there betrayed exactly where they'd been. What he'd written looked okay. He continued.

> I miss you, Mary. I miss you almost more than I can express. I wish I could reach out and touch you right now, but I know this is an experience that both of us must go through alone. I just wish you were with me.

Robert sat back in his chair and looked out the window again. Two more airplanes landed on the brown, grassy field. The sky was clearing.

If he wished for anything, it was to see Mary's face. She'd become very important to him in the short time he'd been in England. He ached to touch and hold her.

He thought about his own family back in Fort Towson and

wondered how his father was doing. Robert considered his brother and sister. They were important, but Mary was different. In the short time they'd been together, Robert had crossed a line that he'd never noticed before. The Walkers back in Fort Towson were kin, but he didn't expect to see them day after day. He could see himself spending the rest of his life with Mary McCoy. He picked up his pencil and wrote.

> Dear Mary,
>
> We saw significant action today, and I can tell you that the war effort is going strong and well. I think we hit our targets and will be able to help the Allied cause. My job is important.
>
> I'm sure that I will receive a letter from you in a few days, but it will take a while to get things going. Don't worry if you don't hear from me for a while. I hope your classes are going well.
>
> Don't miss seeing the movies for me!

Robert looked at the letter again. He'd never been good at writing and found it hard to put his feelings on paper. None of his sentiments came out through the end of a pencil the way that he wanted them to. He wished he could blurt out that he loved Mary and wanted to be with her forever, but that didn't seem like the right thing to write. With an unusually impulsive stroke, Robert simply signed his name and folded the letter. He opened it again and wrote *love* above his name. He needed to let the letter sit for a while and see if something else came to mind.

Robert scooted back from the table and got up. Maybe a walk outside would help his thinking.

~

Robert returned to his barracks and found a few men sitting around their beds, talking, playing cards, and killing time. No one spoke to him, so the lieutenant wandered on back to his bunk and picked up Mary's picture. She was every bit as lovely as he remembered her . . .

"Hey, Lieutenant Walker! They want you over at the administrative building," a major shouted from the door.

Robert looked up from his bed at the small nightstand. His watch said 4:30. He shook his head to clear his mind and get awake.

"Headquarters been looking for you almost ever since you got back," the pilot explained. "Where you been, boy?"

Robert swung his long legs off the bed and stood up. "Been out walking. Didn't know I was on call."

"You're on call twenty-four hours a day, old buddy." The pilot waved for Walker to follow him. "No matter what they tell you, that's the way things work around here."

Lieutenant Walker slapped on his military cap and reached for his coat. "Interesting." He saluted.

The pilot extended his hand. "The name is Major Jimison. I'm from Maryland."

Walker extended his hand.

"The boys at the front office seem to think you've got some sort of hidden talent they can't live without. Want to talk with you really bad."

"Really?"

"That's been the word floating around among the top brass today. By the way, I understand the Krauts hit you a few times this morning."

"Yeah. I got a few holes in the fuselage. Nothing bad."

Major Jimison laughed. "Son, there's nothing good about a hole anywhere in an airplane. By the way, you got a good report from the people flying with you. Said you did the right things."

"You serious?"

"We pay attention," Jimison said. "Not much goes undetected around this place. Like a vacuum cleaner on a rug, we pick everything up that's shook loose."

"Is that right?"

"You don't have to be distant with me, Lieutenant." Jimison smiled. "I work with the intelligence end of this operation. We pay careful attention."

"I see."

"I see?" Jimison slapped Walker on the back. "You haven't even begun to see what we're up to."

Walker stopped and stuck his hands in his coat. "I'm sorry that I'm not entirely following you, Major. I've only been here a couple of days. Still trying to figure out what we're doing."

Jimison scratched his chin. "I imagine when we get through with you this afternoon, you'll have a fairly good idea of what this base is actually all about. Yes sir, we're about to break you in, Mr. Walker."

Eleven

Walker followed Major Jimison into the administrative building and back to the staff's inner offices. The large Quonset hut looked about the same vintage as his sleeping barracks. The place had been thrown together in a hurry. As they walked through the quarters, no one seemed to be paying attention to them.

Major Jimison took Robert into a small office at the end of a long corridor and shut the door behind them. "Okay, Lieutenant." The major crossed his arms over his chest. "Let me tell you exactly how things are. I'm the man from intelligence, and you're the fish I dragged in out of the pond. I already know about everything there is to know about what makes you tick. Got my drift?"

The sudden change of direction and the abrupt assault left Lieutenant Walker speechless. He wasn't sure what to say.

"What I'm about to tell you will be a complete surprise

to you, Lieutenant Walker, but I know the details of your training and experience with G-H materials."

Walker stared.

"You've been sent here to make sure that we bomb right with this new technique recently developed in the USA. Are we on the same page?"

Robert nodded. His mouth hung open.

"Yes, I know this is top secret, but the time has come to turn this technique loose on *der Führer*'s boys. We want to start immediately. Got me?"

"Yes sir." Robert swallowed hard.

"We're going into the inner offices of this base and have a talk with the really big boys. The people who make the decisions on this base. You read me?"

"Yes sir." Robert closed his mouth.

"Be forthright and honest, Walker. That's all you have to do."

"Yes sir."

Major Jimison beckoned with his thumb. "Follow me. The big show in the main tent is about to begin." He walked out the door with Robert in tow. "It's time for you to jump through a hoop or two. Dance a little."

The major and the lieutenant went down the long corridor in total silence. Two military police officers stood guard in front of the door at the other end of the hall. When the major approached, both guards saluted. He returned the salute and said something to one of the men. The guard immediately turned and went inside. Five minutes later he opened the door and motioned for the two men to come inside.

Robert instantly recognized Major General Matthew B. Ridgeway. He was standing behind a desk just beyond a long table that held a large working map of the battle lines in Europe. Walker froze in strict military attention. Out of the corner of his eye, he knew the man to his left was Brigadier General Otto Weyland of the Sixteenth Tactical Air Command that supported the Third Army. He didn't recognize the other men except for General Howerton. He tightened his knees and stood in an even more rigid posture.

"I have Lieutenant Walker, who just arrived from the States," Jamison said. "I briefed him on the purpose of this meeting."

"At ease." General Ridgeway walked toward the map table. "Welcome to our operation, Lieutenant Walker. You'll find us to be an exciting and fast-moving outfit. I understand you were flying today?"

"Yes sir."

"Do you find the operation to be challenging?"

"Definitely."

Ridgeway laughed. "The Krauts do have their own special way of welcoming one to the war." He walked from behind the desk and stood over the table, pointing around the terrain. "We have reason to believe that a significant battle is about to unfold in the area you flew over today. I understand that the Luftwaffe showed up in full force."

"Yes sir."

"Well, the war will get worse." Ridgeway stared at the table as he seemed to talk to himself. "We have reason to believe that Hitler is pushing the Sixth Panzer Division toward the front with full support from the German air force. Possibly as many as eight hundred, nine hundred, maybe a thousand airplanes will be pushed into the assault. You understand what I'm saying?"

Robert wasn't sure how he should respond. He didn't know where Ridgeway was going with his explanation. Robert looked straight ahead but nodded his head.

"We are expecting a significant confrontation in this area of the Ardennes, inside Belgium and Luxembourg." Ridgeway pointed to an area on the map dotted with flags, indicating the line of conflict. "The area is scarred by deep gorges and winding streams. Nothing's easy in there because the forest is thick and formidable. The Our and Meuse Rivers are good examples of how difficult the waterways are to cross. The thickest part of the forest abuts the German border." He picked up a pointer and pinpointed the area on the map. "Hard place to conduct a military campaign in such a morass. If one is looking for a good place to fight, this entire area stinks. We are going to have a difficult time hitting many of our targets because of these conditions."

Robert suddenly understood why he was in this meeting. He had come with knowledge that could make an important difference in the effectiveness of air force strikes. The G-H tracking system allowed bombers to fly over a forest with little visual contact and still hit their targets. His training in Kansas made Robert an important factor in this struggle.

"Do you understand our problem, Lieutenant?"

"Yes sir!" Robert's brisk answer snapped. "I see the issues."

"Good," Ridgeway shot back. "We understand that you know how to use the G-H material, Lieutenant Walker."

"And the most recent Micro-H discoveries, the refinement of G-H and H_2X, sir." Robert relaxed and took a breath.

"Excellent." Ridgeway nodded to the men around him. "This could make a significant difference in our attacks. Tell us how you'd use these materials, Walker."

Robert looked at the table and pointed toward the battle lines. "Today we had difficulty with the interception of Nazi ME-109s against our bombers. Hopefully we were accurate, but in fact I doubt if we hit much of anything."

General Weyland nodded to Ridgeway. "That's been a significant problem. He's right. They didn't make that much difference in hitting the target area today." Weyland turned to Walker. "Show us on the map how this Micro-H material could change things." Weyland handed Walker a long pointer.

For a moment Robert studied the small pieces placed on the map to denote the battle line running from Echternach in the south along the Our River up to the Roer Dams in the north. He placed the pointer in the middle between Our and the Losheim Gap. "Of course, seeing targets in this area is difficult and hard to predict. The use of G-H changes the struggle and brings new accuracy because we are following scientific direction, not line of sight." He moved the pointer back to the front edge of the Forest of Ardennes in Luxembourg. "We must place G ground stations approximately thirty-five miles from the target area.

The vibrations from these machines give the necessary guidance that will allow our B-17s to strike their targets. Once a bomber passes over the sound point station on the ground, the pilot enters into a timed run with the bombardier releasing the bombs through the use of a stopwatch. Blind-bombing devices reduce the necessity of visual attack."

Ridgeway looked at Howerton and Weyland. "Am I not correct that radar bombing is conspicuously less effective than sighting targets visually?"

"Yes sir," Weyland answered, "but what Lieutenant Walker has described puts our bombing assignments on a significantly different basis. The issue is timing, not visual accuracy."

Ridgeway crossed his arms and rubbed his chin. "Hmm, no one is aware of this new technology?"

"Not to our knowledge," Robert assured the group. "To my understanding, I am bringing you the first discussion about this technology on this side of the ocean."

"You have flown using these devices?" Ridgeway asked the lieutenant.

"Yes, I have."

Ridgeway turned to Major Jimison. "Am I correct that these G stations are ready to be planted?"

Jimison nodded. "Yes sir. Virtually no one knows what they are or how the G ground stations will be used, but we have placed the devices with our troops in Luxembourg. The Ninth Armored Division, located in the Ardennes, has the stations."

"How soon can we deploy them?" Ridgeway asked.

"Twenty-four hours should be ample," Jimison answered.

Ridgeway scratched his head and walked away from the table. He turned to his generals. "What do you men think?"

General Weyland raised his hand. "Let's find out. We've got nothing to lose."

Ridgeway looked at the other generals. Each man nodded approval.

"Okay, Lieutenant Walker. Let's see what we can do. Tomorrow we will give you a B-17 bombardier and a crew for you to work with during the day. Other pilots and some of their crew will be part of the instruction time. Your job is to make sure that these men can use this approach accurately and quickly. We want you to train the bombardiers for the attack that will happen at dawn the day after tomorrow."

"Yes sir." Walker saluted. "I will be ready."

Ridgeway returned the salute. "We will be following what you do carefully." The general turned back to the desk behind the table and then stopped. Ridgeway looked over his shoulder at Robert. "Good luck, son. Won't be easy out there."

Twelve ~

Major Jimison and Lieutenant Walker briskly saluted the American generals, turned on their heels, and left the briefing.

"Handled yourself right well in there with the big boys," Jimison quipped. "I thought you'd enjoy my friends."

"Thanks," Robert said. "Bunch of real buddies."

Jimison laughed.

"Why don't you join us tonight at a local pub? You can meet my real cronies."

"Tonight?"

"Sure."

Feeling a strong need to know more about life in England and the war, and feeling more than a bit lonely, Walker agreed.

"Will we walk to town?"

Jimison laughed again. "I have access to a jeep. We'll pick you up at 1830 hours. See you then."

Robert agreed. Waiting for time to pass, he sat down on his bed and wrote a letter to Mary. He tried to tell her everything that he thought would pass the censors. The letter looked good and told her a great deal about the struggle at the front. He sealed the envelope and prepared to put it in the postal drop. Abruptly the sound of the jeep roared up near the front door. The lieutenant grabbed his cap and hurried to the door.

"Hey, meet my buddies," Jimison yelled, pulling his jeep to a stop. "The guy next to me is Captain Brown, and Major Hammonds is in back. Call 'em Bill and Fred."

Walker saluted. "Glad to meet you guys." Hammonds and Brown waved back.

"Hop in." Jimison pointed to the backseat. "We're on our way to a pub in town."

"Where're we going?" Robert asked.

"Over to the Dover Castle," Bill Brown explained. "Ever hear of it?"

Robert shook his head.

"It's about four hundred feet above the port. One of the oldest castles in England. Henry the Second built it in the twelfth century. Got a pub in the basement. Good place to drink a beer and talk."

"Bless good ole Henry," Robert said. "Knew he liked beer, but didn't know he built pubs."

"Stick with us," Brown fired back. "We'll teach you all kinds of things you didn't know." He grinned at Robert.

The jeep bounced down the dirt road leading off the base and on to the small strip of pavement going toward Dover.

The men talked and joked as the jeep wound down the narrow road lined by thick, large trees and piled stone fences. Several people peddled old bicycles along the side of the road. Within minutes, Jimison found his way into the quaint town, down the main streets, past ancient Tudor-style stores, and up the hill. The wind swept in from the ocean and left a salty smell of seaweed hanging in the air. He stopped behind the large gray stone tower, and the four men piled out.

"You're going to like this place, Robert," Jimison assured him. "Real ambiance of the medieval ages, and they've got good food, to boot. You'll like the ale."

"Good." Robert followed the major. "Let's see what the ancient castle looks like."

On the other side of the large wooden door, a massive room opened before him. Brits, as well as Americans, sat around small tables talking. In addition to the small light fixtures attached to the stone walls, candles and a large, smoking torch threw shadows across the room. The cavernous hall felt like a place where men with drawn swords might at any moment leap down from the stone stairs and launch into mortal combat right before their eyes.

"Give us four pints of bitters," Jimison told the man behind the bar. "We'll sit in the back."

"Comin' right up, mate." The old bartender gave a gentle wave and began drawing the drinks by pulling the long-handled taps. "Four big ones for the Yanks."

"Walker's been here two days, and he's already been promoted to being an instructor," Major Jimison told the other men. "Some clout, huh? Treat this boy with respect."

"A real operator!" Brown pursed his lips and rolled his eyes.

"Indeed!" Fred Hammonds groaned deep in his throat. "I'll have to clean up my act."

"Hey." Robert held up both hands. "I'm just a simple Oklahoma country boy. Be good to me."

"Thought you were from Kansas?" Bill Brown asked. "Mid-America?"

"That's where I flew here from, but I grew up in Fort Towson, Oklahoma. Ever hear of that?"

"Fort Towson? Oklahoma?" Fred Hammonds sounded like he knew the place well. He took a long drink from his mug. "Never heard of either."

The men laughed.

"Nah," Brown objected. "Never heard of Fort Towson, but we do know about Oklahoma. You sound like a down-home sort of guy."

Walker smiled. "Yep! That's me. Hometown boy." He felt more at ease than he'd felt since landing on the brown grassy runway the first morning. Jamison's friends seemed like good airmen. Easy to talk to and a good sense of humor.

"You're all in intelligence?" Robert asked, trying to change the direction of the conversation.

The men nodded their heads.

"You know the inside on the inside, huh?" Robert continued.

"Not as much as Jimison would lead you to think," Brown quipped, "but we do know a great deal about what happens around here."

"Yeah, Jimison specializes in the international stuff. We're just local boys."

Everyone laughed.

"You boys ever fly over Europe?"

The three men looked at each other. No one answered.

"Come on. I'm wondering if you guys know what it's like to have the Nazis bearing down on top of you, firing away like they're going to blow you into a thousand little pieces."

"Your friend gets right to it, doesn't he?" Brown said to Jimison. The humor was gone.

Jimison shrugged. "Guess he does."

Silence fell over the group.

Robert looked at the faces of the men and felt embarrassed. "Look, I must have said something wrong. You have to understand that I'm new around here. Excuse me if I hit the wrong button."

Jimison smiled. "Robert, you just put your finger on one of the issues that creates friction between our intelligence unit and the other people in the Ninth Air Force. After it's all said and done, we just gather data. We don't get shot at."

Robert scratched his head. "I see. You must forgive me. I was only trying to get some perspective on my experience today. Honestly. I've never been shot at before this morning. The experience scared me."

Hammonds chuckled. "The other pilots tell us they never worry. They're too tough for anything so negative as a little doubt about what might happen to them. Every day I keep getting the reassurances that nobody flying our airplanes worries about anything."

Robert blinked. "You have to be kidding?"

"Sure, he's kidding," Brown added, "but that's what we hear seven days a week. That sorta talk is meant to put us in our places."

"Tension builds up between units," Jimison explained. "Apparently it's inevitable. Simply happens. Part of the way scared people corral their fears."

"I can't believe that anybody facing a Nazi ME-109 doesn't have more than a small amount of fear rolling around inside of him." Robert pushed back in his chair. "At least they frightened me plenty today."

Jimison slapped him on the back. "That's why you're a good man, Robert. You tell the truth. But let me share something with you about how it is around this base." He lowered his voice and moved closer. "Don't be telling people about your natural fears. These pilots don't want to hear it because every last one of them struggles with the same feelings, and they don't want to admit it. Every last one of them has got to fly over the bad stuff that they don't want to think about. That's the way we keep this base operating. We smile or frown . . . and just drink. Got me?"

"I see." Robert tugged at his chin. "Don't let anyone know about your apprehensions. Humph!" He shrugged. "New one on me."

"Get ready, Walker." Hammonds said, grinning. "You're going to learn a host of things you've never heard of before you got here, and many of those adages won't make much good sense. It's simply the way this war is."

Robert grinned and saluted his new friends. "Cheers!" He raised his mug, and the men toasted him back.

Their conversation continued for another two hours, but behind his smile, Walker felt desperately isolated in this corner of England jam-packed with Americans who lied to each other and could be dead by tomorrow afternoon. Loneliness settled over him, making him want to be silent. For most of the rest of the evening he listened to the other men talk, trying to understand what was going on in Dover. The picture was getting clearer. Much more was happening than the eye could see.

~

Most of the men in his barracks were already asleep when Walker returned. The air was cold, and the long room smelled damp. Lights were already out, and he had to walk softly in the darkness. Old, warped boards creaked, and some of the men turned restlessly in their metal beds. These pilots would fly early in the morning while he waited until after 0800 hours to begin his instruction on using the G-H system. If he could push aside the noise of their getting up, he had a chance of getting an extra hour of sleep. At least he wouldn't have anybody shooting at him tomorrow morning.

Trying to keep from making a sound, Robert eased down carefully on his bed. The pieces of wire squeaked, and he rolled over as quietly as he could. He realized that something was different with Jimison, Brown, and Jones.

An unspoken message had oozed out of the evening at Dover Castle. They seemed to be suggesting that the nature of his assignment was such that he came in a different category from the usual pilot. He brought hidden, secret data that put one of his feet in the intelligence world and the other in flying airplanes. These men weren't simply being friends; they were checking him out, making sure he was on the up-and-up. The truth was that he was probably an intelligence assignment for the evening. Realizing their intention made him feel strange and disconcerted. Maybe his assessment was correct; maybe it wasn't.

He flipped on his flashlight. The day had been so full he hadn't had time to write Mary. He wondered if it was possible to scribble under the sheets in the dim light. The thin mattress seemed far too soft to support the pencil. Robert flipped the small light off and pulled the covers back from over his head. He looked around the room and realized he was the only one awake.

Mary's day is half over, he thought. *I wonder how she is? She'd die if she knew what I lived through today. Nazis shooting at me. Near disaster. I don't care what any of these people think or say, up there in the skies the shooting is terrifying. Only takes one bullet to end everything. Just one. O Lord, I know it's going to get worse. I need Your help . . . Your touch . . . Your protection . . . if I'm going to survive.*

The wind picked up, blowing through the long space between the Quonset huts. For a moment it seemed that each lonely sound had a haunting quality, as if all the men who had died on past flights were outside crying their massive chorus of protest into the gale. The darkness seemed filled with a thousand dead faces.

"Lord Jesus, hear me," Robert whispered. "I don't want to be afraid, but I'm sure going to need Your help. I pray that I don't become one of *them*."

Thirteen

Allied Air Base, England, December 1944

At 0800 hours, Lieutenant Walker stood in the center of a long narrow lecture hall, staring at the thirty men seated in front of him. On the table in front of him were the basic units of the G-H system. The black metal sender boxes sat unobtrusively as little more than ordinary radio-signal sending devices. The reception units for the airplanes looked equally innocuous. He was the only person in the room who knew that these little black boxes could revolutionize Allied bombing raids.

"Good morning, gentlemen." Robert stopped, cleared his throat, and said nervously, "Pilots and officers."

The men looked back at him with blank stares. They didn't seem any more excited or interested than if he'd been selling vacuum cleaners. Most weren't any older than he was. They were simply American boys in a foreign war.

"I'm going to introduce you to a new guidance technique

that can radically improve your percentage of successful attacks on ground targets while flying at even higher altitudes than you now fly."

The pilots looked up with interest in their eyes. He had their attention.

"Please turn with me to page one of the instruction manual in front of you."

The rustle of pages turning filled the room.

~

THE ARDENNES, BELGIUM, DECEMBER 1944

The Nazi assault in the Ardennes began with new intensity. The First SS Panzer Division's *Panzergrenadier* battalions turned their tanks west and started their deadly thrust toward the Allies. Thousands of soldiers marched into the Ardennes forest, and heavy artillery pounded the front line. Field Marshal von Rundstedt's offense was on.

One of the *Panzergrenadier* units, dubbed "The Blowtorch Battalion" for their ruthless night attack with flamethrowers on the Russian village of Pekartschina, surged across the battle line into Allied territory. The panzer regiment, which had killed 2,500 Russians and captured only three, marched forward, eagerly prepared to hit the Allies hard and fast. The Sixth Panzer Division's commander, General Dietrich, had already sent the word to his troops to spread a wave of terror "without humane inhibitions." His command simply meant "kill all prisoners." Dietrich meant exactly what he had ordered.

The 4,000-man force of the *Kampfgruppe Peiper* fielded seventy-two medium tanks and an equal number of Mark IV and Mark V tanks, giving them the fighting strength of one and a half American tank battalions. With their multiple 20 mm guns and assault weapons, the battalion moved during the night, devouring everything in its path. The situation on the front line worsened by the hour. The swiftness of the attack gave the Allies little or no time to respond.

Before the offense began, a rest center, including entertainment facilities, for the Allied troops of the 394th Infantry had been set up in the town of Honsfeld. A stage was constructed, and the men were ready for relaxation. Captain Paul Purdue, in charge of the festivities, had welcomed actress Marlene Dietrich's arrival with great enthusiasm, but the sudden advance of the Germans changed everything, and Purdue hurriedly sent her back out of the area. December 17 proved to be a very bad day for the show.

AIR BASE, ENGLAND

By noontime, Lieutenant Walker believed the Allied pilots had the basic idea of how to use the G-H system. Their task was to learn to pick up the radio signals from the ground and hone in over the G-stations. Once they crossed the exact location of a sender station, the rest of the bombing run became a matter of simple mathematics and coordination with a stopwatch. The bombardier assigned to Walker's flight got the idea immediately and wouldn't have any trouble. While the device remained top secret, the basic nature of the machine wasn't complicated, and its use could be learned quite quickly. By the next day, the pilots he had trained would use the system. Robert felt good about the proposed attack; the men had the idea, and the pilots would be ready.

Not so in Europe.

North of Aachen, Germany

Major General Leland S. Hobbs, commander of the Thirtieth Division, and his unit, were parked in the forest north of Aachen, waiting for assignment when his phone rang.

"Hobbs, is that you?"

"Yeah, who's this?"

"Chief of staff of the Fourteenth Corps. I need to know exactly where you are."

"We're sitting out here in the trees just north of Aachen. Our boys are dug in, waiting for instructions on where to go next."

"Get your boys on the road, General. The war's heating up."

Hobbs frowned. "I'm not sure that I understand what you're telling me."

"I don't have any of the details, but we need you to go south. Probably the trip is only temporary."

"South!" Hobbs snarled. "We've been there."

"You got it. We're concerned for the safety of Malmédy and the Liège highway into Bastogne. I'll be back in touch when I have more insight on what's happening. All hell is breaking loose everywhere." The phone went dead.

General Hobbs cursed and slammed the receiver down.

"What's happening?" his assistant asked.

Hobbs scratched his head. "It appears that *Kampfruppe Peiper* is trying to take Malmédy or they may be aiming at the Bastogne-Liège highway. Looks like they want to put us in a position to block any move on the Liège area." He shook his head. "Tell the men that we're moving out ASAP."

The assistant leaped out of the M-36 tank destroyer and ran down the rows of tanks. "We're moving out!" he screamed at the soldiers. "Move it! We're going back south."

That evening General Omar Bradley returned to his headquarters in Luxembourg City and immediately went to the war room to check on what had happened during the day. Major General Leven Allen stood, waiting and watching Bradley's response. When he looked at the situation map, Bradley instantly saw that the Germans had committed fourteen divisions to the battle. Bradley cursed, worrying where the sudden show of Nazi strength had come from. The Nazis seemed to be rising out of the ground.

"Seems like this offensive maneuver is Rundstedt's all-out attack," Bradley told his chief of staff, Major General Leven Allen. Bradley shook his head. "I still think that Rundstedt's basically trying to force us to pull our strength away from the Third Army's sector."

"Sir," Allen answered, "this thing certainly seems to be heating up today. Could be much bigger in scope than a simple attempt to change how we're supporting our troops. I'm wondering if we shouldn't make contingency plans for the possibility of our having to move back from our headquarters here in Luxembourg City."

Bradley flinched and cursed. "I will never move backward with a headquarters! There's too much prestige at stake!" He stomped out of the room. Allen rubbed his forehead nervously and stared at the floor.

~

Air Base, England

The sun slowly eased toward the horizon as it set for the day. Robert walked briskly through the flying snow toward the administration building to make a full report on what had happened during his teaching. He knew Major Jimison waited for him in the intelligence unit's office.

Jimison looked up when Robert walked in. "Lieutenant! Looks like you've had a busy day. How'd the boys do?"

Walker saluted and sat down. "Quite a day, but I think we'll be ready to go tomorrow. The big question is whether your contacts in the infantry got those stations in place thirty miles from the targets."

Major Jimison rubbed the side of his face. "We put the order out. I hope they got things nailed down."

Walker squinted. "I'm not sure that I'm following you."

"Something big has broken out there in the battle zone today. The Germans seem to be on the move. Our people could have problems."

"You're serious?"

Jimison nodded his head. "Yeah. We're not entirely sure what's going on over there, but the pace of battle has picked up significantly."

A military policeman suddenly appeared in the door. "They're ready for you in the war room, gentlemen."

"Let's go." Major Jimison flipped his thumb. "We'll let our armed escort here take us in. Okay, Sarge?"

The MP saluted and started down the hall. Moments later he opened the door for the men to enter.

Lieutenant Walker immediately realized that General Ridgeway was not there; only Generals Howerton and Weyland stood over the long table. Walker came to rigid attention and saluted. A far more relaxed Jimison did the same thing.

"At ease, men." General Weyland saluted back.

"Please give us a succinct report on what happened today," General Howerton asked Walker.

Major Jimison turned to Robert and nodded.

"Everything went well," Robert reported. "I believe we are prepared for tomorrow's exercise."

"Good!" Weyland turned to Howerton. "That's what we wanted to hear." He looked at Jimison. "What about the placement of the G ground stations? Is that portion of the plan ready?"

"They've been ordered," Jimison hedged.

"I asked if they're ready?"

"I can't speak with precision, sir." Jimison bit his lower lip. "We are apparently experiencing a major German offense in the Ardennes. However, I can report that the troops in that area should have the ground stations operating by tomorrow morning."

Weyland and Howerton exchanged a quick, hard look.

"*Should have* won't cut it, Major. You're telling me that our success tomorrow may well depend on how far this new German advance has gone during the night?"

"I'm afraid so," Jimison said.

The two generals turned back to the long table and looked at the placement of the battle lines. Howerton pointed toward one end of the battle line. "A great deal will be affected by how long it takes General von Luttwitz and his 47th Panzer Corps to cross the Clerve River. They've got about fifteen miles between them and Bastogne. The 28th Division's 110th Infantry is going to be sorely pressed to keep those Germans out. We're looking at a real battle."

Weyland pointed above and below the place where Howerton pointed. "We've got the 112th Infantry in the north and the 109th Infantry in the south. We don't want to get those units knocked out of place, or the 110th will have to fight alone." He pulled at his lip and studied the table. "Could get very tough." Weyland pulled on his chin. "We need the Third Army in there."

Howerton turned around slowly. "Thank you, men. Walker, your assignment in the morning will depend on what happens tonight. Our hope is to be able to use those G-stations as they are being placed right now. Understand?"

Walker said nothing, but nodded.

"We'll see you at 0530." General Howerton saluted, and the two men left.

fourteen ~

The crunch of Robert's boots in the frozen snow left a hollow, empty sound in his ears as he walked back to his Quonset hut. A black sky made him feel empty and alone again. Jimison had been friendly, but he was probably still checking Robert out. His lack of assurance that the G-H sender devices would be in place worried Robert. Success depended on the devices sending out their pinging honing signal. If they didn't fire, the bombers would be on their own. Big problems would follow.

Before the lights in the barracks went out, Robert wrote Mary for the third time in the three days since he'd been in England. He described in vague details what he'd done during the day and told her about his teaching assignment, lunch, supper, his feelings. After detailing a couple of incidents that he thought might make her laugh, Robert hinted at his apprehension about flying the next day. As he came to the end of the letter, Robert told her how much he missed her and added a few more affectionate caveats than he'd done the day before. He wanted to say something more passionate and compelling but wasn't quite sure how Mary might feel about that much ardor. Robert sealed the letter and put it in the wooden clothes locker next to his bed for mailing the next day. Before Robert did anything else in the morning, he'd make sure his thoughts were on their way to America. He was surprised by how much he missed Mary.

Robert lay in the darkness, thinking about the world that rested so very far behind him across the broad Atlantic. What might his father and the family in Fort Towson be doing at this very moment? They seemed so remote out there in that tree-covered southern part of Oklahoma.

Sleepiness crowded in, and Robert knew he'd drift away in a short while. As his mind wandered over the past, he abruptly remembered when his father sold the store to old man Clark. What a row that maneuver created with his mother. He recollected Pa and Ma fighting over that one. In fact, the sale of the family business was about the only time he recalled really hearing them battle it out in front of the kids over something they disagreed on. His mother didn't want his father to let go of the store, but what else could the man do? The Depression had taken everything to the bottom, and old man Clark came over from Arkansas looking for such buys. The geezer had a bagful of money. No, Pa had done the only thing he could do to save the family. That time Ma was wrong.

Robert's thoughts of Fort Towson slipped away. The past was the past. He had to worry about tomorrow. What went wrong yesterday was gone.

~

DECEMBER 17, 1944

Well before dawn, Lieutenant Walker and the pilots flying to Europe were up and on their way toward the mess hall. Robert had left his letter in the mail drop and was mentally hunkering down to prepare for the long day. The difficult assignment would take considerable stamina. By 0530 hours, they walked into the briefing room in the administrative building. No one was certain that the G-stations were in place, but the squadron was to fly with the plan of attack as originally devised. The commander detailed the obvious, pinpointed their targets, and sent them on their way.

Outside the windows, the first rays of sunlight suggested that December 17 looked like it was going to be a cold, blustery day. The temperature had dropped during the night, and the winds had blown harder than usual. Snow whirled through the walkways between the buildings and shifted into growing drifts. The crew pulled their collars up around their necks and wrapped scarves around their faces. This day would be particularly demanding and unforgiving.

In the crew dressing room, the men put on parachutes and finished getting ready without saying much to each other. Word had fairly well sifted down from the command center to the troops that something big was breaking at the front, but no one seemed exactly sure what it was. The American pilots sensed the unsettledness and were uneasy about the day ahead. Solitude seemed to be the best way to face the test.

Lieutenant Walker led his crew out through the blowing wind toward the B-17, already loaded with bombs. Snow bounced off the glass dome covering the cockpit; the howling wind encouraged the crew not to linger on the ground beneath the bomber. They climbed inside and each person settled immediately into his assigned area. The tail gunner and the men in charge of the machine guns on top hurried into place. The only sound in the fuselage was that of equipment being placed for operation. Robert slipped behind the panel of dials and switches. For a moment he stared out the window, trying to order his thoughts.

"O God," he whispered to himself, "help me today. Please put Your hand around this airplane and keep us from being destroyed by the enemy. Help me to not be afraid. Amen."

A flurry of snow hit the windshield and sprayed the white dust across the dome. Another blast of cold air spread the frozen powder down the side of the nose of the airplane. Robert took a deep breath and pulled the sides of his leather helmet around his cheeks and under his chin.

"Guess it's time to warm this baby up," the copilot next to him said. "You ready, Lieutenant?"

Walker nodded his head. The engines turned, and a roaring noise filled the cabin. After a few adjustments, the B-17 began rolling forward. Other bombers pulled across the snow-covered runway, and P-38s fell into place. The die was cast; they would soon be on their way.

Walker looked up and down the line, making sure everybody was there. The bombers appeared to be in the right order, and the lineup was proceeding smoothly. Nothing seemed to hinder their flight.

Robert switched on the intercom. "Okay, men, we're ready to go. Should be off the ground in a few minutes. Buckle up. This is going to be a big flight."

Walker's airplane picked up speed as it taxied down the runway, and the roaring noise of the engines filled the cockpit. Robert pushed the throttle forward, and the big engines rolled to complete capacity. The airplane's tail lifted slightly, and suddenly its wheels were off the ground. They were in the air and off to Europe.

~

Lieutenant Walker's navigator followed closely the same flight plan Robert had flown earlier. Going straight across the English Channel, the squadron eventually turned slightly toward Belgium and bore due east, high above the clouds. The squadron settled into the higher altitude in close formation. Flying without incident or interruption, the airplanes maintained radio silence, as they had been ordered to do back at the base. The vastness of the sky opened before them with the brilliance of the rising sun casting red and yellow over the clouds. The hue of color glided over the tops of the white clouds, and the scene felt peaceful.

"Is everything in place?" Robert motioned for the navigator to come closer. The airman scooted next to the pilot. "Are we in good shape?"

The navigator nodded. "We're ready," he shouted above the roar and winked.

"Try tuning in the G-station and see if you can pick up anything yet."

The navigator returned to his station and began adjusting a special radio receiver.

Robert flipped on the intercom for contact with the bombardier. "You ready?" he asked. "We're getting close. Won't be long."

"Roger," the bombardier echoed back. "I'm sitting here waiting for the big okay from our radio man."

"Keep your radio on," Robert answered.

"Hey! I've got the signal." The navigator shouted into his microphone. "The system's working!"

"Excellent!" Walker said. "In a few minutes we should be thirty miles from the front line and our target area. We don't want to break radio silence. At this point, we'll assume the other bombers are doing the same thing. Let's get ready to zero in on the target. You know the instructions, men," Robert radioed the crew. "Here we go!"

Robert again read the instrument panel, making sure that everything was set and ready. The sky looked large and empty except for his squadron. No fears and anxieties out there over the billowing clouds. This attack wasn't going to be so hard after all. He'd simply set the course from the G-H system, fly in, and the bombardier would drop the bombs. They'd turn around and fly back out. Just that simple. The Nazis were too busy fighting down there to even pay any attention to him until it was too late. Robert took a deep breath and smiled for the first time that day.

"We're approaching the G-station," the navigator boomed across the microphone. "Get ready. When we are on dead center, I'll signal by saying *now*. We'll be there in a few moments."

Robert thought about his struggle to qualify to fly two very different combat airplanes. The commanders in Kansas had mentioned that jet airplanes would be coming in the future. He wanted to fly those wild machines, too. Flying was in his blood. No question about it. Robert Walker had been created to pilot airplanes. He loved what he was doing.

"Almost there," the bombardier said. "Hang on, boys." A few seconds later, he shouted, "Now!"

Walker pushed the control stick forward, and the airplane began a gradual dive. In a few moments their airplane would plunge through the clouds that wrapped the planes like puffs of cotton. The feeling of speed thrilled Walker as the white and gray sailed past his cockpit.

When the airplane suddenly shot through the bottom of the clouds, Robert could see the ground below. Tanks were firing, and a battle appeared to be in progress. He took a second look. Their squadron was flying over German tanks and trucks!

"Shouldn't be!" he mumbled to himself. "The battle line is supposed to be in front of us, not underneath."

"You sure that our maps are right?" Walker yelled at the navigator.

The airman nodded his head and stuck his thumb up.

Walker looked again. No question about it. The squadron was flying over truckloads of enemy soldiers and guns. As best as Robert could guess, the Nazis had broken through and were pushing west. The battle down below wasn't where it should be.

"Get ready," the bombardier's voice echoed through the intercom. "We're almost over the target!"

Guns began firing at the sky. Explosions shook the airplane and filled the sky with smoke. Robert's heart started pounding, and he gripped the stick even more tightly. Abruptly, from out of nowhere, a German fighter appeared above them, his gun blazing.

The bombardier began dropping the bombs. Walker steadied the airplane. Their deadly cargo must hit the targets regardless. Robert glanced in every direction and saw another ME-109 coming from above them.

"Enemy at ten o'clock! Get 'em!" He screamed into the microphone. He flipped on the radio. "Don't let these guys ambush us. We're under attack!" he called to the squadron flying near him.

Immediately the P-38s were all over the sky, and the dogfight was on. Trying to avoid being distracted by the attack, Walker steadied the B-17 and began turning back toward the west, but the groundfire increased. Realizing that a higher altitude was a necessity, he pulled back on the stick.

Just as the bomber started gaining altitude, two Nazi

ME-109s came at them from one o'clock. Suddenly the airplane jerked violently. Robert heard fabric tearing and the sound of plastic shattering. Instantly he shut his eyes and covered his head. The fire of machine guns increased, and then the sound was gone.

Walker turned to speak to his copilot, but the man was slumped over the instrument panel. Robert reached for him, but the man slipped sideways and Robert realized that most of the man's throat had been ripped out. Blood covered his instruments and ran down the front of the man's flight jacket. The plastic window covering the copilot's side had been shattered.

Robert caught his breath and ground his teeth. The plane was veering to the right and shaking violently. He tried to stabilize the craft.

"Help me," Robert screamed at the navigator. When no one answered, he turned to shout again. Behind him the man was lying on the floor with crimson red holes shot in his jacket.

The engines shook again, and fire streamed from the motor on the right side. Robert realized the B-17 was sliding into a downward dive and he was losing control.

"They hit our gunners!" the bombardier shouted into the microphone. "This plane is going down."

Robert's training suddenly took over. "Yeah, we're hit!" he yelled, "and I don't know how long I can keep the airplane steady. Get to the exit! We've got to get out of here now!"

Fifteen ~

OKLAHOMA, FEBRUARY 2000

By the start of the second week in February, Andrea had finished cleaning the garage and had done most of the jobs around the house. It was time for her to go home to Denver. Three days later, Mary Oliver sat down at her desk to write her recollections of her college years. She put an old black Underwood typewriter in the center of the leather pad covering the wooden desk and piled white paper on one side. Her fingers felt as decrepit as the machine looked.

January's snow and ice had disappeared from the dead dry grass, but the raw February winds blew hard. Little piles of snow still filled the brick-edged flower gardens. Mary watched the black smoke curl up the living room chimney from the snapping burning logs before she turned back to her typewriter and started writing.

She typed slowly, but in thirty minutes she had turned out several pages that described her earliest memories in her little farming community. Yet the more Mary wrote, the more disturbed she felt. A dark emotion seemed poised inside her, ready to explode. Although she couldn't get her mind around the disturbing, throbbing impulse, something deep and foreboding was trying to force its way out of her soul.

Mary tried to push the contorted feeling aside and made a quick verbal sketch of her last two high school years. Writing little about her private life, she described events in her rural high school. She only hit the highlights, writing about a few friends, basketball, a single boy she'd once thought cute, little else. Mary knew that her initial draft meant nothing more than setting the stage for what happened in college. She mostly wanted to describe her years after she'd left home, but words didn't come easy. She fumbled, trying to keep her mind focused. After typing five pages, Mary felt slightly better. She stopped and took a quick read to get a sense of things.

"Obviously rough," Mary finally said to herself. "Just doesn't sound right." She nervously ran her hand through her hair. "Painting, I can do. Writing, I cannot do." Mary dropped the pages on the desk and shook her head in disgust. "This stuff stinks."

One inescapable thought kept pushing through and raising itself. Mary didn't want to think about the question but couldn't keep the impulse back any longer. The uncertainty had to be answered. *What had happened to Robert?*

One minute he had been kissing her good-bye; the next he was gone, disappearing into eternity. She had tried to bury the pain, but after all these decades, the abruptness of his leaving, the finality of his disappearance, still haunted and dismayed her. The feelings exploded in her head with roaring bewilderment. Mary stared into the fire and thought honestly about his leaving for the first time in five decades.

~

KANSAS, DECEMBER 1944

Mary awakened while the sky was still black. From her upstairs window she could see large aircraft already flying overhead in what looked like an endless wave of bombers and transports heading toward Europe. Robert was in one of those airplanes.

Freezing wind blew in her face and chilled her. Mary felt as though her future was flying off and disappearing beyond the horizon.

Old Mr. Hobbs, her landlady's husband, had died eight or nine years earlier. According to Mrs. Hobbs, nothing had changed since the funeral except that the wallpaper had gotten a bit more yellow and frayed. Mrs. Hobbs often mentioned that the pale yellow paper had been hanging on the walls for nearly fifty years. High ceilings and glass-knobbed doors in every room left further clues to the house's age. The upstairs floors creaked when she walked, so Mary sat quietly, looking out the upstairs window, which opened out over the prairie that turned into endless wheat fields. The cold wind blew her red hair back, making her feel alone and lonely.

At the other end of the horizon, P-38s and B-29s filled with pilots trained for the front lines took off. The aviators must feel as completely lost as she did. The man Mary loved was gone, flying away. At that moment the minister's words returned to Mary: "It is I; be not afraid." Yet fear still throbbed and inched its way through her like a parasite boring into her muscles. Anguish and apprehension gripped her heart.

~

In the beginning Robert and Mary had written to each other faithfully. The first letters Mary received were scribbled on regulation paper that arrived as photographs, having been screened for security purposes. Robert had written the first one as he flew toward the White Cliffs of Dover. In turn, Mary wrote every day and mailed her letters each evening to make sure they left in the early-morning mail. Then Robert's letters stopped. After the middle of January nothing came again.

At first Mary assumed that the postal service must have a hitch in their machinery, but that assumption quickly died. Local newspapers told the story of a great battle swelling up in the woods across Belgium and Luxembourg. The Germans poured in men and machines in endless waves, and the fighting was fierce. Robert's letters indicated that he would be flying over that part of Europe. She concluded that he must be caught up in what the newspapers began calling the Battle of the Bulge.

Mary sat down at Mrs. Hobbs's old kitchen table and pulled the *Sterling Daily News* close to read the headline story:

PATTON SPEEDS TO THE FRONT

> Reports from the Allied front indicate that General George Patton is rushing the Third Army into place to support current attempts to stop the Nazi advance, which is aimed at splitting the Allied thrust across Luxembourg and Belgium. Casualties remain high during one of the worst winter weather storms of recent years. Freezing conditions have proved to be difficult for Allied and Axis efforts.

Stories in the local paper were always sparse and didn't say much. Mary turned the page and read another description of General George Patton's bold attempt to swing his troops into the fray. The story left her with many unanswered questions. A similar headline story shouted that this confrontation might be a turning point in the war. She folded the paper and restlessly ran her hands through her hair. Mary was frightened.

On Sundays people prayed in church and talked endlessly in the restaurants about the conflict. When Robert's letters stopped coming, Mary found it even more difficult to hear people speculate about what was happening at the front. Many nights she cried herself to sleep, worrying that Robert might be caught in the crossfire. Maybe he had been hit . . . trapped . . . pinned down . . . captured.

Mary finally decided to call the chaplain who had contacted her about Robert's appendectomy, and she made the thirty-minute drive to the base to talk with the major. Mary cleared security at the gate and drove onto the base. Because of her previous trips, she knew where the chapel was located and quickly found the chaplain in a white board chapel near the center of the base. He was sitting in his office, which was located in the front of the building.

The chaplain welcomed her to his office. "Come in, Miss McCoy. Nice of you to come and see me." The room was meagerly decorated, with scant furniture scattered around. "Please take a seat."

"You remember me?" Mary smiled.

"Of course." The major pulled a chair in front of his desk for her and hurried around to sit down. "You're the young lady who came to see Lieutenant Walker in the hospital." The officer pursed his lips and frowned. "A difficult time for a young pilot. Your visits proved to be most helpful."

"Thank you." Mary forced a smile. "Glad to know that I did some good." She cleared her throat and wrung her hands. "I have another reason for coming today. As time went by, Robert and I became—how shall I say it?—much closer."

"Yes." Chaplain Miles nodded. "I understand."

"And then almost overnight, the army sent him to Europe. His leaving came so quickly that eight hours after he told me, Robert was gone."

"Happens like that," Miles said. "Hard on everyone, but many times the army's security demands quick action."

"That's exactly what Robert said."

"Certainly." The chaplain's face suddenly took on an obviously forced smile. "How far along are you now, Miss McCoy?"

"Beg your pardon?"

"I'm talking about your problem."

"My problem? You mean our problem."

"Yes, of course." The chaplain stiffened. "But you obviously carry the weight of this issue."

"The weight?" Mary nervously pushed her hair back. "You mean because Robert's disappeared?"

"Disappeared! I think that I'm missing something here."

"I came today because Robert seems to have vanished. I haven't heard from him for, well, over a month."

The chaplain took a deep breath. "Ohh, I see." He cleared his throat. "Yes, I see where you're coming from . . . now."

"I need your help, sir." Mary bit her lip. "I'm deeply concerned."

"Most certainly." The man sank back into his chair and looked out the window as a bomber taxied across the field. "Well! I'm going to have to do some searching." He scratched his head. "I'll have to find his file, his records. Maybe, just maybe, I can get some other addresses for you. Could I call you back in a week?"

"Thank you so much." Mary smiled. "I'd be ever so grateful for any leads you might give me."

The chaplain immediately stood. "I'll call you the second I have information."

Mary returned home, but the chaplain didn't call within a week, or two weeks. Three weeks later he sent her a letter.

Dear Miss McCoy,

The United States Army regretfully must inform you that Lieutenant Robert Walker is missing in action. We have no details that can be shared except to report that his airplane was shot down while flying over the European war theater.

You might find some consolation by speaking with his mother, Mrs. Samuel Mills, who lives in Pasadena, California. I believe you can locate her telephone through information.

Please accept my personal condolences in this matter.

Sincerely,
Chaplain Raymond Miles

Mary's hand shook as she read the letter for the third time. She folded it carefully and put it back in the envelope. It felt and sounded as sterile and removed as she'd found Chaplain Miles to be. No help there.

Impulsively Mary grabbed the telephone off the kitchen wall and put in what she knew would be an expensive phone call. Ten minutes later a California woman answered the phone.

"Mrs. Mills?" Mary asked.

"Yes." The woman sounded very far off.

"I'm looking for a Mrs. Samuel Mills who has a son that

is a pilot in the U.S. Air Force. A Lieutenant Robert Walker."

"Who is this?" The woman's voice turned harsh, and the pleasantness disappeared.

"My name is Mary McCoy. I am a . . . very close friend of Robert's. I live in Kansas."

"I see." She sounded tentative and almost angry.

"Mrs. Mills, I have received a notice from the army that Robert is missing in action and—"

"Yes, I know," the woman cut Mary off.

"I am very concerned. You don't know me, Mrs. Mills, but—"

"No, I don't know you, and I never heard Robert speak of you. I am sorry, but I don't make many friends and am cautious about any phone calls that I receive under these circumstances."

"Of course." Mary tried to keep her voice from sounding strained. "I simply wondered if there was anything that you could tell me."

"I'm sorry, but I can't. Thank you for calling." Mrs. Samuel Mills hung up. The line went dead.

Mary stared at the receiver and then hung up the telephone. The quietness sounded like death.

Mary was shocked. Mrs. Mills hadn't asked Mary to phone her again, and she clearly sounded like she didn't want Mary ever to do so. Either the woman was extremely strange or something else was wrong.

Oklahoma, February 2000

Five and a half decades had passed. Long ago Mary had lost the address of Robert's mother, who, like Robert, had dissolved into thin air. Mary looked down at her kitchen table.

Mary kept staring at the tabletop and tried to make the entire story fit together in her mind, seeking lost pieces still floating around in the past. She gaped at the shiny vinyl tabletop as if she could stare holes through the bright surface. The longer Mary looked, the more the layers of her past peeled back, revealing the doubts and lingering feelings that were waiting underneath. Dimensions of Robert's story drifted back. After thirty minutes, Mary felt a tear run down her cheek.

Mary brushed the tear away, but more followed. Soon the side of her face was wet, and her silent weeping wouldn't stop. She began crying harder and more loudly. Pain poured from her eyes. Mary began to shake violently, and her anguish exploded with quick, whimpering cries. She could not stop, and she cradled herself with her arms across her chest.

After several minutes, Mary stopped and caught her breath. A chilling realization settled over her. She had been crying as if she had just gotten the letter telling her that Robert Walker had died in combat yesterday . . . rather than having disappeared fifty-six years ago.

Sixteen ~

Mary shut the door to her old Oldsmobile and started across the church parking lot. Saint Stephen's Episcopal Church had stood on the corner of Tenth Street and Maple long before the Olivers moved to town. The high steeple of the red brick building towered over all the other structures in town. Whether people attended or not, they knew the place. No one could miss it. Over the years the venerable old church had become one of Burlington's most important landmarks. Mary guessed the present structure was built in the early 1920s. While the town wasn't large, the congregation remained one of the largest in the area. Mary and George had attended services there virtually every Sunday since they moved into the town more than twenty years ago. The plain wooden front door welcomed Mary like an old friend bidding her to enter.

"Good morning, Ann." Mary pushed open the office door and spoke to the receptionist.

"Mary!" Ann Trimble turned around from her computer. "Great to see you."

"Good to see you, Ann." Mary smiled politely. "I'm supposed to talk with the pastor. Is he in?"

"Sure." Ann reached for the phone and dialed Reverend Ed Owens. "Father Ed? Mary Oliver's here to see you." She listened several seconds and hung up the phone. "Just go on back. He's expecting you."

Mary trudged down the narrow hall toward the pastor's offices at the back of Saint Stephen's administrative wing. She knew without looking the names of all the former rectors whose pictures lined the wall. Every time she walked this drab hall, Mary thought that someone ought to take down the portraits and donate new carpet. The old gray hunk of wool had more miles on it than any carpet should, and most of the rectors were ugly old coots anyway.

When Pastor Ed Owens had first come to town, Mary and George hadn't been too excited, but ten years had passed and she'd become one of Ed's biggest fans. He'd done a good job at George's funeral and had kept an eye on her to make sure she was recovering in an acceptable manner. Always on a first-name basis, Ed helped her when matters got sticky, but Mary worried that he might not understand why this problem bothered her so much.

"Mary! Come in." The pastor stood when Mary walked into his office. Ed's stomach hung over his belt, and his hair was thinning. He looked like a rather typical small-town rector.

"Sit down." He came around his desk quickly and offered her a padded antique maroon office chair. His tight clerical collar made his neck seem larger. "Glad you came by today." He sat down in front of his desk. "Always good to talk to you, Mary. How's your heart doing?"

"Oh, just fine." Mary sat on the edge of the chair. "I simply needed to chat with you a while, Ed." Mary glanced around the room at the book-filled shelves. The man had enough books to cover any problem she could ever have. "Need your perspective."

"Worth what it costs you." Ed laughed. "Andrea got back to Denver okay?"

"Oh, yes. Fine. She's been gone nearly a week now. Flew home. We had a fine time together."

Ed smiled. "It's always great to have the children come and spend a few days. Our daughter will be home from college for spring break in another month or so." He winked. "Means even more to have them go back after a few days." Ed laughed.

Mary forced a smile. "I need to tell you a story, Pastor." Mary looked at the carpeted floor for a second, trying to organize her thoughts. *The person who fixes the hall rug should donate carpet for this room as well,* she thought. Mary took a deep breath. "I'm afraid it will take a little while to tell you my story."

"Take as long as you wish." Ed relaxed in his desk chair. "I'm here to listen. Got all afternoon."

"Let me start at the first." Mary launched into her story, describing the diary, yearbooks, and letters that Andrea had uncovered in the garage. Mary had no trouble covering the details and gave the pastor a general picture of her college years as well as how she came to teach at Sterling College. After ten minutes, she explained who Robert Walker was and how he vanished. Almost immediately Mary was surprised by how emotional she became. Simply talking about Robert caused the past to come to life and shook her. "The whole situation is very upsetting to me." Tears welled up in her eyes, and she reached for a handkerchief.

"Let me see if I understand you correctly." Ed rubbed his chin. "This is a man who's been gone for over five decades but has, in a way, come back to life for you? As you wrote about him, you were emotionally overpowered. Have I got that much right?"

Mary felt her stomach churn. Listening to the pastor's description of what happened made her feel uncomfortable and crazy, but his explanation made her even more emotional. She could only nod.

"And your trying to write about this Robert Walker person causes more sadness to follow?"

"Uh-huh." Tears started down her cheeks, and Mary sniffed. "I know that I sound a little, a little foolish." Mary choked. "But that's why I'm here, Ed. I don't understand why, after all these years, I would feel more emotional about this man than I did when he disappeared! It's like . . . like he died yesterday morning!"

The pastor nodded understandingly. "Mary, significant

events in our past that have touched us deeply don't simply disappear. You obviously cared a great deal for Robert. I sense that you've gotten back in touch with feelings you didn't let yourself experience years ago."

"I need to tell you something that isn't pleasant to hear about George." Mary caught her breath. "My husband." She exhaled deeply. "He always seemed to be threatened by Robert. They never met, and George only knew the little that I told him about Robert, but he insisted that I never mention Robert again. I suppose after we had a confrontation about my old boyfriend, I pushed everything out of my mind. After George's death, I realized that I hadn't let myself even think about what had happened to Robert." Her tears made her stop and blow her nose. "I just buried the story." She sniffed and shrugged. "I know that Robert must have died in the Battle of the Bulge." Mary took a deep breath. "I guess that I thought my unspoken conclusion was the end of the matter." Mary bit her lip. "It wasn't."

"No, your emotions didn't agree," the pastor observed. "They went on hold for quite a while but didn't stop working. This old relationship is still alive in you, Mary."

Mary began weeping again. "Isn't this strange?" She dabbed her eyes with a handkerchief. "A grown woman crying about a dead boyfriend from eons past? I think I'm nuts."

"No." Ed shook his head. "Not at all. Everyone at some time or another has the strange experience of going back to a place in their past and knowing deep, strong feelings about what's there. Sometimes we're nearly overwhelmed by the scope of what is still alive in us."

"Makes me feel absolutely crazy." Mary kept wiping her eyes. "Ridiculous!" She blew her nose again.

Ed squeezed her hand. "Mary, I'd go home and read that diary, write what you're thinking and feeling. You don't have to show the material to anyone, but you do need to let your emotions come out. Grief has been buried inside you for decades. Let yourself grieve over this man. It's truly okay."

"Grieve?"

Ed nodded. "My sense of what you're telling me is that Robert died and you didn't allow yourself the opportunity to let those old feelings settle. Consider what would have happened if, when George died, we'd never had a funeral? Think about how you might feel if you'd never viewed his body." The pastor paused and let his suggestions sink in. "I believe you'd feel rather strange today. Disconnected. Probably have a hard time believing he had died. Right?"

"I guess. Just never thought about it in that light." Mary looked at the gray rug again and shook her head. "All of this seems so strange to me."

"You're experiencing what is called displaced grief, Mary. Why don't you go home and attempt to let yourself feel the loss? My hunch is that, after a few days, your feelings will settle down and that everything will get back into place." He nodded his head. "The whole experience may turn out to be extremely valuable for you. Think of this time as making peace with the past."

Mary patted her cheek with a tissue and dried her eyes again. "Ed, I've simply never lived through one of these episodes. I guess what you're telling me makes sense. I'll certainly try to do what you said."

"Give yourself a week or so. Work on what you're writing for your grandchildren. Don't feel bad about whatever comes up. Let it happen. Experience the old feelings and go on to the next issue that life gives you."

"Thank you, Ed." She stood up. "I'll give it a try and see what happens." Mary started to the door. "I'll let you know what develops."

"Good, Mary. I know you'll be okay. Things *will* get better."

She waved feebly and walked down the long hall, using her cane to steady her gait, trudging past the gallery of former pastors, not feeling quite as irritable. Just more broken.

Seventeen

Mary Oliver looked across the kitchen table and muttered to herself, "Every letter that I sent in 1945 was returned." She ran her hand over the pile. "They're all here."

She glanced at the clock on her stove. Two o'clock. Since her talk with Pastor Ed three days earlier, Mary had read her entire diary six times. Scattered across the kitchen table in front of her was everything she still had that once was associated with Robert. One question remained: How had Robert died?

Father Ed Owens was seldom wrong, but this time he hadn't been correct. Far from leveling out, the issue was growing in importance.

Mary remembered that shortly after the first of that year everything had come back, marked UNOPENED, RETURN TO SENDER, or ADDRESS UNKNOWN. Not one letter indicated that anyone knew what had become of Lieutenant

Walker. "Missing in action" was the final communication from the War Department.

Mary turned to the last page of writing in her old diary, in which many empty pages still remained. She picked up her pencil and wrote on the top of the first blank page, "February 10, 2000: Reflections." For a moment she compared her present handwriting with her style decades earlier. The former writing appeared bolder and more assertive, but anyone would have known that the same person wrote both pages.

She picked up the pencil again and began writing a sketchy description of her feelings, thoughts, and frustrations, detailing the overwhelming task of finding how this man vanished. She wrote no more than half a page, then stopped. Mary shut the little gilded diary and pushed it away. The clock only said 3:00 P.M.

Three days later Mary Oliver returned to Father Ed Owens's office. They talked for a few minutes about her heart condition and a few small matters around the church. Mary sensed that his cordiality only marked time until it was appropriate to get down to the real business of the day: what had become of Robert Walker?

"You're probably wondering how I've done emotionally since I was last here," Mary said.

"Yes. How have things gone?"

"Not well."

"Really?" The pastor looked surprised. "Sorry to hear that."

"This diary business has truly thrown me for a loop." Mary shook her head. "The kids would say that I'm not a happy camper." She rolled her eyes.

Ed rubbed his chin and studied her face, saying nothing.

"I can't seem to get this problem out of my mind, but I'm not doing much to solve it either," she confessed and pushed her hair back with her hand. "I feel upset most of the time."

Ed kept rubbing his cheek and pulling at his chin. "The man disappeared, you say?"

Mary nodded.

The pastor drummed on the arm of his chair for several moments. "Hmm." He looked out his window. "I wonder . . ."

Mary didn't know what to say. She sat there looking bewildered at the minister.

"Mary," Ed spoke softly and slowly, "something occurred to me after you left last week. I've thought about this a number of times since then. Maybe it's an irrelevant question, but I don't remember you telling me the answer when we talked last week."

"Yes?"

"How do you know that Robert Walker is dead?"

The question struck Mary with the force of a lightning bolt. "What else would he be?" she mumbled.

"Just because you didn't hear from the man doesn't mean that he died."

Mary blinked several times. "I don't think I understand."

"Many things could have occurred. He might have been injured for a long time. He could have had amnesia." The pastor held up his hands as if preparing her for what he was going to say. "Possibly, he decided the easiest way to end his relationship with you was . . . to never contact you again."

Mary stared.

Ed shrugged. "Mary, you're a lovely person, and I hate to tell you, but people do things like this every day of the week."

Mary swallowed hard. How did she know? No one ever told her that Robert was dead. The assumption had grown out of that pile of old letters. She had simply believed that he was dead.

"Am I making any sense?" Ed smiled gently. "What I'm wondering is, what if the man's still alive?"

Mary put her hand to her cheek. *Alive? Robert Walker?* She felt like the wind had been knocked out of her.

Ed looked at her, waiting for her to respond.

"Alive?" Mary finally said softly. "From the beginning I thought Robert was injured or captured, but my conclusion simply grew up by itself. I assumed he was dead. No one told me."

"Could it be that you've been looking at the wrong end of things? Is it possible you've looked back about five decades too far?"

"But, but where would I look to find out?"

"I've got a hunch that the Record Management Center for the Department of Veterans would be able to help you. They keep good records of what happened to people who served in our military overseas. Did you ever contact them?"

Mary shook her head. "Never heard of them."

"I think there's an office in St. Louis. You could call information and get their number. See what they can tell you."

Mary thought about the letters. Each had a number that matched Robert's ID tags. She knew where he'd been stationed before going to Europe as well as the military base near Dover, England. As a matter of fact, she knew a great deal about him.

Ed rubbed his chin again. "I had a cousin who liked to work on tracing her family history. She found many ways to ferret out information. Used to tell me that some of this military stuff was the easiest material to get if you knew how to go about it. What do you think, Mary?"

The shock of discovering that Robert could still be alive had undone everything in her. Mary's only response was to nod.

"Why don't you work on this angle and see where it takes you?"

Mary swallowed again. "I just believed he was dead," she said again. "Robert Walker might be alive somewhere in this country," she said incredulously.

"If he is," Ed said, "I'd bet you'll find him."

Mary pushed back from the pastor's desk and stared at the dull carpet for a moment. "I'll try," she said and forced a smile. "I will certainly try." When she left minutes later, she felt unstrung. She marched resolutely down the hall, not seeing anything around her.

Eighteen ~

The cold winter night settled in quickly after the sun went down, but Mary's mind wasn't on the evening twilight. She kept returning to her conversation with the minister earlier that day. Could Robert Walker still be alive?

A television program droned on in the background, but Mary stared at the fire. She watched the smoke and flames curl up the blackened stone hearth and float up the chimney. The crackling and popping of the burning logs drew her away from the moment at hand and into a world that was gone. As wood turned to ash, old memories came to life again. The constant depression of the past week disappeared, and Mary felt a growing sense of intrigue and curiosity. Another memory came to mind.

A year had passed after all communications with Robert ended, and Mary remembered how difficult and painful each of those months had been. The Sterling community was sympathetic with anyone facing her difficulties. People gave her kind words of encouragement, and the college students seemed concerned. The love of her friends sustained her.

Then George Oliver abruptly appeared out of nowhere. She remembered seeing him first at the church one Sunday, and then he showed up again during coffee time when the regular members were encouraging college students to become involved with the church's program. One minute she was standing in the corner, watching people talk; the next minute George was next to her, finding out who she was, flirting, smiling like a used-car salesman closing in on an indecisive customer.

With the persistence of a bulldog, George hounded Mary constantly after that Sunday. Going to a movie, eating out, or taking a drive, he seemed omnipresent. Eventually a relationship began. Mary didn't mention Robert but sensed that George knew far more about her than she did of him. George picked up every possible detail about her life from across the community. As the weeks went by, he showed up more and more often.

One spring evening Mary recognized that decisions had to be made. The war in Europe would be over soon. Robert was gone and would never be coming back. Over time, she had become fond of George. The man worked hard, went to church on Sunday, and they had much in common. Even though she wasn't passionately in love with him, they could build a good life together. Only one recourse seemed open before her. Mary decided to accept the proposal of marriage that would surely come shortly.

Three months after the marriage, Mary realized she was pregnant. George was ecstatic, and life certainly appeared to be going down the right path. The pregnancy unfolded without problems, and life in Sterling became much better. The college appreciated her work; George seemed happy most of the time if the subject of Robert didn't come up. What more could she ask?

~

As Mary gazed into the fire, an old incident suddenly returned. She had been seven months along in her pregnancy at the time. They'd had a few bad incidents, but she had gritted her teeth and gone on. George had changed jobs and was doing well in a promising new company called Kim-Co. The war was over, and business was booming and soldiers were returning. Because of her condition, Mary hadn't been teaching, and her delivery date wasn't far away. On that morning she had needed some thread for a dress she was making and decided to walk to the downtown business area in Sterling to pick up a few things.

The weather felt wonderful, and she thought a walk would help her condition. Mary put on a light topcoat that certainly couldn't conceal how very pregnant she was. She giggled at her huge stomach in the full-length mirror. Not much time left before delivery. Mary started down the street at a good clip, exercising her legs and making her blood flow. People waved and nodded when she passed by. The world felt good.

Six blocks from the Oliver house, the business area with shops and stores opened up on Main Street. Mary walked down the street toward the mercantile store where she always purchased thread and cloth. Halfway down the block, she had the strange feeling that someone might be watching her. She didn't feel threatened, but sensed a person was staring . . . somewhere . . . She kept walking, looking at everyone in front of her. No one seemed to be paying her the slightest bit of attention. Perhaps someone behind her might be watching from some hidden corner, but she didn't want to turn around quickly and appear obvious.

Just ahead she saw a green metal can standing at the edge of the sidewalk. Mary felt in her pocket and discovered an old candy-bar wrapper. She stopped at the trash can, dropped the wrapper in, and looked back over her shoulder.

Across Main Street a man was sitting in a 1940 Chevrolet, staring at her. Mary turned around and kept going. He wore a hat pulled down low, and his face couldn't be seen well. Yet she had seen enough. A cold realization ran up her spine. She would swear that man looked like Robert Walker!

Mary caught her breath and swallowed hard. It couldn't be! Yet, he looked *exactly* like Robert. She shook her head. Surely not! By the time she reached the corner a half-block away, Mary knew that she couldn't let things remain as they were.

Mary abruptly stopped and turned around. To her shock, the car was gone. One minute the man was staring, the next he was gone! For a second she felt like a cold knife had cut through her a second time. She'd walked only a few feet, but the man had vanished!

Mary caught her breath, and her hand grabbed her side. She realized just how pregnant she must look. From a distance she had to look like a moving barn. If the man had been Robert Walker, he had seen her obvious condition. Mary felt dizzy and lightheaded. She leaned against the light pole on the corner and breathed hard.

Mary stood on that street corner for maybe ten minutes. Cars came and went, but she neither waved nor spoke to anyone. She eventually concluded that what she thought she had seen was a mistake. She turned and crossed the street, fighting the nagging idea that the man had been Robert Walker.

Now as she remembered the incident, Mary looked up at the big picture of George over the mantel. What in the world would he have done that day if he had known Robert had come to see her in Sterling?

The recollection heightened her sense that Father Owens was right. Robert was alive. She'd made a vow before God and the people in that little church in Sterling to be faithful and true to George. She'd kept the course, often with great pain and struggle. No one could fault her, but that day was done; it had died the day they placed George in the ground.

In the morning, she'd call St. Louis.

Nineteen

The warm April sunlight beamed through Mary Oliver's kitchen windows, and the struggle of her winter heart attack felt long behind her as spring began. Pain in her chest came and went every now and then, but she definitely felt better. Mary looked at the letter lying in front of her from the Record Management Center for the Department of Veterans in St. Louis and for the third time read the letter that had come a week ago. The letter explained that they did have a record of the service of Robert Walker. To her shock, the story of Walker's military career ran from September 23, 1942, through his retirement from the Air Force on March 9, 1960. Mary stared at the data on Robert's chronological listing of dates. He had been a prisoner of war from December 1944 through the spring of 1945, but Robert Walker had not returned home to live in the United States. The report indicated that he had continued to fly over Europe until 1951. For reasons that made no sense to her, Robert appeared to have lived in Europe after the war, doing some kind of work for the military.

In 1951, the report said Walker had gone to Tokyo, Japan, where he served with the Air Force for another three years before being sent back to Washington, D.C., where he seemed to have worked around the Pentagon.

"I just don't understand it," Mary said to herself. "Everything seems so strange . . . and yet so right."

Mary picked up the card that had come in today's mail. After she discovered how to contact the Record Management Center, Mary found that the center would share Walker's record of service but not give her any indication of where he lived. Any mail sent to Robert would be forwarded to him without disclosing his address. In turn, she had sent a letter to Robert but requested that the post office send her a certification that her letter was received by Walker. In this April morning's mail, the green slip had come back from the local post office confirming that Robert Walker had indeed received her letter. The slip said he got his mail in a little town not too far from Washington, D.C. Robert Walker was alive and living in Chaptico, Maryland!

Mary turned the postal form over and over. More than fifty-six years had passed since she'd heard from this man. Both of them had lived a lifetime filled with friends, children, marriage, a host of things that turned living into life. At least Mary had, and she assumed the same was true for

Robert. Surely his life had been as good as hers had been. Maybe better.

Mary thought back over the many years she'd lived with her husband. George Oliver had been a strange man. He liked to give the image of a highly successful negotiator and businessman. Although glib and quick to say anything that sounded clever to him, he made enemies and never realized how uncomfortable his assertive flirtations made women feel.

She'd never been sure of what George really did when all the doors were closed. Maybe he was faithful, maybe he wasn't. She had no reason to accuse him of anything more than being insensitive and overly aggressive. Nevertheless, he'd embarrassed Mary and made her nervous more times than she could count, and he left the appearance of being a womanizer. In the end, life with George Oliver proved to be more uncomfortable than she wanted to think about. He was dead and gone, taking all her suspicions with him to the grave. The past was gone, finished, done with. Today was a new day.

Mary sipped her mug of coffee and looked out the window. The constant Oklahoma wind blew the winter's leaves across her yard, and she knew that in the near future someone would have to do a great deal of raking to get ready for the spring Bermuda grass to come back. Probably there'd be a neighborhood boy around who needed a couple of bucks. Yet she no longer had much interest in the flowers and plants. Mary had one thing on her mind. She wanted to find out who lived in Chaptico, Maryland. Was the man *her* Robert Walker?

Mary took her cane from the side of the table and stood

up. She'd heard about this new service at the town library that allowed people to use their local computer system to access information all over the world. All she needed was a little help to get started, and this was the moment. If ever there was a time that she needed what she'd heard this system could produce, it was now. Surely someone would show her how to use this newfangled piece of equipment.

Within minutes, Mary pulled up her Oldsmobile in front of the library. She marched in with total confidence that there shouldn't be any problem. After a little help from the librarian, and thirty minutes later, Mary was at the place on the Internet that she needed to be.

Within a couple of minutes, the screen filled with information about Chaptico, Maryland. It was an old colonial town of around thirteen hundred citizens surrounded by many residential areas that made for a much larger local population. The data indicated that the Roman Catholics and Anglicans had fought it out there more than three centuries earlier. The place sounded quaint and filled with interesting little side streets. A nice place for a spring visit. In fact, an excellent town for an *immediate* visit.

Mary held the telephone tightly against her ear and listened to the travel agent explain. She shook her head as the woman talked. "Yes," Mary said dogmatically, "I need to go to Washington, D.C., in two days, and I know a ticket is available."

"It's not that, Mary," the travel agent argued. "You're talking quite a bit of money, flying so quickly and all. Can't you simply wait a week?"

Mary shook her head. "I've made up my mind, Alice. I want to leave the day after tomorrow and fly from Oklahoma City. I'd hoped to have a little time to get up to the city before the airplane took off, but I'll do whatever is necessary."

"I know about that trouble you had several months ago. I was just concerned that you would feel—"

"Alice," Mary warned. "Either you write me this ticket or I'll go back to the computer and come up with my own arrangements. Ya hear?"

"Okay, okay. Let me work on the best schedule, and I'll call you back in about ten minutes."

"Thank you." Mary crisply dropped the receiver into the phone cradle. "You'd think I wanted to go up there and see the president or something, don't you know." She hobbled out of the living room and back into the kitchen.

Mary plopped down in a chair by the round kitchen table and ran her hands nervously through her hair. *Never done anything like this in my life. Rent a car and all that! Heaven help me. I'll have to drive through that terrible traffic up there. Terrifies me just to think about it.*

Her mind went into neutral, and Mary stared out the window at the clouds rising over the trees. Before long the tornadoes and the spring rains would be coming. Life was so predictable in Burlington. Flying off to find this unheard-of town called Chaptico didn't fit what anyone did in a small Oklahoma town.

From the Internet map it looked like she'd have to drive across Highway 50 going to Annapolis, then take a toll road across the Chesapeake Bay and go north up toward Chestertown to find that little town. It couldn't be too far away from the Bay, maybe an hour's drive or so. Other than too many cars driving down the highway, Mary felt sure she'd have no trouble getting there.

The phone rang. She jumped.

"Hello?"

"It's Alice. I got everything lined up, but I tell you the price on these tickets is—"

"Thank you," Mary cut her off. "I'll drive over and pick them up this afternoon."

"Oh, don't do that. I'll bring them by your house on my way home from the office."

"Whatever is the most convenient for you, Alice."

"Mary, I'm not trying to be an old maid, but I have to ask if you've talked with your daughter, Andrea, about making such a long trip. After all—"

"Yes, Alice. You *are* being an old maid. I'll look forward to seeing you shortly after five." Mary hung up and smiled.

Twenty ~

WASHINGTON D.C., APRIL 2000

The American Airlines plane came in for a smooth landing at Dulles Airport and pulled to a stop on the runway. A large vehicle drew up to the side of the airplane, and the exit door opened. Passengers hurried into the large metal buggy and a few minutes later filed into the terminal. Mary hustled along as fast as her cane would carry her, and in fifteen minutes was sitting in a car rental agency with keys in hand. She looked out at the small Ford and wondered if she'd lost her mind. Never before had she done anything like this.

"Your car's ready, ma'am." The service attendant pointed to the red car. "You can take a right turn out the back and be on your way to Highway 50."

Mary looked into his dark black eyes. "You sure that car's safe?"

"The Ford?" The boy laughed. "You got to be kiddin'."

Mary shook her head and smiled. "Just want to make sure."

"You're ready to roll whenever you want. I'll put your bags in the backseat."

"Thank you." Mary slipped him a couple of dollars. "I'm sure that I'll be fine." She carefully walked down the steps to the parking lot.

Chaptico, Maryland

After an hour and a half of strenuous driving and a few hair-raising moments, Mary pulled into the outskirts of the small town of Chaptico, Maryland. The long bridge across the Chesapeake Bay at Annapolis had bothered her, as had the press of traffic, but the pressure proved bearable. Only a sign seemed to separate the town from the housing sections surrounding the village. The village still looked like a page out of a Washington Irving story. The streets looked old, with giant oak trees in front of the colonial houses. Some side streets were brick. Everywhere she looked, Mary saw white houses with large columns holding up little porches. She rolled down the window and felt the crisp air. Even though it was April, the air still felt cold enough that it might snow that night.

In the center of the town, Mary found a large, old-fashioned square, much like the one she remembered years ago in Sterling. A large band shell dominated the dry, grassy area, and it looked like a place where people might come in summertime to listen to concerts.

She drove around the square. No one waved, but the town

felt warm and inviting. A nice place. Must be dripping with history. Somebody had to know about Robert Walker. He couldn't be living far from the center of downtown.

Mary pulled up in front of a small grocery store and pulled the key from the ignition. The sign above the door read THE CAPTAIN'S TABLE: GROCERIES AND SPIRITS. She was seventy-eight and should be concerned about wandering somewhere she'd never even visited before. Possibly she ought to worry about falling. Breaking a leg. Having another heart attack. Real possibilities, but then again something could happen in Oklahoma. Being in Maryland didn't make the problem any more or less likely!

Mary adjusted her glasses and looked at her reflection in the rearview mirror. She'd come a long way from the college art teacher she had been. The years registered in her eyes, and the wrinkles in her face. Maybe she *should* have called Andrea and talked the trip over with her. On the other hand, Andrea would have wanted to come, and who knows what that would have meant?

Robert Walker had received her note several days ago. He hadn't called or written. Maybe he was married and had a lovely wife at his side. If so, she'd shake hands, wish them the best, and be gone. Then again, Robert's wife might have died. Maybe she'd left him. Who knew? Mary's first task was to find out where the man lived, and the grocery store seemed like a good place to start.

Mary walked in and casually made her way around the place. The building was at least two hundred years old and decorated to look like George Washington could be shopping in the next aisle. The place was small but was a nice, country market with a large produce department. "Natural" seemed to be the theme of most of the items in the store.

She ambled back to a counter loaded with apples, oranges, grapes, and lettuce. For a few moments, Mary picked through the produce until she found a couple of apples that looked like they'd suit her taste. She put them in a little plastic sack and started looking for a clerk old enough to know the community. A teenage boy was stocking shelves, but he was probably too young to be of help. A middle-aged woman, maybe in her fifties, stood behind a cash register. Mary watched her talk with people for several minutes. The woman seemed to know everybody and talked with them as if they were her good friends. The grocery checker appeared to be exactly what Mary was looking for.

"Good afternoon. See you found our apples." The lady smiled.

"They looked very good." Mary returned the smile.

"You'll like them. They recently came in from Florida." The clerk picked up the apples and put them on her scale.

"You've lived here long?" Mary asked.

"Actually, I was born in Chestertown," the grocery checker said. "Been around this little town virtually my whole life."

"How interesting!" Mary beamed. "Seems like such a nice little place."

"Well, we're actually not very small. Don't have many people living in Chaptico proper, but the area is just crawling with folk. We seem to get bigger every year. People are moving in like we're going to have a housing shortage."

"So it's possible to live here quite awhile and still be a stranger?" Mary frowned.

"Afraid so. Many of these people are so transient that they go through in a hurry. That's the way the world's become. Used to be that folk stayed where they moved in."

Mary forced a smile. "You're right. Times certainly have changed."

The lady rang up the cost of the two apples. "Anything else?"

Mary pushed a few coins across the counter. "Actually there is. I'm looking for an old friend who lived here for some time. Have you ever heard of anyone with the name of Robert Walker?"

"Walker? Colonel Walker?"

"Colonel?"

"That's what we called him because he was an old Air Force pilot."

"Yes! That's exactly who I'm looking for. Would you have any idea where he lives?"

The woman rubbed her chin. "I think he lived about five or six blocks from here." She scratched her head. "Just a minute." She turned around and pushed a button on a small microphone. "Jim? You up there?"

"Yes," a distant voice answered.

"I need the address of the colonel? You know. Bob Walker. Got a phone book?"

"Just a minute."

"That's our manager," the woman explained. "His office is in the back, and he keeps the phone book in there. Afraid that I'll sneak a peek." She laughed.

"I can't tell you how much I appreciate your help," Mary said. "You're saving me a world of trouble."

"Glad to do it."

"Marge?" the voice on the intercom boomed. "The phone book says it's 2356 Easton Street. Around the corner and two blocks over."

"Hey, thanks." The clerk flipped the microphone off.

Mary grabbed a pencil and scribbled the address on a piece of paper sitting on the counter. "Just a few blocks from here, you say?"

"Sure. You turn at the corner at the end of the square and go two blocks. Easton turns off that street, and you go to the right."

"Wonderful!" Mary beamed. "You have certainly been helpful."

"My pleasure. Have a nice visit."

Mary picked up the apples and started toward the door.

"Marge!" the man's voice echoed from the intercom. "Why you looking for old Bob Walker?"

The cashier turned around and pushed the button. "I'm not. A customer is looking for him."

Mary stopped and turned around, listening to their conversation.

"Don't send her to the house," the man demanded. "Remember? Old Walker's in the hospital."

Twenty-One

CHAPTICO, MARYLAND, APRIL 2000

With the directions to the hospital clearly fastened in her mind, Mary Oliver left the grocery store and drove in the opposite direction from where Robert Walker's house should be. She took the street at the opposite end of the square and went up the highway toward Chestertown. Approximately ten miles later, she saw a large three-story brick building ahead. The sign on the side of the road said it was a hospital. Mary slowed down and pulled into the parking lot.

The building looked like it was about fifty years old and had probably been built at the end of World War II, when no one expected the growth the area had known in recent years. She could see that a wing had been built on the back to allow for increased capacity, but the place kept the same quaint country look as the town of Chaptico.

Mary found a parking place near the front door and

turned off the engine and sat quietly. Robert was in that building on one of those three floors. Suddenly she realized that in her joy at finding out where her Robert Walker was, she'd overlooked asking if he was married. She was about to walk inside without the slightest idea whether she'd find one or two people. Mary felt very old and out of place. She clutched her cane tightly.

What in the world was she doing? More than half a century ago, she'd had a relationship with this man who then disappeared. Probably the whole time they were together meant absolutely nothing to him. Maybe he wouldn't remember her. She swallowed hard and clutched the handle of her cane more tightly. Perhaps she ought to get back in the car and drive to the airport. Just forget all this nonsense. The intelligent thing to do was go back to Oklahoma and dispense with this bizarre set of circumstances.

But then again . . .

The worst that could happen would be that the Walkers would tell her that she'd wandered into an unwelcome situation. Quite possibly Robert would be interested in what had become of her. A polite conversation wouldn't harm anyone. She needed to go ahead and find out how he was doing in this place. After all, she'd paid a considerable amount of money for the airplane ticket. Mary shut the car door and walked determinedly forward.

"Can I help you?" a nice lady asked at the reception desk.

"I'm looking for a patient. His name is Walker. Robert Walker."

"Oh yes." The receptionist smiled. "Bob is upstairs." She

punched the keys on her computer. "Let's see . . . yes . . . 212. He's in room 212. The elevator is just ahead of you."

"Thank you." Mary clutched her cane securely and walked slowly toward the elevator about thirty feet away. Her heart beat increasingly faster, and for a second she felt dizzy. A sharp pain shot across her chest. She caught her breath and took hold of a doorknob. Mary fumbled through her purse until she found her nitroglycerin tablets. After about a minute, the pain subsided, but she still had to take a deep breath. She pushed the button on the elevator and the door opened.

Mary studied the wall signs on the second floor. She saw that room 212 had to be to her left. Walking at a snail's pace, she inched toward 212. The door was closed.

Mary looked around, but no nurse was in sight. She would have to open the door by herself. Maybe she shouldn't. What if Robert was embarrassingly indisposed? She knocked gently and then pushed the door open a crack. Mary put her eye to the opening and peeked in. She saw a man lying in the hospital bed under the sheets, but no one else was in the room. She couldn't see his head. Everything appeared to be in place. No reason not to go in.

She knocked slightly again and pushed the door open. The man in the bed didn't move. His back was turned away from the door, and the sheet almost covered his face. His snow-white hair was tousled against the pillow like a frenzied wig. Robert's hair had always been coal black. The whiteness took her aback, and for the first time Mary realized she hadn't let Robert age in her mind. He had to be much older than she'd allowed for.

With slow but definite steps, Mary shuffled forward, waiting for something to happen, but nothing did. She walked around to the far side of the bed to look at his face. He suddenly turned over without waking up. At the end of the bed was a strip of masking tape with *Bob Walker* written across the top. He had to be the man from her past.

Mary studied the face. The man had a double chin, and his cheeks sagged. Folds of skin came down over his eyes, and his hairline looked farther up his forehead than she remembered, but as Mary stared, another face shifted back into focus. Years ago in a military hospital, she had watched the other man wake up after an appendectomy. As Mary stared, this face slowly but surely became the face of Robert Walker. Time had worn the edges, but the center remained the same. Underneath the extra skin and the shifted layers of the chin, she could see the man she'd once loved. He *was* Robert Walker.

Mary settled into the chair and studied his face again. Robert had changed a great deal, and yet he was still the same person. Whatever time had done with either of them, an essence, a uniqueness, a substance of their personalities, remained. Something that had been him wasn't changed by time. The question was what time had done in this man's heart. She had no idea.

After about fifteen minutes, Robert moaned and rubbed his forehead. He opened his eyes. His eyes were still dark but edged with a lighter color. He stared at the ceiling without saying anything.

"Robert?" Mary said. "Robert, are you okay?"

He slowly turned his head. "Robert?" He blinked his eyes. "Most people call me Bob."

"Do you need anything?"

"No, no, I'm fine." Robert kept looking at the ceiling.

"Just checking."

"No one's called me Robert in a long time," he said.

"But that's your name."

"Yes, yes, it is." Robert turned his head slightly and glanced at Mary. "No one calls me that much these days."

"I guess they all call you Bob."

Walker nodded his head. "Yeah."

Mary took a deep breath. He looked frail. She'd lost weight after the heart attack, but Robert looked like the pounds had been worn off of him. The man was not in good health.

"You're with the hospital?" Robert asked.

"No," Mary said. "I'm here visiting."

"That's nice." Robert closed his eyes for a few moments. "You must be here from a local church."

"No. I came to see you."

Robert turned his head and looked at her. He blinked. "Thank you. That's nice."

Mary squinted. He didn't seem to have any look of recognition. Nothing about her had touched anything in him. Everything was gone.

"Do I know you?" Robert asked.

"You did once."

"Oh." Robert pushed farther up in bed. "You'll have to

forgive me. I don't have my glasses on, and I don't do very well without them. Can't see distances well."

"Your glasses!" Mary's hand came up to her mouth. "Of course! You need glasses to see me. Where are they? I'll get them for you."

Robert reached for the table beside the bed. "Just a moment. I'll find them in here somewhere." He opened the little drawer and reached inside. "Just a moment," he said again. Robert took out a pair of old wire glasses and put them on his nose. "Takes me a minute to get things into focus." He smiled. "Let's see. When did we meet?"

Mary scooted closer. "My name is Mary Oliver," she began. "I'm sure you won't know me by that name."

Robert squinted. "You used to have a different name?"

"Yes. When we knew each other, my name was Mary. Mary McCoy."

Twenty-Two

"Mary?" Robert Walker's mouth dropped. He shook his head. "Mary McCoy?"

"Yes." Mary smiled. "I, uh, I've changed a bit."

Walker took hold of both sides of his glasses and pushed them more tightly into his face. "I can't believe my eyes. Is it really you?"

"Afraid so." Mary tilted her head and shrugged. "I guess I've changed quite a bit."

"No!" Robert shook his head. "No." He rubbed the side of his face. "It's just that I didn't have any idea . . . I had no idea that you were coming." He looked around the hospital room as if trying to find something.

"You didn't get my letter?" Mary frowned.

"Your letter?" Walker shook his head. "No, I didn't get a letter. Of course, I've probably got a good patch of mail piled up at my home. I haven't seen my mail in several weeks."

Mary took a deep breath and put her hand over her mouth. "My goodness, I didn't even think about that possibility. Of course, my letter would be over there in Chaptico!" She shook her head. "Didn't even consider such a thing, don't you know. Well, I wrote you about a week ago."

"A week ago?" Robert's voice rose. "Can't believe it. Mary," he said again. "Here you are. In this room. After all these years."

Nothing was said for several moments. Silence hung heavily in the air. "We haven't seen each other for virtually five and a half decades," Mary finally said. "Quite awhile, wouldn't you say?"

Robert nodded his head and dropped back on his pillow. "Simply can't believe my eyes," he said more to himself. "After all these years," he mumbled to himself again, "here you are . . . again."

"I was concerned to know how you were doing," Mary said factually. "The last time that I saw you in Sterling, Kansas, you were a handsome young pilot getting ready to go to Europe." She reached over and flipped on a switch by the bed. A wall lamp came on with a soft, indirect glow above Robert's head. "You were going to make the world safe so we wouldn't have to worry about Hitler getting us. Remember?"

"Mary," Robert said and sat up again. "I can't believe my eyes. How are you? Really?"

"Some days I'm better than others. Now and then I have a few pains." Mary forced a smile. "I use a cane, as you can tell."

"Come closer," Robert beckoned. "I can't believe it's truly you."

Mary moved her chair even closer to the hospital bed. "I've put on some weight," she hedged. "Well, a lot of weight, and I know that my face sags somewhat. I probably don't look anything like I once did."

"Your hair hasn't changed a bit." Robert smiled. "Same red hair you always had. Just can't believe that I'm looking at you." He shook his head and took a deep breath. Robert looked pained and put his hand on his chest.

"You don't feel well, do you, Robert?"

Walker shook his head. "Things have been rough lately." Robert took another deep breath. "I've had a heart bypass operation, Mary. Five days ago the doctors replaced four of my blood vessels, and the pain has made it hard to sleep."

"Know what you mean." Mary shook her head. "Hurts, huh?"

"Other things as well," Robert added and looked away. His eyes clouded over. "Been a tough time."

Mary studied Robert's face carefully. Time had worn lines around the sides of his eyes and down his cheeks. The bags under Robert's eyes looked dark. His jowls sagged, and his forehead looked knurled. Robert's color looked dull, faint. He wasn't doing well. His body looked worn and tired. Time had taken a considerable toll.

"I'm simply amazed that you showed up on this particular day," Robert said.

"Why?"

"Today's been a lonely time."

"How?"

Robert hung his head. "A lot's happened to me, Mary.

Difficult situations and unexpected hardships. Experiences that caused me a considerable amount of anguish." He shook his head.

Mary waited a minute, trying to find the right way to ask her question, but nothing seemed natural or casual. She finally couldn't wait any longer and blurted out, "You must be married?"

Robert turned his head slowly. "I was," he said. "But Donna died," he mumbled under his breath. "About nine months ago. She always enjoyed smoking, smoked a lot. Then she started coughing continually, and the doctor finally diagnosed her as having developed lung cancer." Robert sighed. "Donna was only sixty-six."

Mary took a deep breath. "I see." She nodded her head. "I'm sorry to hear that your wife is gone."

"I have a son. Peter. But he lives in England. You see, Donna was from a small town about twenty or thirty minutes from London, a village named Woking. I lived there for a while after the war was over." He forced a smile and shrugged. "Peter lives there now."

Mary nodded solemnly. "I guess both of us have had a life filled with all sorts of experiences that we would never have imagined or thought possible back in those days when we lived in Sterling, Kansas." She forced a smile. "Many unexpected events."

Robert looked back out the window. "Mary, I simply can't believe that you are here. I am so pleased to see you."

"You really are?" Mary frowned.

"Definitely."

Mary shifted her weight in the chair and pushed her leg nervously to one side. “I understand that you live in Chaptico now?”

Robert nodded. “I worked in Washington for a while near the end of my career and sort of got used to this area.”

“Never wanted to go back to California? To Los Angeles?”

Robert shook his head vigorously. “No. Never.”

“So you drifted up here?”

“Donna always like Chaptico—the trees, but most of all the history of the place. We’re rather saturated with colonial period events around here.”

Mary forced a smile. “The town looks very nice.” She cleared her throat. “I always wondered what happened to you in the war. Your letters stopped. My mail came back to me marked MISSING IN ACTION. Everything went from day to night almost overnight. *Wham!* You were gone.”

Robert nodded his head. “Yes, I disappeared. You see, I switched dogtags with a dead man, and that made me look like I’d gone up in smoke.” He turned back to Mary. “I was captured.”

“Captured? I often thought that could have been a possibility.”

“My airplane got shot down during the early days of the Battle of the Bulge. I bailed out, but the bomber blew up in the air. I ended up floating down into the middle of a battlefield.”

Mary nodded her head slowly. “Exploded? I’ll be darned.”

“Turned out to be a very difficult time for all of us.” Robert stared up at the ceiling. “At times I didn’t think that I would survive. Never experienced anything like that war period again in my life." Walker shook his head.

"Well, after four months, I had to conclude that you were dead." Mary sighed. "At least that was what the Air Force led me to think. I didn't hear a word after the fifth month and finally decided that I had no other choice but to go on with my life. Believe me, the decision wasn't easy."

"I took the dogtags with the name of Private Guy Robert Jones," Robert continued talking, "because I knew secret information and was afraid the Germans would squeeze the facts out of me." Robert smiled. "Seems like a million years ago."

"Secret information? Yes, the last night I was with you in Sterling, you talked about having been trained in using classified paraphernalia. What was it?"

"In today's world, the bombing guidance device that I brought to the war would look primitive, but the system must have helped back in 1945. The war didn't last too much longer after we kept Bastogne from falling."

"What really happened to you, Robert?" Mary leaned closer. "Would you tell me the story of how you were captured and what followed?"

Robert reached out for the table next to him, fumbling across the top as if to pick up something. "They told me that I have to stop smoking, but it's hard. I sort of automatically reach for a cigarette." He smiled at her. "You know how habits are."

"You didn't smoke when we went together. Did you?"

"No, but I spent too many years flying under difficult circumstances and got used to needing a little pick-me-up."

Mary studied Robert's face, looking for hints of stress and strain. "Too many years?" she asked.

"After the war, I flew over Russia, testing their radar system."

"Russia?" Mary's eyes widened. "Good heavens! What a scary thought. Robert, you've done some very brave maneuvers."

Walker's sober look didn't change. He only nodded.

"Look. I want to know how you disappeared. Tell me the story of what happened to you over in Europe. Would you mind?"

Walker settled into his pillow and looked straight up at the ceiling. "Seems like it happened just yesterday, not fifty-six years ago. Feels even more real than things that happened to me a couple of months ago." He nodded gently. "Sure. I'll tell you the story." He thought for a moment. "The story . . . the story happened like this . . ."

Twenty-Three

Over Belgium, December 1944

The two Nazi ME-109s disappeared into the horizon. Robert had been hit hard, and the airplane was in deep trouble. He unsnapped his harness and pushed himself out of the pilot's seat. The copilot and the navigator were dead. He didn't want to take another look at them.

"We're what's left, Captain." The bombardier hurried toward him. "Everybody else is dead."

Robert nodded.

Smoke had already filled much of the fuselage, and the airplane started turning toward the right. They were already descending. If they didn't get out quickly, Robert would be running uphill.

"We've got to get out now or we won't be able to." The bombardier ran back to the center of the aircraft and pulled the lever that released the side door. "Better hurry."

"After you. Take off."

The airman made a feeble wave and jumped without looking back.

Walker stopped and took a long last look at the men slumped on the floor. He mumbled a prayer under his breath and then leaped through the door. At first he felt as if he were gently floating in the cloud-filled sky, but he knew the sensation was deceiving. He was plunging toward the earth like a rock. He reached for the ripcord, counted, and pulled, and the chute immediately flew out, jerking him upward. Cold air filled his nostrils; his feet dangled beneath him.

Robert turned to watch his airplane fly pilotless across the sky. The B-17 appeared to be ambling leisurely downward, leaving a long black train of smoke, when suddenly the airplane exploded in a brilliant ball of orange fire and gray smoke. A wing broke off and hurtled toward the earth. Thirty seconds more, and the bombardier and he would have died in the flames.

"Thank You, Lord!" Walker shouted above his head. "Thank You, God! I'm still alive! Bless You!" He shook his fist in the sky. "Bless You!"

The parachute drifted lazily toward the ground as the German and Allied airplanes continued the dogfight above Robert. Roaring gunfire and explosions filled his ears. He guessed that they must have still been flying over Belgium or Luxembourg. Hard to tell at the speed they were flying. A small village lay to his left. Far off in the distance he could see the bombardier's chute about to hit the ground. The wind must have caught the man's parachute and blown him much farther north. Wherever he looked, the countryside was a battleground. Trucks, tanks, and artillery moved up and down small hills and across flat fields. Blasts and explosions increased in magnitude as he came closer to the ground.

A few moments later Walker landed in a field. He hit the snow-covered dirt and immediately rolled on the ground to collapse the parachute. Robert got out of the harness quickly and dragged the massive chute into the bushes. To his back, towering pines edged the field. He listened carefully but heard nothing except gunfire in the distance. Robert gathered up the parachute and crammed it under a pile of brush to cover the white nylon. The gesture probably didn't make any difference on a battlefield, but he did what he had been taught.

Robert crouched at the edge of the field and listened carefully. He heard the roar of machinery off in the distance, but nothing seemed to be close. Periodically rifles fired. The bombardier couldn't be too near him, but he would surely try to link up with him. A shiver of fear ran down his spine. He was alone.

Hope I'm in the Allied sector, he thought. *The town over there's got to be my best bet for survival. My bombardier will undoubtedly show up there. Don't have much choice but to walk out there. Got to be careful. Very careful.*

Robert started toward the town, staying in the clump of trees that edged the field. His flight suit provided ample coverage, but he couldn't afford to let himself get very wet. A cold northern wind blew snow in his face. His gloves helped. The ground was covered with snow, and he tried to avoid stepping in any drifts. He glanced at his watch to check the time. It was 0800 hours.

Fifteen minutes later, Walker found himself at the edge of the small village, but the place looked deserted. He maneuvered around the side of a house but saw no one. An eerie silence settled over the streets as if the village were empty. It looked like the entire town had been overrun. He crept forward, wondering whose army controlled the streets.

Windows had been shot out of many of the houses, and a few buildings had been burned to the ground. Yet the village still looked quaint, like a picture from a travel brochure. Behind a small house, he spotted a dead horse. No motors from a truck or car cut into the quiet. He could see ahead what appeared to be an old pub or a restaurant of some kind. Food might be left inside. He crept along the front wall, listening, not making a noise. Then, reassured, Robert broke into a run and dashed inside. Something knocked his feet out from under him, and he smashed to the floor. A heavy metal rod poked him in the back. The pain paralyzed him.

"Don't move!" a voice growled in his ear.

Robert's heart beat so hard he could barely speak. "Don't shoot!" he spit out.

"Who are you?" the voice sounded closer to his ear.

"I'm an American." Robert knew that his dogtags would tell the man at least that much. "Please. Don't shoot." He felt whatever stuck in his side move away. The pain immediately eased.

"What do you know! He's one of us!"

Robert rolled over and looked up. An infantryman stood above him with a rifle pointing at his face. He glanced around the dark room and saw five soldiers. "Americans!" he gasped.

"Yeah, the Jerries ran over us last night. We holed up in this town."

"Where am I?" Robert asked slowly.

"Bullingen," the soldier answered. "We're in Belgium."

"Thank God." Robert sat up. "I thought I was dead."

"Don't be so grateful. You may be in the middle of German-held territory," a man at the back said. "We're not sure what's happened."

"How'd you get here?" the soldier standing above him asked.

"Got shot down," Robert explained. "I was flying a bombing mission when the Nazis attacked my B-17. Killed all but one of the crew." He looked up at the soldier standing above him. "Who are you guys?"

"We're Canon Company of the 394th Infantry Regiment of the 99th Division," a man in back said. "Just glad to be alive today. We lost a good number of men out there last night. My name is King." He extended his hand. "Private First Class Albert King."

"Thanks." Walker shook hands and gently waved around the room. "I'm Lieutenant Robert Walker. I'd be delighted to travel with you boys for a while."

King laughed. "Hey. You've got the rank on us. Sure. We were just sitting here having a party anyway."

The other men laughed.

"You got a weapon?" King asked.

"Just this pistol." Robert pointed to his hip. "They didn't issue anything heavier."

"Need to find you a rifle out there somewhere because I'm sure the Krauts will be back sooner or later."

"Good idea." Robert stood up and brushed off his pants. "You boys know if anybody else is in town?"

"We've got men scattered all over the place, but the attack last night knocked out our communications and separated us from the rest of the company. We aren't able to get the word out of here that we're pinned down."

An explosion roared in the middle of the street, and glass blew in every direction. Robert hit the floor just as a wave of smoke poured across the room. A second and third explosion shook the building, and he crawled under a table.

"Watch out!" Private King called from his corner. "Keep your head down."

A couple of minutes passed, and quiet returned.

"I think the Germans may be getting ready to shell us again," King said. "We need to get into a more substantial building."

"There's a stone church about a block over there on the next street," one of the men said. "Maybe we ought to make a run for it."

"Good idea," another man said. "By the way, my name is Desmond. Desmond Allen." The man saluted.

King stood up. "This lull is an opportune time to make a

run for it. Follow me." King grabbed his rifle and ran out the front door.

The men followed, with Robert bringing up the rear. He gawked at the huge hole that had blown part of the main street away. From off in the distance rapid rifle fire echoed down the street. Another group of soldiers answered.

"Over there!" King pointed around the corner. "There's the big church. Run for it!" He took off. The men hurried behind him.

Robert looked around again, hoping to see the bombardier, but he saw no one. The infantry company ran toward the big stone church and disappeared inside behind a mammoth set of wooden doors. Robert inched around the corner and got ready to run. At that moment he saw an American soldier just feet from the church's front door. The soldier was crouched down beside a barricade with his gun aimed toward the opposite end of town. The man seemed to be guarding the church. Robert ran for the soldier, cleared the street, and dropped down beside the man. The soldier didn't move. "Hey, I'm one of your guys." Robert gasped for air.

The man didn't answer but leaned forward with his gun aimed straight ahead.

"I said I'm an American."

The soldier didn't move.

"Can you hear me?" Robert asked, but the man didn't respond.

Robert inched up next to the soldier and touched his shoulder. Nothing happened. He reached up to push the helmet back, feeling the man's cold skin. Blank eyes stared straight ahead. There was no blood, only a hole in the center of his forehead three inches above his eyebrows. A bullet had hit the man squarely in the front of his head, instantly killing the soldier hunched against the barrier where his gun lay.

Nausea engulfed Robert, and he fought for air. The cold winter wind slapped his face, and he took quick, deep breaths. Robert knew there was nothing else to do but take the man's rifle and get inside the church. But when he reached for the carbine, trying to loosen the man's hands frozen around the gun, he felt the cold and hard skin. Touching him added to the nausea, but Robert had to pry the soldier's fingers loose from the gun.

Robert pulled the man's ammunition belt from him and took his steel helmet. The soldier's stiffened body didn't move, staying in the crouched position. Robert trotted back to the church and shut the door.

"What took you so long?" King asked caustically.

Robert only shook his head.

Twenty-Four

Throughout the remainder of the afternoon and the early evening of December 17, Bullingen remained under intense fire. Bombs exploded around the village, and shells landed in the streets. Robert and the five men of the 394th Infantry Regiment stayed hunkered down, occasionally returning rifle fire but not always sure of their target. They might be shooting at their own men, so they mainly hid and watched. No one saw Germans, but they had to be out there somewhere, maybe on the edge of the village. Walker traded off keeping watch at the windows. As the sun set, the machine gun fire subsided and quiet fell over the freezing, snow-covered Belgian village.

"I think we need to build a fire in here," one of the infantrymen said for the fourth time.

"Where's the smoke gonna go?" Al King finally asked. "You expect it to simply disappear because we're Americans or something like that?"

"There's a hole up there." Desmond Allen pointed at the roof. "See? Up there in the top." He kept gesturing toward the high ceiling. "The smoke'll go out up there."

"Don't work that way," Al insisted. "Way too far up there."

"Even if it don't, a little smoke beats freezing to death," Allen argued. "This place's goin' to be an icebox. Gonna be rough tonight."

King nodded. "Now you're making sense. Yeah, that's why we need a fire, regardless of what the smoke does." He looked at Robert. "You bring a bed roll with you, flyboy?"

"What do you think?" Robert answered. "I just dropped in out of the sky with what I got on."

"How you going to sleep tonight?" King asked. "Remember? That's part of what we do when the lights go out."

Robert looked around the church. Chairs were turned over and crowded in a wrecked huddle in the middle of the old sanctuary. One of the altar rails across the front of the chancel had shattered when a hunk from the ceiling fell down. Wasn't much left to select for warmth. In one corner a remnant of a curtain hung from a pipe. Walker shook his head. "I don't know. Don't see anything left around here."

"That's what I thought," King said. He looked around at several of the men. "Anybody got extra blankets for our lieutenant? We're not going to let our new leader freeze."

No one looked at King.

"I asked if any of you men had anything you can share with our pilot?" King looked around the room. "Those bombs affect your hearing? I'm talking to every one of you. He's got rank, you know."

"Nobody's got anything extra, Al," a man finally said. "We're lucky to have what we carried in with us. You know that."

Private King shook his head. "You boys ain't going to let Walker get cold tonight, now are you? I suggest you have a discussion among yourselves about how you will work him in between a couple of you or share a spot with your blankets over him. Understand?" King turned back to Walker. "We'll come up with something. Don't worry, Lieutenant."

Desmond Allen piled some broken chairs together over pages from a hymn book. The soldiers built a fire on the stone floor underneath the hole far above in the ceiling. Smoke curled up and dispersed among the massive beams that supported the roof. A few wafts of black smoke floated out.

"Notice how quiet it's gotten?" King asked Robert.

"Yeah, nobody's shooting."

King nodded his head. "Maybe the Krauts have retreated."

Allen crawled into the conversation. "Hey, possibly our boys took the town back. What do you think?"

Robert raised an eyebrow. "Hope so. I'd hate to believe the Germans had this place in their hip pocket."

"Quiet's a good sign," Allen concluded.

"I need a good night's rest," King added. "Let's hope we can sleep."

Robert kept warming his hands over the fire. Allen crawled back to the broken window to maintain the watch. Robert knew he was an easy target sitting around the roaring fire, but the wind blowing in the windows got colder, and freezing wasn't a great alternative either.

Robert eventually found a place between King and another soldier. He put some cushions he'd found underneath him and covered himself with the curtain that had been hanging from the old pipe. The fire put out enough warmth to break the bite of the freezing night to allow Robert a troubled sleep.

A huge explosion shook the building and knocked the men apart. Robert found himself uncovered in the midst of falling plaster. He grabbed his head and hunkered into a ball. Plaster crashed around him, and a chandelier smashed into the floor. Another bomb went off, and the walls of the church quivered. Somebody kicked the fire out to kill the light. More black smoke blew in the broken windows. Now wide awake, men grabbed their rifles and crawled toward the broken windows. Increasing machine gun fire filled the streets. Robert glanced at his watch and discovered it was almost 0100 hours. While he had slept, another day and a counterattack had begun.

Gunfire ripped across the front of the church and cut into the heavy door. Splinters flew everywhere. Infantry fire answered from down the street. For a moment Robert struggled to grasp what was happening. The Germans must have returned and started invading the village. He pulled up the rifle he'd taken from the dead soldier and started crawling.

Hunched against the side of the window in front of him, Walker recognized the large shoulders of Private King. The infantryman's steel helmet bordered the man's eyes; his rifle was propped up on the windowsill. Smoke blew into the soldiers' faces from a fire burning on the edge of the church's cemetery. Inching forward on his elbows and staying close to the floor, Walker scurried toward King. The smell of smoke filled Robert's nose, and he could hear movement outside in the street.

Just as he reached the window, King reached over and covered Robert's mouth. The infantryman shook his finger and motioned toward the other side of the window. Not far outside Robert could hear an unusual sound. He pressed his ear against the windowsill and listened carefully. The strange sound was the German language.

The Jerries couldn't be more than a hundred yards down the street. Icy fear gripped Robert's fingers. His heart pounded, and a cold sweat broke out across his forehead. The tips of his fingers dug into the wooden side of the rifle.

Private King again put a finger to his lips, and then he crawled away. Walker slipped his rifle up on the ledge and gripped the trigger more with terror than assurance. The Germans seemed to be making a systematic search of the buildings along the town's main street. They had to have already encountered other American gun crews and must have killed them. Robert stared down the sight of his gun barrel and swallowed hard. He had no idea where to shoot.

Moments later King and several men returned to the window with a large gun. Walker recognized the M-2 60 mm mortar that was capable of launching a real blast. For several moments King worked at hoisting the large gun onto the windowsill and positioning a man behind it ready to fire straight at the Germans.

The private leaned over next to Robert's ear. "Grapeshot," he whispered. "We don't have much left, but we're close enough that this'll give them something to think about for a long time." King put his hand on Walker's wrist. "Don't fire until after we shoot."

The three men silently watched the black forms working their way toward the church. Walker could see the distinctive shape of the Nazis' pointed helmets, the barrels of the *Wehrmacht*'s MP-43 rifles. The enemy was getting dangerously close, and the Americans needed to do something quickly. Robert clutched his rifle in resolute terror.

Private King held his hand in the air. He leaned toward the window, listening. The crunch of men walking through the snow filled the night. The Germans must have decided they had the village and so they came out of hiding to walk the streets. At that moment, King abruptly dropped his hand, and the gun blasted with fire and smoke.

Germans screamed and yelled at each other. Instantly the 394th Canon Company fired from every possible corner of the church building. Robert shot at whatever he saw moving. After several minutes, the Americans stopped. To Robert's surprise, the streets were silent. Off in the distance, he could hear men running, falling in the snow, getting up, running again. After several minutes even that sound died out. The Germans were in retreat.

Robert slipped back against the wall. Despite the cold wind, beads of perspiration dotted his forehead. His heart pounded like a bass drum in a Fourth of July parade. He was breathing hard. The acrid smell of smoke filled his nose and choked him. How in God's name had he ever gotten into this terrifying mess?

Twenty-five

During the early morning hours of December 18, gunfire and exploding bombs punctuated the night air, but no Germans returned to Bullingen. Fearing discovery, the Americans didn't rekindle the night fire, and bitter cold settled over everything inside the battered church. Much to his surprise, Robert eventually went back to sleep and didn't awake until dawn.

The sound of a truck roaring up in front of the church awoke the lieutenant. Walker rubbed his eyes, making sure that he was where his aching back told him he must be. The truck's engine shut off, and the front door of the church opened. Two American infantrymen came in.

"Trust you boys had a good night's sleep," one of the soldiers called from the door.

"Ha-ha," Private King answered. "Your company just drove over to pay us a little social visit?"

"Not quite," the other soldier answered. "We got a truck-load of dead and dying men. We thought you might have a few contributions for us."

"You boys are really comedians." The private stood up and stretched. "Now tell me what's really happening."

The soldier at the door walked into the center of the church. "The name is Private Brown," he began. "My buddy's name is Alexander. We're telling you the truth," he said bluntly. "The Germans cut us off last night. Really whacked up our company. We got some wounded men, but most aren't going to live long. Truck's full of dead soldiers."

No one said anything. The men of Canon Company exchanged glances.

"You guys got any kind of communications hookup to tell us how to get out of here?" Alexander asked.

Private King shook his head. "Krauts blew ours away two days ago. All that we're sure of is that the town is called Bullingen."

"Bullingen?" Brown turned to his friend at the door. "Oh man! We're totally lost."

Alexander hit the doorframe and cursed. "We either took a wrong turn or the Germans have completely sealed off the roads out of here."

"I'll be honest," King answered. "I'm not sure how you guys even got in here. Last night the Nazis just about took the town away from us. We're not even sure where the rest of the regiment is. We're stuck in the middle of a German offense that nobody seems to have stopped yet."

Brown pulled up a broken chair and sat down. "Here's

what we know to date. We had around eighteen hundred men in the 395th Regiment that were killed in the last several days. We and the still-living out there in that truck may be all that's left of the support troops in this area!"

Private King looked around at the men with him. No one spoke. "Look, Brown. We may be all that's left of the 394th. None of us knows for sure where the Germans are, but we've got to get out of here. Make sense?"

Brown nodded.

Alexander started counting heads. "I'd suggest that we get you boys on the back of our truck and try to make a break toward the west. Maybe our troops are closer than we think. Maybe we can outrun the Jerries."

"You said the truck was filled?" King asked.

"We'll have to decide what to do with the dead." Brown stood and started for the door. "We need several of your men to help us clear out a space."

Alexander nodded. "Yeah. Either that or we let the Germans come back in here and grab you."

King stood up. "We picked up a downed pilot." He pointed at Robert. "Counting him, there's six of us in here. We'll all go out and help clear space." He turned to Robert. "I think we'd better turn you into one of us and dress you as an infantryman. If the Germans catch us, that's the only way they'll leave us together. If you have any secrets in your head, the Krauts will squeeze them out of you. We'll find the clothes outside."

"Sounds good to me," Desmond Allen answered and turned to point. "You're actually in charge here."

Robert looked at King. "Al knows what he's doing. I'm with him. I'll take care of what you need an officer to do, but King knows the best way out of here." Robert looked around the room. "Anybody disagree?"

No one answered.

"Then I'd suggest you boys get your gear and let's follow King." Robert pointed to the front door. "Let's go."

The remnant of the 394th assembled their equipment and hurried through the splintered front doors.

Snow had fallen again during the night, covering many of the holes in the street. The soldier that Robert had taken the rifle from the day before was now frozen solid and covered with snow. Eerie silence had settled over the town. The sky offered only a misty gray-white ceiling of low-lying clouds. Most of the soldiers in the truck looked like they had been hit with everything from gunfire to meat axes. Blood soaked through bandage-covered heads, arms, and legs. Few men moved.

Without an order being given, the men of the 394th climbed into the truck and began removing the dead. One man collected dogtags. A few of the bodies were already frozen. In a few minutes, Walker had his change of clothing. The pants felt stiff and hard where the blood had frozen down the leg. He picked up one of the sets of dogtags and stuck it in his pocket.

"We can't bury these men," Private Desmond announced. "The ground is frozen, and it would take all day. If we're serious about escaping, we've got to do it now."

Brown and Alexander nodded.

"No question about it," Private Brown agreed. "We're going to have to get out of here during this lull. If they start bombing us again, they'll blow us into a million pieces. I say we take the road leading west and drive as fast as we can."

Private King nodded. "Get in the back, men. We're leaving now."

Brown and Alexander hurried to the cab and started the truck. The roar of the engine echoed across the silent village. Walker was the last one in, sitting on the edge of the tailgate and trying to avoid looking at the devastated.

The truck bounced down to the end of the block and turned toward the west. Everywhere Robert looked, he saw burned-out houses. Rubble covered the town's streets. The truck picked up speed. In a few minutes they'd be out of Bullingen and into the countryside. Walker clutched his rifle and ground his teeth. They were nothing more than a moving target.

As the military truck approached the edge of town, an explosion erupted twenty feet from the truck, covering the truck bed with dirt and sending a spray of dust in every direction. More dust and debris fell into the faces of the injured. Walker ducked and covered his head. Another explosion raised the front end of the truck, and the vehicle came to a stop.

"Take cover!" one of the infantrymen yelled. "Over there, by that house." He leaped from the truck and ran for shelter.

"Hide behind a rock, a fence post, anything!" King screamed and jumped out of the back of the truck.

Somewhere up ahead a machine gun blasted away. Bullets sprayed the road and sent pieces of rock and dirt flying.

"I'm going for it," Alexander yelled out of the driver's window. "Hang on! We're leaving!"

The truck roared to life, pulled out of the hole in front of it, and shot down the road. About two hundred yards beyond the village, Alexander had to slow down to negotiate a left turn. The truck had only barely started to veer when a machine gun opened up. Instead of turning, the truck careened off the road and slammed into a tree. Seconds later the cab exploded, sending a blast of fire skyward. The machine gun fired relentlessly for a full minute and then aimed at where Canon Company was hiding. When it stopped, one of the men in Canon Company had been hit in the leg.

"We're surrounded," Private King told the men hiding together at the edge of town. "We can't go backward or we'll walk into the whole German army. You can see what's ahead. They've trapped us."

Robert slid down the side of the house. In the pit of his stomach he again felt the terrible sense of isolation and fear. No one needed to say anything. Their plight was obvious. The Germans had either killed or caught his bombardier, and all he'd done in Bullingen was delay the inevitable. The Nazi offensive had caught the Allies by too great a surprise. No telling how far it had gone by now. Maybe the Krauts were already ten miles in front of them.

"We don't have much of a choice," Private Allen shouted

to the group. "We can stay and fight until we're all dead, or we can surrender. Truth is, we're desperately outnumbered."

Nobody said anything. German artillery opened up again from the same area where the first shots had hit the truck. Machine gun bullets raked the road and houses. Robert huddled against the ground.

"What do you say, men?" King looked around at each of the soldiers. "No one wants to do it, but it looks to me like surrender is the only way we'll come out of this alive."

The men of the 394th Canon Company looked at each other but didn't speak.

Finally Robert stood up. "We've got no choice unless we want to commit suicide. No one wants to run up a white flag, but we either do it or they'll kill us before the hour's out. Let's surrender."

The men stood up one by one and laid their rifles down. Two of the men helped the wounded man try to walk. Al found a piece of white cloth and hooked it onto a long stick.

"We did our best," King said. "No one can fault us. Let's go see what the Germans have to say."

The men fell into a line with King leading the way holding his white flag up in the air. The rest of the crew walked with their hands on their helmets. Robert brought up the rear, watching the men in front of him trudge down the snow-covered road, trying to walk in the ruts cut through the snow by the truck. Fortunately the ice stayed frozen and they didn't slip through the crust. Flames continued to consume the vehicle now only a hundred yards ahead of them. The soldiers walked forward in resolute silence.

The six-man unit was only thirty yards from the burning truck when two young German soldiers stepped out of a clump of bushes. Maybe fifteen or sixteen years old, the boys smiled and pointed their guns at the troop of Americans.

"Good morning," one of the boy soldiers said in excellent English with a British accent. "How are you?"

"We're surrendering," Private King answered.

The two boys immediately spoke to each other in German, apparently discussing what to do next.

"Please follow me," the boy said and motioned with his weapon in the opposite direction from the burning truck.

King said nothing but followed.

"We're prisoners," Robert said to the man in front of him.

The soldier cursed. "Yeah, prisoners of war! Can you believe it?"

Twenty-Six

MARYLAND, APRIL 2000

"You were a prisoner of war!" Mary exclaimed. "Good heavens! I would have died if I'd known they had captured you." She caught her breath and gently fanned her face. "I suppose not knowing was easier than having to live with the knowledge that the Germans had captured you. What a terrible thought!"

Robert smiled. "Yeah," he said softly and took a long drag off the cigarette. "I guess that I don't need to tell you that I was frightened to death. I didn't have any choice but to walk up that long road to where the Germans were waiting for us."

Mary looked out the window. The afternoon would be over before long. Everything looked peaceful and serene. Life went on as if it had been this way for a thousand uninterrupted years.

"Seems quite lovely out there," Robert said. "Who'd

believe that all of that nice, quietly ordered way of life was paid for by the lives of people who died in World War II? Today most people don't even remember much about what happened."

Mary studied Robert's face. Time had taken its toll, but she still saw the handsomeness. "I remember, Robert." She cleared her throat. "I remember our time together in Sterling."

Robert nodded his head. "Yeah." He answered softly.

"It was the best time in my life." Mary's voice quivered.

He looked away and didn't answer. Robert had turned his face so she couldn't see his eyes. Mary waited for what seemed an interminable amount of time, but she didn't speak.

"Maybe I ought to go on with the story." Robert finally turned around, and his eyes looked reddish.

"Sure." Mary shook her head. "I want to know everything. Please tell me what happened next after you decided to surrender. I know you were frightened out of your skin."

Robert took another puff. "Wasn't easy," he said, "but the five infantrymen and I kept walking down that long road out of Bullingen with our white surrender flag blowing in the cold wind. We looked like lost chickens wandering off to be slaughtered."

~

Belgium, December 1944

In front of the Americans, the sounds of bombing increased and machine gun fire became heavier. The hard snow crunched beneath their feet, and no one spoke. The Allies trudged down the twisting old road with the two German soldiers following, their rifles pointed at the Americans. Eventually the German soldiers led them inside a long split-rail fence surrounding a stone farmhouse. From the burned-out vehicles scattered around the yard, apparently the farm had been used by both the German and Allied armies for stationing troops and vehicles. A battle had been fought over the farm, but the house hadn't been destroyed. The boys insisted the six Americans sit down in a cleared rocky area in front of the snow-covered farmhouse. The men relaxed and started talking.

"How's our boy doing?" Robert asked.

"Hey, Mason's making it great." Desmond Allen tried to sound encouraging.

Robert glanced at Al King. The infantryman shook his head and looked away.

"Good!" Robert answered Allen, but he knew the situation was grave.

The bleeding on the American soldier's wounded leg seemed to have increased during the march down the road. His torn pants looked black where blood had dried, but he continued to bleed and couldn't walk without someone supporting him on each side. The white-faced young man stretched out on the stone pavement in pain.

The Americans broke out a few cigarettes and started smoking, passing the cigarettes among themselves until the Lucky Strikes disappeared in smoke and ashes. Their youthful guards didn't seem to mind. No one spoke to the Germans.

"He looks bad," Walker said quietly to Private King. "Your man needs medical attention."

King nodded. "He won't get it," the soldier answered glumly. King took a deep puff of the cigarette and handed it to Robert.

Robert took a drag. "What's next?"

"I'm not sure." Al King tightened his jaw and shook his head. "These people are tricky. Might shoot all of us."

Robert jerked. "Are you serious?"

Al cursed. "It's possible. They've done it before."

Walker swallowed hard. "Maybe we should try to make a break for it?"

"Nah, we went through that scenario back in Bullingen. The Krauts outnumber us and are everywhere. We'd be dead men for sure. We're stuck until we see what happens."

Walker eyed the German boys, who were standing with rifles pointed at the Americans. King was probably right. Not much possibility of getting away without running into more Germans. They'd made their decision and would have to stick with it.

"How'd you get here?" Robert leaned close to Private King.

"Here in Europe?"

Al smiled. "You'd never believe it," he said nonchalantly. "They like to a killed me, getting me into this war. I was one of them shipload of soldiers that sailed over on the USS *Excelsior*. The brass put us down in the number-three hold, packed in there with everything from anti-track troops to administration personnel and medics. You wouldn't have believed it! Only had enough space to stretch out horizontally. Crammed in da boat like a pickup load of pigs."

"Tough, huh?"

Al smiled out of the side of his mouth. "Let me put it this way. During that first week at sea, virtually every man in that hold was sick. Must have been seven hundred soldiers throwing up about twice a day. We were so sick, we used the good ole handy-dandy steel helmet I'm wearing to vomit in so that we wouldn't have to stagger up to the latrines. Got a sense of the smell of our facilities?"

Walker cringed. "Yeah."

"I was sick the first five days. Didn't even eat." King shook his head. "Thought I'd starve to death. Fortunately, candy bars sold for about sixty cents a carton so I got by, but dat was a tough trip."

Walker looked at the Nazis standing above them. The soldiers obviously understood everything being said in English and listened carefully. They seemed to be more curious than intrusive. He looked away in disgust.

"We ended up landing at Liverpool on a cold rainy night. Walked off the boat and onto an English train. Best deal of the trip. We had ten men per car on coaches made for thirty men. The Red Cross passed out all the candy and doughnuts we could eat. We settled onto those soft seats and played poker all night. Rode through the English countryside like royalty."

Robert looked around again, hoping to find something that might suggest a way of escape. Nothing had changed. No way to run without getting shot quickly.

"Where'd you end up?" Walker asked.

Al grinned. "Headquarters trucked us ta a town called Beaminister in Dorestshire and put us up in private homes. Me and my buddies ended up in an English manor house built around 1650." The private suddenly laughed nervously. "You wouldn't believe how nice we had it in that ancient mansion." He shook his head. "We set up a theater in Beaminister and a PX in one of the old store buildings. Real life of Riley in that burg!"

Walker smiled and thought about Sterling, Kansas. The little town now seemed like a glorious retreat center. He could see Mary directing the college's dance when he and his buddies walked in for the first time. People smiled when soldiers passed by and treated them with deep respect. Children waved. Women liked them. Life was kind and easy. No chance of getting shot there. But Sterling was a million miles away.

King continued. "Eventually they shipped us down to Southampton and loaded us on the USS *LST Number 1*, a veteran of five invasions. Couldn't believe it. This time they even put us up in the sailors' quarters. Had white sheets and Navy blankets. You'da thought we were da generals."

Robert kept watching the German guards. Although they were boys, the two soldiers looked more than ready to shoot. No point of rushing them and getting someone killed.

"Unfortunately, a storm blew in and we were on the boat for five days. Guess what? I got sick again." King swore.

"Yeah," Robert said. "I could feel that one coming."

"Eventually we put out to sea and crossed the English

Channel, landing at Le Havre. Waded in just like we were taking the place, but the Allies had already leveled the big city. Wasn't a house standing, and every pier had been smashed. Some of the houses were still on fire. The civilians were gone. Nasty sight."

Robert nodded. "Nothing nice about a war."

King nodded his head. "You got that one right." He glanced at the guards and spit sideways.

Up the road a German soldier appeared out of the woods, walking toward them. The SS grenadier's leather overcoat nearly covered the man's hands and stretched down over the top of his black boots. The side of his green steel helmet flared out, covering his ears and the back of his neck. He carried a Schmeisser MP-40 machine gun.

The soldiers saluted the man and immediately broke into an excited discussion, sounding as if they had virtually wrestled the American soldiers to the ground after lengthy hand-to-hand combat.

"Oberst Otto Kolb," the Nazi introduced himself. "You are now prisoners of the Fifth Panzer Army." Kolb walked among the six men, looking at each one. "If you give us any problems, you will die instantly," Kolb explained in excellent English.

Oberst Kolb walked back to the two boys and said a number of things in German. The soldiers nodded as he spoke. Kolb turned back to the Americans. "Get up!" he ordered.

The four men stood slowly. One soldier stood next to the wounded man.

"Up!" Kolb barked.

The wounded soldier held up his hand and waved futilely. Slowly the hand fell back over the man's chest.

"Only those who can walk and have no wounds can go with us," Kolb announced indifferently. "The rest stay here."

"Just a moment." Walker stepped forward. "I'd like to say that—"

Kolb swung his machine gun within inches of Walker's face. "You no longer have the right of free speech. You are prisoners of the Third Reich. Shut up." Kolb said something to his two young comrades and then swung the barrel of the gun forward. "March!"

The boy soldiers pointed down the road and signaled for the Americans to follow them. The five Allies fell in behind. Kolb brought up the rear.

Robert turned and looked over his shoulder. The wounded American soldier had one hand on his chest and the other over his eyes. Blood still ran down the man's leg. He raised his hand from his chest and saluted slightly. Walker gave a return salute and then looked away. He could do nothing but march on.

Twenty-Seven ~

When the five Americans began marching away from the farm, Walker noticed that it was 1600 hours. Noise of battle increased as the sun set, and the wind picked up again as the squad wound through the thick forest. Robert knew the temperature was below freezing. Snow hung on the tree limbs, and it looked as if nothing had thawed all day. Eventually two other German soldiers joined the march as guards. The Germans were not taking them in a straight line but were constantly winding, as if following an unseen obstacle course. After about four hours, the squad stopped for a short rest break. By this time the sky had turned black, but the moon was bright.

"Know where we're going?" Walker asked a private named Gene Tivey.

Tivey looked around to make sure one of the Germans

was close enough to hear. "I think the Krauts are surrounded. Allies seem to be everywhere out there."

Walker nodded. "That's what I figure. I think we've been walking in the midst of our troops."

Tivey shook his head and walked on. "They ain't got us for sure yet," he said over his shoulder.

Abruptly a group of men with their hands on their heads came out of the bushes in front of them. Of the ten Americans, four soldiers were bleeding and having a hard time walking. Three German soldiers surrounded them, herding the men with their rifles. The roar of an engine broke out of the trees, and a *SdKfz-251* half-track rumbled into the clearing. A smell like kerosene hung in the black smoke trailing behind the half-track. Six Germans sat inside with backpacks and guns in hand. The half-track lumbered past, with the soldiers staring over the side at the Americans standing in the darkness, looking at them more in curiosity than anything else.

"Achtung!" the oberst in charge of the half-track yelled at the Americans, but no more was said. The vehicle ground on past the prisoners up the road the Allies had just come down. Only exhaust fumes lingered behind.

The four wounded men sank in the snow, blood oozing from their wounds. The other six stood around them, hugging themselves and rubbing their hands, trying to keep warm. Two hours passed.

"I suspect that we are now inside German-held territory," King whispered to Robert. "I'm not sure exactly where we are, but we can't be too far from Bullingen except that we've gone farther back to the east. We could have walked toward Eisenborn, but I think we're closer to the German border."

Walker nodded. "That's my reading. The German border."

One of the soldiers pushed part of a cigarette between King and Walker. "Take a puff," he said. "Gonna be very cold tonight."

One of the German boy soldiers walked into their group. "We must walk again," he continued in good English. "Please stand." He walked on.

Walker watched the young man's confident gait, functioning way beyond what his age should have allowed. He seemed so self-assured, buoyant, happy. Robert waited for him to come back by. "How'd you get in the Panzer Army?"

The boy stopped and whirled around. His eyes sparkled. "I was a Hitler Youth! They recruited me." The seeming innocence slipped from his eyes, and only arrogance remained. "Understand?" he sneered. "I am one of *der Führer*'s men."

Walker nodded. "Yeah, I got the picture."

"Let's go," the young Nazi ordered. "We march again." The soldier swung his rifle under Robert's nose. "Now!"

Walker fell in the line of eleven men. The four wounded soldiers struggled to stand up.

"Leave the wounded behind," the boy soldier commanded in English. "Only those who can walk are allowed to march with us."

"Wait." One of the wounded men reached out. "We can make it."

An older German soldier gave a harsh order in German and motioned for the Americans to walk on in the night. Another German soldier pointed his machine gun at the four wounded men and forced them to stand in place while their comrades marched away. The man's eyes looked cold and resolute. Walker didn't look back this time but marched forward. After five minutes of walking in the darkness, he heard the rapid fire of a machine gun behind them. Robert ground his teeth and kept walking.

Another couple of hours later the eleven men suspected that a large number of troops was probably directly in front of them. Rifle fire and machine guns filled the black air. The ground shook as large mortars hurled deadly blasts into the night sky. Rockets exploded, showering explosive phosphorous in every direction. *Panzerfaust* rocket-propelled projectiles flew over the trees. Machine guns blasted away over the next hill. Antiaircraft ground guns kept firing into the heavens. Two *Panzerkampfwagen V Panther* heavy tanks roared up the road, causing the eleven men to step aside and stand in two feet of snow as the Nazi death machine clanked past.

Minutes later the squad of prisoners crossed behind the German assault line and had no question where they were. Everywhere they looked, the Allies saw German vehicles. The Germans firmly and unquestionably held them captive.

"What time is it?" Tivey asked Walker.

Robert glanced at his wrist. "It's 2215 hours."

King pulled closer to the group. "It's really cold." Steam rolled out of his mouth. "Freezing."

"Think they'll let us live?" Robert asked.

King nodded his head. "The Nazis killed the wounded and would have done us in if that had been their purpose. We're lucky. We landed with a moderate group of Germans."

A couple of large shells shot past them. Moments later explosions shook the ground, sending balls of red fire straight up in the sky. Tivey, Walker, and King huddled closer together. The sky lit up with another explosion, and the roar deafened them. Smoke poured into their nostrils.

"We must be standing right on the attack line," Walker concluded. He looked at the Germans standing with their guns trained on them. "These boys mean business. I don't think they'll keep us here very long."

King nodded. "Yeah. They'll start us walking again when they round up a few more prisoners."

The German guards yelled something. The three men separated and stopped speaking to each other. Fifteen minutes later, the German guards ordered the men to move out. The prisoners backed away from the gunfire, and they marched due east. They were tramping toward Germany.

After an hour of marching down an old farm road, the roaring noise of battle subsided. The battered road eventually connected with a larger, paved highway. Constant traffic from troop-carrier vehicles had worn through the snow and made the walking much easier, but Robert's feet still felt the biting cold. He trudged on, saying nothing, pulling his thick coat next to his body.

During the next hour, the noise of battle became even more distant. Overhead the skies began to clear. Robert pulled his neck scarf more tightly over his ears and marched onward, looking upward at the sparkling stars. How strangely familiar the sky looked. A million tiny lights flashed above him. He might as well have been back in Oklahoma. Christmas was only a few days away, and his family would be thinking about him not coming home. He'd miss the best day of the year. Maybe tonight someone in the Walker clan would be looking up at exactly these same stars, with no sounds of bombs or guns. Just a quiet, gentle Oklahoma sky stretching across the horizon as far as anyone could see.

When he had been a little boy, Robert, his brother, and his sister loved to chase each other during the summer nights when the blue black sky sparkled with a million stars. They'd hide behind the trees and try to scare each other. The night air was humid and warm. He could still feel the grass tickling his toes as they tagged each other. Hide-and-seek wasn't only a game; it was a test of courage. The point was to find out who'd get afraid and retreat first. That objective was always the test, and Robert never lost. His sister didn't tumble easily, and his little brother could be tough, but neither had his staying power. Their game was played under a dark sky that looked exactly like the one above him. If he could only touch them once again . . .

Around 0100 hours the squad stopped for a short break to accommodate the needs of the German soldiers in the center of some quiet town. No lights or candles dotted any windows; everyone was already asleep. The Germans sat the Americans down in the town square, standing around them with their guns pointed at them. Snow piled up around their feet.

Al King scooted close to Walker. "I'd get rid of those dogtags with your name on them. If they find out you're an officer, they'll separate you from us. No tellin' where you'd go. Probably will give you very rough treatment during the interrogation. Might be easier to be some guy who's already dead."

"Thanks." Robert nodded his head and looked away. For the first time he realized the Germans would kill to obtain his knowledge of the G-stations and the new bombing patterns. If they were able to drag this data out of him by torture, it could affect the course of the war. At that moment Robert knew that he could no longer be an airman. His only hope was to turn into an infantryman. He couldn't see any other way to safeguard the information except to switch dogtags.

"You need to make the switch with as much secrecy as possible," King added. "These Nazi guys don't miss much."

"Yeah," Robert finally said. "Good advice." He walked away from King and sat down alone, burying his head in his hands. Moments later, he slipped his dogtags off his neck and dropped them down his pocket. In the dark it wouldn't be hard to get the other set around his neck, but he wasn't really ready yet to exchange his identity. He gave another look to make sure who he was supposed to be. *Guy Jones,* the tags said. *Private Guy Jones.* He dropped the tags back in his shirt.

One of the German soldiers hurried back to the group

and began shouting. The Americans stood up. Time to move out. The march started again. After a couple of steps, Robert was overwhelmingly aware of how hungry he was. He had not eaten in more than twenty hours, and fatigue gnawed at his legs. Under his breath, he kept praying for strength not to stop or fall. Although hunger abruptly exceeded his fear, Walker's captors pushed on. The oppressors marched forward at a steady rate, not allowing for any slack. Robert's stomach ached, and he feared stumbling and falling in the dark.

Robert periodically looked at his watch. No matter the lateness of the hour, the Germans didn't stop. Eventually the eleven-man squad came to a large barn already surrounded by Nazi troops. Someone unlocked the wooden door and pushed the men inside. Peering into the darkness, Robert recognized that many other men were sleeping on the ground. No one spoke or moved as the eleven marched in. The wind's power of destruction had been broken by the high walls of the barn, and the straw felt warm. It felt like the temperature of the barn was above freezing.

Walker dropped to the straw on the ground, cratering it, and for a moment he felt overcome. His stomach hurt and his legs ached fiercely, but at least he was alive. A crack of moonlight cast a long strand of light across the ground. Robert stuck his wristwatch into the moonlight. It was 0400 hours.

Twenty-Eight

A nurse entered the room. "Bob? Colonel Bob Walker?" she asked.

"Sure. That's me."

"Need to take your temperature and make sure that you're doing okay." The nurse smiled at Mary. "We have to check on our boy here every now and then to make sure he knows we're paying attention to him. Otherwise, he's as good as gold."

"How is he doing?" Mary asked nervously.

"Colonel Walker is making excellent progress. He'll be going home before long. Won't you, Bob?" When he opened his mouth to reply, she stuck in a thermometer.

"That's one way to get him to cooperate," Mary observed.

"Don't worry about the colonel," the nurse said. "He always does what he's supposed to. Bob's an excellent patient."

"Of course," Mary agreed.

The nurse pulled the thermometer out. "Looking fine,

Bob. I don't see any signs for concern anywhere." She picked up the chart at the end of the bed. "Let me make a note for the doctor." The nurse scribbled several things. "That ought to take good care of you."

"I hope so," Bob grumbled.

"Go on with whatever you were doing," the nurse answered and walked toward the door. "You have a good afternoon now."

Mary watched the woman disappear. "Sounds positive, Robert."

"They'd say the same thing if my temperature was a hundred and ten degrees," he snorted. "They try to make you feel good regardless of what the truth is."

"Of course," Mary agreed. "Are you getting tired of talking?"

Robert looked up at the ceiling for a moment. "Yes," he finally said. "Yes. I think that I'm running out of energy."

"You've been talking a long time."

Robert took a deep breath and exhaled. "Feels like it all happened only yesterday"—he shook his head—"not more than half a century ago."

"I hope you realize that you are filling in the blanks that have lingered in my mind for years," said Mary. "When you get tired, simply stop. That's what I always say."

"Probably should." Robert closed his eyes. "I seem to get tired easily these days."

Mary smiled. "The last thing that I want to do is tire you. Why don't you just take a little nap?" She waited for an answer, but nothing came. After several seconds, Mary said, "Robert?" No answer.

To her surprise, Mary saw that Robert was sound asleep. "My, my," she said softly. "He *was* tired."

As quietly as possible, Mary gathered up her things and slipped out the door. Evening was coming quickly, and Robert needed his rest. Walking down the hall, Mary realized for the first time how completely exhausted she felt. The length of the trip and the strain of the overwhelming emotion had drained her. By the time she reached the car, she was ready to fall asleep.

For a few moments, Mary sat behind the wheel. She remembered seeing a Motel 6 up the road that should be as inexpensive as anything else. She turned the car key and backed out.

~

When Mary awoke, the sun was shining brightly through a crack in the curtains of her small room. "Oh my." She pushed herself up in bed. "What time is it?" Mary picked up the small alarm clock. "Eight o'clock!" She hurled the blanket back and leaped out of bed, rushing to the shower. "I've overslept."

Thirty minutes later, Mary hustled out of the room. "I can grab something to eat at the hospital," she talked to herself. "Food will be fine over there, don't you know." Mary was on her way back to Robert more quickly than she'd done anything in years.

After a quick bite in the cafeteria, Mary hurried upstairs. She glanced at her watch. In exactly twenty-two minutes, she had gone from the motel to the hospital, had breakfast, gone up the elevator, and was standing in front of Robert's room. She took a big deep breath, knocked, and gently pushed the door open.

"Come on in," a man's voice said.

Mary peered around the corner. Robert sat propped up in bed, freshly shaved but still a bit on the peaked side. "You sort of disappeared last night."

"Well." Mary fidgeted for a moment. "You went to sleep so soundly that I didn't see any other way but to—"

"Sure." Robert gestured for her to come on in. "I'm glad to see you. Sit down."

Mary pulled up a chair. "You look like you've already had your morning shave and shower."

"They start early around here, but it fits my regular schedule well."

Mary sat down and pulled at her chin. "I always wondered what it would be like to see you in the morning. Fresh, shampooed, all spiffed up for the day."

"What do you think?" Robert reached over to pick up his cigarettes. "Do I pass?" He smiled. "Sorry. I picked up this nasty habit and can't seem to give it up."

Mary smiled. "We've all got these little quirks. I'm sure you'll come to observe mine."

"Hope I get the chance." Robert smiled.

Mary blushed. "Uh . . . we need to start your story from where you left off last evening."

"Oh yes. I was telling you about our troop of men walking through the cold night. What a terrible evening."

"I'm sure that it was." Mary settled back into the chair and stuck her legs out. "Please don't stop now. I want to hear everything that happened to you."

Robert closed his eyes for a moment. "For three days and nights we remained locked in that dilapidated old country barn. Can you imagine?"

"No." Mary shook her head. "No, I can only listen."

BELGIUM, DECEMBER 1944

Occasionally they heard a truck drive around outside and then leave a short time later. They heard the Germans talking outside but little else. Except for Robert Walker, the prisoners came from either the Ninety-ninth or Twenty-eighth Infantry Divisions. The men talked, fretted, and prayed, but no one came in or went out of the barn. Although the soldiers heard the guards walking around outside and feared what could happen, the Germans did nothing but march back and forth with guns hanging from their shoulders. It had been five days since Walker had eaten anything or drunk any water.

As night fell on December 22, 1944, the large wooden side door of the old barn creaked open. Five German soldiers walked in with guns aimed at their prisoners. The Americans froze in place.

"*Achtung!*" one of the guards called across the barn. "*Aufstehen!*" He tried again in broken English. "Stand up!"

Immediately another unit of soldiers walked through the door, carrying large metal vats.

"Line up with your helmets held out," the guard in charge ordered. *"Spoise. Abendessen!"*

The Americans instantly grabbed their helmets and rushed to line up in front of the steaming containers. Without a word being said, the men stumbled past while the guards ladled thick bean and potato stew into their helmets. The Allied soldiers quickly found separate areas of the barn to wolf down the food. Once the vats were empty, the German soldiers quickly retreated and left the barn as the last soldier kept his gun trained on the prisoners.

"Oh man!" Walker told Al King. "I could have eaten for the rest of the night."

King huddled in a tight ball on the ground. "Yeah, the stuff was amazingly good." He rubbed his stomach.

"Couldn't believe it," another soldier said. "If they'd just fed us a day ago." He shook his head and bent forward, saying nothing.

But as the evening wore on, most of the men felt pain and cramping set in. The food didn't set well. Worry and no food for five days caused their stomachs to churn and burn. Some men felt sick; others hurt. A few vomited. Without any lights, the soldiers finally drifted into sleep. Somewhere in the middle of the night, King felt a hand shaking him. Robert heard their voices.

"Al? Al? Are you awake?"

"Huh?" The private rolled over and saw a man standing over him. "What's happened?"

"I need your help."

"Who is it?"

"Desmond."

"Can't you just sleep?" King rolled over the other way.

"I got a big problem."

Al turned back over and sat up. "What?" he whispered. "What's the matter?"

"I messed my pants."

"You did *what*?"

"I ate too much or something. What am I going to do?"

"Listen!" Al pounded the hay on the ground beside him. "Throw the pants out the window and go back to sleep. Understand?" He put his hands over his head and curled up in a tight ball. "Get out of here. Don't wake me again."

~

The first light of dawn broke through the cracks in the wooden barn some time shortly after 0700. No one moved for a while. Al King finally stirred and sat up. A few feet from him a soldier was sleeping without his pants.

"Desmond? Where's your pants?"

The soldier stirred and rubbed his eyes. He slowly sat up and looked around.

"Desmond! Where's your pants?"

Pulling his white legs up next to his chest, the soldier shivered and shrugged. "You told me to throw them out the window last night."

"You did that?"

"That's what you said."

"How do you plan to find another pair of pants this morning?" King stood up. "You thought that you'd run down to the local mercantile store?"

Desmond scratched his head. "I don't know," he muttered.

"Good Lord!" King shook his head. "Anybody in here got an extra pair of pants?" He shouted across the barn. "Desmond will freeze to death if we don't find something for him to wear."

After several minutes of searching, a soldier from Nebraska with the Twenty-eighth Infantry Division came up with extra pants, and Desmond hurriedly put them on.

"I can't believe you." King walked away shaking his head.

Men began walking around, stretching, trying to get their bodies moving. Robert watched Desmond for a few minutes and wondered if their time of incarceration might be coming to an end. The fact that the Nazis fed them was a clue. The Germans would either kill them soon or move the soldiers to some other place. Robert knew the moment had come to get rid of his own dogtags. He walked to the side of the barn and began digging with his heel, opening a hole along the side of the barn. Squatting down, Robert dropped the old dogtags in the ground and pushed dirt back over the top. He looked around to make sure no one was looking and then swept a handful of hay over the area.

Lieutenant Robert Walker was gone. Private Guy Robert Jones would live on.

Robert walked over to Al King. "From here on out, my

name is Private Guy Robert Jones." He pulled the tags out. "That's what my ID says."

"Good. I'll spread the word to the people around here who already know you." He walked away and started talking to a group of men who were standing around Desmond.

Sounds of vehicles pulling up echoed through the front door.

The Americans could hear the Germans doing something outside the barn. Ten minutes later the large double doors swung open. The guards had changed. Germans dressed in black uniforms stood outside with machine guns in hand.

"God help us," King said under his breath. "The SS has arrived."

"March!" a noncommissioned officer (NCO) shouted. "Make one line! Now!"

The men grabbed any gear they still had and hurried outside, lining up singularly in a long line with their hands on their heads and standing behind each other. Immediately the SS began systematically frisking each man. Al and Robert stood in the middle of the line waiting. In about five minutes the Nazis reached Al and began searching him.

"Ein armbonduhr!" the *Unterscharführer* said to the Nazi next to him and yanked Al's watch from his wrist.

Another NCO, a *Hauptscharführer*, took the watch and looked at it carefully. "Government issue," he told Al. "Legitimate loot. We will not return this to you."

Al nodded.

The NCO put Al's wedding ring back in King's hand as well as his black billfold. "We will not take these items from you."

"Thank you," King muttered. "*Danke.*"

The *Hauptscharführer* pulled out Al's dogtags and read them. "You are infantry?"

"Yes sir."

"Good." The NCO smiled and dropped the dogtags down his shirt and continued on down the line.

In another ten minutes the search concluded, and the SS troops ordered the men to start marching. For some reason, no one noticed Robert's watch. Periodically an SS trooper hurried the march along by striking the men with rubber truncheons and rifle butts. As the sun rose the temperature improved, but the day stayed cold.

Eventually the first group of SS troopers was replaced by other soldiers, but the Americans continued marching. Walker studied the SS officers with their autumn-pattern smocks over field-gray tunics. The officers' collars had been pulled up and out to display their medals of rank. Officers wore caps that buttoned in front and could be pulled down over their ears. Binoculars hung from their necks. Most of the time their captors looked sullen and emotionless, saying nothing. The SS officers generally acted hard, as if a brutal streak ran down their backs and they were marching animals over some cliff.

Abruptly Nazi infantrymen roared past, bouncing down the frozen road piled atop a *Panzerspahwagen SdKfs-234/1* armored car. Robert could see a 20 mm gun turret mounted on the armored car and aimed at them. The soldiers stared contemptuously at the Americans marching down the road but said nothing. The *Panzerspahwagen* hurried on as if keeping an appointment with the god of war somewhere on a battlefield off in the distance.

In midafternoon the Nazis allowed the Americans to sit down. The group fell to the ground in exhaustion. A few men talked to each other, but most sat with their heads between their knees.

"How long you think we've been walking?" a soldier asked Robert.

"I'd guess more than thirty miles."

"Go for about thirty-five," King added, leaning into the conversation. "I got the mileage off several signs we passed along the way."

Robert nodded. "I'd buy thirty-five miles. Just don't know when this is going to stop. My feet are killing me."

"There's a town not far ahead," the soldier pointed in front of them. "Let's see if that place offers any relief."

King nodded. "I hope." He looked up. "Uh oh, here comes the big man."

"Marsch!" the NCO yelled. "*Un!* Now!"

The Allies slowly returned to their feet and started out once again. They did not stop in the town, however, but kept marching toward the east, struggling down the snow-covered, paved highway. An hour later a larger town came into view, and the herd of prisoners straggled into the village. As the sun set, German citizens lined the streets and watched the Americans file past. Periodically someone yelled a threatening jeer, but most people stared silently. The parade didn't stop until it came to the jail in the center of the town.

Robert looked up at the tall buildings, reflecting another world, another time, another era. The place looked more like a castle and had to be two or three hundred years old. He felt that an aura of evil hung over the building, as if maybe the Inquisition had started in the basement. Above his head he could see a massive stone edifice with bars on the windows. Men seemed to be crammed against the steel railings over the windows. Several waved. The dungeon looked slightly crowded.

Abruptly the line started moving again. SS troops forced the Americans up the rock stairs and down the dark halls of the jail, which smelled putrid and damp. Many of the American soldiers at the front of the line disappeared as they were herded into cells that still had some space. Everywhere Robert looked, he saw men crowded together like Vienna sausages in a tin can. Looking up, he realized there were only two men in front of him.

The SS guard yelled something at the men in the cell in front of them. No one moved. The guard raised his machine gun and blasted away at the ceiling. Plaster, powder, and smoke flew. Chips of rock fell on Robert's head. Instantly the crowded room of men parted for Robert and his friends to enter. The second they were inside, the cell door slammed behind them. Walker felt the bars cramming into his back. The rest of the prisoners behind him marched silently on down the hall.

Robert caught his breath and looked at the tired, bedraggled faces around him. "Sorry for the inconvenience. Where you boys from?" he called out across the cell.

"Twenty-sixth Infantry Division," someone said.

"Second Division," another voice answered.

"Eighteenth," a man standing close by added.

"Thanks," Robert answered. "We're mostly the Twenty-eighth and Ninety-ninth Infantry here."

No one seemed to care. Robert turned to Al. "Can you move?"

"Not a hair."

"We supposed to sleep like this?" Al asked a man in front of him.

The soldier turned his head and spoke over his shoulder. "You're lucky 'cause you came in last. You're on the outside. Guess what it feels like to be the men in the middle."

Al drew a deep breath. "Man, this is the worst place we've been in so far."

"Wait until midnight," the soldier in front added. "You ain't felt nothing bad yet."

Twenty-Nine ~

As night settled, cold wind gusted through the broken windows of the jail, blowing the smell of the men, the latrine, and the filth of the prison across the drafty building. The stench caught Walker in the face, making him feel nauseous. He swallowed hard and turned away from the breeze, but the small crowded cell was even more difficult to endure. Elbows hit him in the arm and shoulders, in the chest. Robert couldn't move. If he let his mind wander and started reflecting on what he saw around him, fear would creep into his mind and distort his thinking, only adding emotional weight to his having to stand continually. Every ounce of strength he could muster would be needed to keep from slipping into despair. He had to fasten his mind on other things.

Robert kept reminding himself that he was now Private Guy Robert Jones, American 394th Infantry. The name

Robert was fortunate, making his task easier, but he worried that he'd slip and forget who he'd become.

Robert tried to turn his mind elsewhere. For a while he thought about Mary and what she might be doing, but his seven hours ahead meant she was probably finishing the day at the college. Not much to ponder there. He shifted his thoughts to home in Fort Towson and what people were up to there. Eventually, Robert thought about his mother.

The divorce had torn his world to pieces. One day he came home from school and Ma had disappeared, her clothes cleaned out of her closet and the suitcase gone. Robert had languished in pain for weeks.

Only later did he begin to hear the rumors. Seemed Ma was really upset when Pa had to sell out the business to old man Clark and they fought over the transaction. Robert never found out the gory details, but apparently the marriage quickly started on a slippery slide. A man showed up from somewhere and wanted Ma to go to California with him. The only thing Robert ever understood was that Ma just left. No hints, no warning, no nothing. His mother simply took off.

Robert still winced when he thought about her vanishing in the night. She'd written a couple of letters, but the contact had been marginal. With time her absence chewed away at his sense of self-confidence and certainty that life was predictable and dependable. Matters got scrambled in his mind, and everyday events felt uncertain. Just like his being forced to stand in some German jail when only a few days earlier he had been asleep in a warm bed in England.

Life seemed to be nothing but the unexpected exploding in his face.

The effects of the day's exhausting march pounded through his body, causing his legs to ache, his back to hurt, and his ravishing hunger to return. The men around him talked about food, but fatigue continued to work in his bones as all light faded. He couldn't decide if the tiredness in his muscles was worse than the gnawing in his stomach. Finally he knew that he couldn't stand up any longer. Robert slid down the side of the jail cell. No one could hold him up.

Robert leaned against the iron bars as he huddled on the floor. He rubbed his calves and the back of his thighs, but the pain wouldn't stop. If he couldn't stretch his legs out, cramping would soon start. The constant murmuring of hungry soldiers filled the cell. Men talked, fretted, and tried to distract each other from their pain. His head began to throb.

No one was fed; no water was given out.

Night fell over the entire town, and blackness filled the jail. A few lightbulbs kept the corridors barely lit, but the crowded conditions bathed the cells in darkness. Somewhere around 2200 hours, Robert dropped into an exhausted stupor, but an hour and a half later the jostling of the prisoners awakened him. At least the prisoners kept each other warm.

Before the break of the next day, the Allied prisoners were abruptly taken down the back steps of the city jail, and the march through the frozen streets started again. The men struggled to keep from succumbing to exhaustion.

The number of Allied prisoners had grown during the night, and Robert caught only occasional glimpses of men he had met earlier. During most of the early morning hours, the prisoners trudged silently through forests and villages that all took on the same anonymous white look. Snow covered everything. Robert concentrated on keeping his legs going and trying not to think about the cold or the biting wind or his empty stomach.

Somewhere near the middle of the day he thought about his sister. Lou was five years younger and was still in high school. Today she'd be riding in a car down Main Street, drinking a malt, and talking to some boy. Lou would be warm, wearing a heavy winter coat. Her black hair would hang down the back of her neck, and she would probably be wearing a wool pullover. She wouldn't have to walk through frozen snow for more than a few minutes. Her feet would stay warm, and her fingers would not hurt.

And he thought about Mary, teaching in a warm college classroom of warmly dressed students who were learning to draw and discovering how to paint. In the center of the room a large vase of flowers would be . . . warm.

The march halted. Robert could see seven green tents and many German soldiers lining the road. Nazi troops appeared to be hurrying the Allies into lines in front of the tents. No one spoke except for the SS troops shouting back and forth at the Americans. Robert had no idea what they were saying. Within moments, he found himself standing in a line behind six American soldiers. He hugged himself and blew on his stiff fingers. The man at the front of the line disappeared inside the tent, which looked large enough to hold four or five men.

Fifteen minutes later, the SS trooper beckoned for him to enter. To Robert's surprise, a heating stove roared in one corner of the small tent. He sat down in a chair waiting for him and felt his legs sag. Relief surged across his body. On the other side of a small field table, a German officer scribbled on a notepad. Robert rubbed his chin as he glanced around the barren green canvas room. He had not realized how thick the stubble on his face had become. Days had passed since he had last shaved. For a minute he fumbled around trying to remember just when had been the last time. Time blurred the past few days together.

"Ah, you are noticing your beard," his interrogator began in excellent English. "It does look as if you could use a barber." The German spoke with a slight English accent and smiled broadly.

Robert nodded but said nothing.

"Allow me to welcome you to Germany," the Nazi began casually. "We hope you enjoy being with us." The officer lit a cigarette and blew smoke over his head. "Perhaps you'd appreciate a smoke." He held out the pack in front of him.

The heat of the cigarette felt wonderful. Robert's fingers ached, and a little warmth would help limber up his joints. He reached out and took the cigarette, holding one hand above the curl of smoke.

"Good!" The SS officer smiled. "You will like these cigarettes. Excellent tobacco." The Nazi settled back in his chair, a fixed grin across his face. "I am interested in how you feel about your government assigning you to participate in such a sacrificial patrol."

Robert tried to make sure he understood what he heard.

"You are aware that the Allies sent you and your fellow soldiers out on a sacrificial mission, are you not?"

Robert frowned, not certain how to answer.

"Yes, it is true." The German continued smiling. "The other members of your squad have given us a great deal of information already." He held out his hand. "Might I see your dogtags?"

Robert slowly pulled the chain out of his shirt and held them in front of the German. The Nazi wrote the numbers on a piece of paper with the name Jones and his rank.

"American infantry," he mumbled as he wrote. "A shame that you would be used in such a meaningless use of manpower. So many of your fellow soldiers have had your same difficult experience. I am certain that you are feeling the pain this morning. Patrol-ordered slaughter is such an unfortunate thing." He smiled again.

Robert knew that he was being manipulated, and he tried to look blank. The warmth, the cigarette, the seemingly innocent comments suggesting that he was dumped on the Germans were nothing more than a ruse. But Walker remained one up on his interrogator; the SS officer hadn't recognized that he was wearing the wrong dogtags.

"Would you like to share the name of your destination when we captured you?"

"The Geneva convention only requires me to give you . . ."

"Of course, of course," the German officer cut him off. "I am well aware of those parameters. I thought we might be able to offer you better accommodations if we knew more about your assignment." He smiled again.

"I am only an infantryman," Robert shot back.

"Yes, yes." The German kept smiling. "Perhaps you would like a drink of water." He looked into Robert's eyes. "Yes, I can see that you would appreciate some water." He poured a small glass and pushed it across the table.

Robert stared at the glass but didn't move.

"Go ahead." The officer shrugged. "Be my guest."

Robert tried to raise the glass slowly but found himself abruptly gulping it down.

"Good. I thought you'd find the water enjoyable. I have more things that can be shared with our friends. The issue is one of your settling in for a little discussion. Do you understand me?"

Robert nodded. "However, under the Geneva conventions I am only required to report . . . "

"Of course, of course," the German officer's voice took on a slightly bored quality. "We've been over that fact. You must understand that other members of your patrol have already talked with us in some detail."

Robert looked straight ahead but said nothing.

"They have given us the nature of your assignment. All the details. You must understand that we know about the 394th Infantry Regiment, Canon Company, including the fact that Captain Frank A. Arnoldy of Minnesota is commander and First Lieutenant Binkley P. Brown of Houston,

Texas, is your executive officer." The Nazi continued smiling. "Surprised? You see, we have all the information."

Walker stared straight ahead.

"Sorry, old man. We know everything there is to know about you. During the thirties I spent years living in the United States. I know your people from top to bottom." Without losing his smile, the German reached over and took the cigarette out of Walker's hand. "I know that you sailed over here after landing in Liverpool. We basically have all the details of your travels in our notes."

Walker felt himself blink but kept looking straight ahead.

After several moments of total solitude, the German stood up, with his hands behind his back. "May I congratulate you on not sharing information. You have done well, but I must also tell you that should you prove to have other material that we need, our officers have very effective means of prying that data from you. You will find their techniques, shall we say, much more painful than mine. Are you sure that you have nothing else you might wish to share with me?"

Walker said nothing.

The SS officer opened the back of the tent and pointed out. "Good luck, Private Jones."

Walker walked back outside. The wind had picked up slightly and was blowing large flakes of snow through the air. Robert tucked his hands under his armpits and waited in the freezing snow.

Thirty ~

Maryland, April 2000

Robert stopped talking and stared straight ahead. In the silence, Mary studied the lines on his face. His wrinkles looked deep, and stress seemed etched around his eyes. He had seen hard, difficult things.

"How did you stand the extreme cold?" Mary finally asked.

Robert blew a long stream of smoke across the top of his bed. "I don't know." He ran his hand nervously through his hair. "I suppose there was no other choice if I was to survive. I simply made myself keep on walking."

Mary bit her lip. "You thought about dying?"

Robert nodded his head. "Fear was my motivator. If anything kept me moving, it was unrelenting dread. Frankly, I really didn't expect to make it through that first night's march. I thought that I'd stumble and someone would shoot me."

"I prayed for you every night, Robert. I didn't even stop until after the war was over, and then I had to assume you were dead."

Robert nodded his head and his eyes watered. "Ahem." He tried to clear his throat. "Thank you," he muttered.

"I wanted you to live." Mary's voice cracked. "I finally reached the place where I couldn't think about what happened to you anymore." She forced a smile and felt a tear run down her cheek. "I'm sorry." Mary wiped the tear away. "I didn't mean to get so emotional."

Robert nodded and looked down at the covers.

Mary sniffed. "Do you feel like going on?"

"Sure." Robert took another puff of the cigarette. "I can talk some more."

GERMANY, DECEMBER 1944

Tired soldiers milled on the back side of the interrogation tents, waiting for the rest of the men to complete the screening process. The Germans stood around the edge of the group watching. Most of the time their rifles hung loosely from their shoulders. The Americans were too tired to attempt a break. When the Germans spoke to each other, their breath circled up in frosty puffs. With the temperature below freezing, the Allies had to keep moving to fight off the terrible effects if the chill cut through their boots. Walker spotted Al King hovering in the center of the circle of men, hugging his arms around his chest.

"You all right?" Walker sidled up to the infantryman.

"Just a tad on the cold side," King quipped cynically. "Did you tell Mr. Nazi in there everything he wanted to know?"

"Afraid not."

"Too bad. Then you'll have to walk with us to the next stop." King kept rubbing his hands together. "Terrible cold out here."

"What do you think they wanted?"

King shrugged. "Probably a good look at our dogtags. I imagine they're trying to figure out where our troops are positioned. Keep our units identified."

"You got it," Robert clipped. "They're also trying to spread a little discontent along the way to see if we'll fall for it."

"Yep." King nodded his head. "That's my reading."

"EinschlieBen!" an SS trooper shouted at the men. *"EinschlieBen!"*

"Don't talk anymore," Robert said under his breath.

Silence fell over the group of men. In five minutes the last Allied soldier trudged out of the tent and the long march started again. Without a word being spoken, the Americans fell into a single line winding down the highway, tramping through the snow with their German captors marching alongside them.

Periodically the SS soldiers descended on the group, shouting and striking the Americans. *"Sich beeilen!"* a German yelled somewhere behind Robert in the line. *"Beeilen!"* another SS trooper picked it up.

Walker increased his pace. "Those SS idiots want us to walk faster." Robert growled under his breath.

The men picked up the tempo. Walking faster kept him warmer, but Robert's hunger chewed away at his endurance. He had to fasten his mind elsewhere than on the road in front of him.

Once again Walker's thoughts returned to Mary and the last night they had been together in Sterling's city park. For a moment he could almost smell her fragrance and feel the warmth from the touch of her hand. That night she had told him, "Be not afraid." Her words echoed through his mind. He could see the tears in her eyes and hear her voice quiver. He replayed the scene again and again. He imagined that he could feel her warmth.

"Schnell!" echoed from somewhere near the back of the line. *"Schnell!"*

Robert tried to walk a bit faster but knew he'd stumble and fall into the snow if he did. They'd probably shoot him. Robert made himself think about Mary again and started another rerun of his last night in Sterling. If he could simply keep his mind locked there, maybe the walk would be endurable. Maybe he wouldn't stumble. Maybe . . . At least the thoughts made him feel warmer. Maybe . . .

The hours dragged past, but near the middle of the afternoon, the shape of a large city appeared on the horizon. Robert's feet had become numb, and he felt little below his knees. His fingers burned. Robert soon saw signs indicating that Bonn was only a short distance ahead of them. His mouth felt unbearably dry, but the pace of the forced march didn't slow even when they reached the outskirts of the city. He bent down, grabbing at the snow and shoving a handful into his mouth.

People stood on the streets and stared at the frozen Americans hustling down the icy road. A few women hurled insults, but most said nothing. Their stares looked blank and empty. Eventually the Allies were herded into a small city square and surrounded by Germans with rifles and submachine guns pointed at them.

Robert studied the new soldiers guarding them. Most of the Nazis wore two-piece pajamalike white camouflage suits over their woolen uniforms. The camouflage seemed to be water-repellent and quilted in a light fashion to provide extra warmth. Arms, ankles, and waist areas had been sealed shut with drawstrings. The Nazis had already collected the Allies' highly prized rubber overshoes. In sharp contrast, the Americans looked bedraggled and forlorn.

"Aufmerksamkeit!" an SS trooper shouted. *"Marsch!"*

Immediately the line of troops started out of the square and back down the street. Fifteen minutes later the line of men trampled inside a barbed-wire-covered gate. Scattered across the wide compound Robert could see many wooden barracks. Towering above the prisoners in high wooden towers, guards trained their machine guns on the men who walked doggedly below. Many other prisoners were already locked inside the wide expanse. Wherever he looked, Walker saw prisoners of war. Some were French and quite a few more British, but most were Americans.

Robert listened carefully to what he could hear of the

guards babbling to each other and soon decided they had come to Stalag VI-G inside the city of Bonn. After thirty minutes of waiting, the exhausted men were marched into a barracks. Without anything being said, the soldiers crumpled into stacked wooden bunks and fell on the slats. For the first time in days Robert could stretch his legs straight out and feel his muscles relax. Sheer fatigue overwhelmed him. Sleep swallowed him in a single gulp.

The movement of a man crawling over him woke Walker, and he looked around the long room for the first time. Robert had fallen into such a stuporous sleep that he had not really looked at the barracks when he had come in. Although men were crowded together in bunks reaching up to the ceiling, the building wasn't nearly as packed as the jail had been. The room smelled stale and flat like bad deodorant, but at least the place wasn't freezing. He sat up on the bare wooden slats and watched the men who were walking around. Most looked as beaten and tired as he felt. Feeling returned to his feet.

"Know what today is?" a soldier asked him.

Robert thought for a moment and shook his head.

"It's Christmas Eve."

"You serious?"

The soldier nodded his head. "Can you believe it? We're going to spend Christmas Eve in a German prison."

Robert rubbed his forehead. The days had slipped by

without his having a sense of time. Attempting to survive had pushed everything else aside. Christmas Eve? Could it really be?

"I've got a surprise for us!" a man at the other end of the building called across the barracks. The soldier stood up and cupped his hands over his mouth like an announcer, "We can celebrate Christmas now!"

Men slipped off the bunks and trudged to see what the soldier was talking about. Robert's legs ached, but he knew that they needed to be moved and exercised. Walker peered over the men kneeling in front of him. From somewhere out in the exercise yard, one of the soldiers had found a single branch from a tree. He had crammed the branch into a crack in the floor and it stuck up like a lonely exile. A few pieces of faded paper had been twisted around the twigs.

"Here's our Christmas tree!" the soldier standing beside the branch exclaimed. "Bring on the turkey. We can celebrate!"

Someone clapped, and the men cheered. "Hurrah!" rang across the room, and the men laughed.

"Wonderful!"

"Exciting."

"Merry Christmas!"

Robert hadn't heard laughter since he had left England, and for a moment he was shocked. But the sudden explosion of joy broke the spell of the frozen nights and the hungry days. He thought he might cry.

A couple of men grabbed each other and started a makeshift dance around the tree. Other men laughed and clapped, and the forbidding gloom of the barracks disappeared.

From some other barracks, a man began singing, "God rest ye merry gentlemen, let nothing you dismay . . ." The noise in Walker's barracks died away as the men stopped to listen. The carol faded out, but from another building in the compound other men began singing, "Noel, Noel, born is the King of Israel." Across the length of Stalag VI-G, noise came to a halt, and the sound of the men's voices settled over camp.

Much closer to Walker's quarters men began singing, "Silent night, holy night, all is calm, all is bright." He tightened his jaw and felt the rumble in his stomach. A tear edged toward the corner of his eye. He blinked it away.

"Round yon virgin mother and child," the men sang in low haunting tones. "Holy infant, so tender and mild."

Walker turned away from the Christmas tree and wandered back to the row of beds. He sat down on the end of a bunk and tried not to weep. In the middle of the building, Robert could see the straggly paper-covered tree. In this seemingly godforsaken prison, God had shown up. Hope had sprung forth like a tree in the spring. Never had he ever expected to find a window of promise in such circumstances.

Thirty-One ~

Maryland, April 2000

Robert had been talking for hours. When lunch came he ate little, and Mary nibbled on what he left on the plate. Telling the tale seemed to energize Robert and relieve his pain. He eventually stopped talking for a moment and lay silently in the bed.

"I remember Christmas so well that year," Mary said. "Christmas of 1944. Of course, I didn't know that anything had happened to you yet. I went home to my family and told them about this wonderful soldier who had come into my life. They teased me and wanted to know everything. I expected that you were gathering around a fireplace in some pub, having the time of your life."

Robert shook his head. "The tree was so small and fragile, and yet it helped me go on."

"We had turkey and dressing," Mary added. "Of course everything was rationed, but we had more than enough. I would have been glad to have given you my share if it had been possible."

Robert smiled. "Thank you." He looked away. "I haven't talked much about this time. I find it difficult to remember some of those moments. They were hard."

Mary looked at the floor. "Take your time."

"I'll try to go on." Robert's voice had become quieter and much lower. "Not easy, you know."

BONN, GERMANY, CHRISTMAS 1944

On Christmas morning across Bonn, the promise of new life echoed throughout the city. The bells of a neighborhood church rang out the blessed message of the morning. The hopeful sound vibrated and resounded across Stalag VI-G, waking the men, telling them that Christmas had come again. Even their capture couldn't keep out the promise.

No guards shouted or yelled at the prisoners. Sentinels didn't demand they stumble out of their bunks. Looking at each other as the warm rays of sunlight fell across the bunks, the men sensed that the festive day brought a relaxation of demands and rules. Calm hung peacefully in the cold morning air as if God had ordered a reprieve.

Several German soldiers wearing woolen overcoats hanging down to the ankles of their high black boots appeared in the doorway of the barracks and motioned for the men to line up. Walker understood little of German and only got the general drift that they would be going outside. Without pressure or harassment, the line of Allied soldiers marched between the wooden barracks until they entered a large mess hall that smelled of food. The pain of an empty stomach hit Robert and left him feeling weak, but the long room was warm and smelled heavenly.

Walker immediately fell into the line of prisoners, walking past Germans serving soup. He said nothing but stared at the steaming vat of soup and the trays of sliced bread standing behind the kitchen crew. The aroma made him feel weak in the knees. He wanted to leap at the bread, grab it, and fill his pockets.

"*Suppe?*" the German soldier said and handed him a wooden bowl.

Robert nodded. "Soup!" He couldn't help but grin.

The German ladled up a bowl of cabbage soup, and the next soldier handed him one piece of bread. Robert immediately scuffled off to a corner of the room where he could eat in solitude. Pieces of cabbage floated wonderfully across the top of the bowl. An aroma of nourishment settled over him with the enticement of a French perfume drifting down a lovely Parisian lane on a spring evening.

Remembering what had happened the last time they'd been fed, Robert made himself eat as slowly as possible. The warm cabbage broth trickled down his throat like a gift from heaven. He could feel and hear his stomach moan and growl. Robert savored each bite of the brown-crusted bread as if it might be his last.

For the first time in days, Robert felt genuinely human again. The subtle quietness of the room offered him a sense of his own dignity. At the moment he might have been eating at home in Fort Towson.

"You okay?" Private Al King asked from behind Robert.

Walker looked at his friend. King hadn't shaved in days. Dark black circles hung under Al's eyes, and his skin seemed unusually white.

"I said, are you *okay*?"

Robert nodded his head. "I'm alive. After what we've lived through this week, that qualifies for okay."

Al smiled. "Good answer. I hope this soup doesn't hit us like the last meal we ate. Went through me like goose liver through a duck. I thought I'd die by nightfall."

Robert raised an eyebrow. "Eat slowly. That's all I can say."

"Can you believe that today's Christmas?"

"Strange, isn't it?"

"Feels like I'm on another planet." Al shook his head. "Ain't never experienced a holiday like this one. Man, can you believe this place?" He shrugged. "I just want to come out of this alive."

Robert took another small bite of bread. "At least we're warm for a change." He leaned closer to the private. "What are you hearing about the war? What's happening out there?"

"Apparently the Germans made a major foray into Belgium in the sweep where they got us. They've taken many prisoners. We're by no means alone in this thing. Sounds like they've rounded up thousands."

"Got any idea how far they went in their offensive thrust?"

Private King shook his head. "Some of the Germans seem to think they've already taken Bastogne, but I doubt it. Nobody that I'm listening to seems to know the real story."

"We've gone rather far into Germany," Robert said. "Bonn isn't exactly on the border, you know."

Private Gene Tivey walked up and nodded to both men. "I could eat a bucket of this soup. How about you guys?"

Robert shook his head. "Not if you don't want to be sick as a dog. Remember last time?"

"Only speaking figuratively," Tivey said. "I thought the Krauts were trying to starve us to death. Must be their way of celebrating Christmas."

"You'll certainly lose plenty of weight before this thing is over." Robert finished eating his piece of bread. "Stewed cabbage isn't exactly what you need for genuine energy and protein."

Tivey smiled. "Well, if nothing else, Merry Christmas, gentlemen."

King laughed. "Merry Christmas? Now that's a one-liner to remember all day." He shoved the last piece of bread into his mouth. "By golly! Merry Christmas to every last one of us!"

The men split up, and Robert shifted over to a window, finishing his soup while looking outside. Even though only a few spoonfuls waited in the bottom, he treated every drop as precious. He looked out across the large assembly field in front of the entry gate. Strands of barbed wire covered the fence tops. German troops stood poised on mounted towers with machine guns aimed inside the camp. Stalag VI-G would be a very difficult place from which to escape. They'd be there until the Germans decided to the contrary.

As the blackness of night fell over the camp, Robert stretched out on the top bunk snuggled between two soldiers. On both sides of the bunk, rows of men stretched the length of the room. Around the packed building, men lay similarly squeezed together. Even though he was still hungry, Robert felt better than he had for days. At least his body could stretch out.

He thought about the wild adventure he'd been on since coming to England. The experience had jerked him around like a child on a roller coaster. England was filled with customs, practices, and habits totally different from anything he'd known in his life. People talked with strange accents and sounded contrary to what his ears expected. The wet climate had proven to be vastly different from anything he'd anticipated. In fact, the experts had said the temperatures were the coldest Europe had known in decades.

Everything had occurred with a speed beyond Walker's wildest expectation. It seemed that he had no more slipped into a familiar B-17 before the Nazis dropped on him like bees diving into a honeycomb. When he was in training he had thought about being shot down, but he had never expected it to really happen. Then he was drifting down through the sky on the end of a parachute. Robert remembered again the man he'd found in Bullingen, shot through the forehead and frozen in place. His cold, empty stare worked like a crowbar prying away at Robert's sanity. The image haunted Robert and made him shudder. Robert wondered what happened to his bombardier. Maybe he was a prisoner too. Maybe he was dead.

The secret of the G material and the new attack plans came back to mind. Robert wondered if they'd made the difference he had hoped for. By now the Allies should be hitting their targets with greater accuracy and consistency. At least changing his dogtags had protected him from even being questioned. The Germans saw him only as an ordinary GI trying to survive.

Robert's mind had been focused during the forced journey on nothing more than surviving. And he knew that the Nazis could decide to shoot all of them. He felt as if the giant of overwhelming fear marched along at his side like a wretched companion. Tonight his situation felt better, but tomorrow hell might return.

Robert rolled over on his back and stared at the dark shape of the long flat bunk above him. The air remained stale but warm. He knew the other men had the same fears and doubts. Regardless of what they said or didn't say, no one was any different. Each man felt dread and apprehension.

"O Lord," Robert whispered without making a sound, "thank You for being with me through this terrible time. I wouldn't be alive tonight if You had not made my life secure. Thanks for Christmas and what happened on this day so long ago. Please speak in my heart the simple command 'Be not afraid' so that I may sleep tonight in Your peace. Amen." He closed his eyes and in a few moments drifted into deep sleep.

Robert slept through the long night and awoke in a fairly

positive frame of mind. Guards were blowing whistles and demanding that the prisoners get up. They'd soon be coming through the barracks. He stretched and stood up, feeling relatively well. Yesterday's soup hadn't made him sick. He shaved with a razor shuffled among the men in the barracks, and his face felt smooth again. He hoped he'd get a hot shower before too long.

The door to the barracks flew open, and German soldiers hurried into the room, swinging their rifles in every direction. "*Aufmerksmakeit!*" the man in charge demanded. "*EinschlieBen!*"

Silence, except for the noise of the American soldiers falling into a straight line, settled over the room. Another German SS officer entered the building. Tall and blond, the man wore a black uniform that boasted the insignia of his office. He surveyed the Americans contemptuously, walking up and down the row of prisoners as if giving them a silent condemnation. The officer walked deliberately yet arrogantly across the creaking boards.

"You look reasonably healthy," he said in excellent English. "In a few minutes you will be loaded in boxcars and sent farther east. You are officially prisoners of war and will be treated with the respect due this lowly position, if you seem to warrant the same." He stopped and looked coldly at the men. "Should you give us any reason or excuse for punitive action, you will be shot immediately. Understand?"

The officer turned on his heels and marched out of the room. One of the soldiers shouted, "*Marsch!*" Robert once again marched out into the ice and snow.

Thirty-Two

MARYLAND, APRIL 2000

Robert stopped talking about his war experiences and turned toward Mary. "You came all the way just to see me?" he asked abruptly.

"Well, yes. Of course." Mary shrugged. "Who else do I know around here?"

"Just to make sure that I was alive?"

Mary gestured with her hands aimlessly. "Certainly." She frowned. "What other reason would I have for coming?"

Robert shook his head. "Because you cared?"

The question caught Mary off guard, leaving her feeling slightly embarrassed. "Certainly I cared," she said defensively. "I always cared, Robert."

"And why did you care?" he pushed.

Mary struggled for an answer. There was no use in being coy. They were too far along in life for that sort of maneuver. "I loved you, Robert," she blurted out. "Wasn't that obvious?"

Robert frowned for a moment and pursed his lips. "Time does strange things to your mind. The pressure of capture makes a few days seem like weeks. I lost all sense of time and felt like they had imprisoned me for years. Strange." He nodded his head and looked down for several moments. Finally he looked at Mary again. "You know, something inside me always kept me hoping that you loved me."

"Well, I did, Robert." Mary jutted her chin out defiantly. "My life situation changed, but I didn't stop loving you."

"That's very good to know," Robert grinned as he replied. He settled back against the pillow and looked up at the ceiling. The grin remained.

"You're not going to stop talking, are you?" Mary asked.

"Oh no." Robert shook his head but kept looking up. "No. I was in the middle of telling you about the Germans marching us back outside in the snow."

"I'm ready."

Robert looked over at her. "You're quite a woman, Mary, determined and very interesting." Robert chuckled. "Let's see if I can pick up where I left off."

GERMANY, LATE DECEMBER 1944

German soldiers marched the Allied prisoners toward the train tracks at the opposite end of the camp. The slackness that Christmas had brought totally evaporated only a day later. Without food or water, the men of the 394th Infantry, Ninety-ninth Division, Canon Company disappeared into cattle cars. Behind them, Walker could see the large assembly area emptying out. In front of them, long lines of trains waited to whisk them to some unknown destination.

Robert maneuvered to stay in the center of the men. The unlucky ones on the outside and the edges got hit and knocked around with rubber clubs, but the ones in the middle were protected by the sheer numbers of soldiers pressing around them. Robert was learning.

"Sich beeilen!" SS troops yelled at the men pouring in front of them. *"Schnell!"* the Nazis screamed at their prisoners. The Allies hurried onto the large wooden boxcars. No one offered any form of resistance. *"Es lilig haben!"*

"Oh!" the man next to Robert observed. "They're putting us on old forty-et-eight boxcars."

"What's that?" Robert asked.

"That's what the French called these things in World War I. They were built to carry forty men and eight horses or mules. Get the picture?"

More than sixty men had already been herded into the boxcar in front of him. The men behind him pushed him on. No time to hesitate or wait, unless he wanted to get smashed on the head. He stepped across the cement loading dock onto the train. The pressure from behind forced him onward, and Robert nearly tripped.

"Watch," the soldier continued. "They'll put a hundred men in here before we move out of this place." Other soldiers struggled past, and the man disappeared with the men being pushed to the far side of the train car.

Robert felt the pressure of prisoners pushing around him on every side. The SS would pack the car full before the door shut. He felt the side of his shaven face. At least he'd added a touch of humanity during the stay in Bonn. No matter what happened, he was shaved.

Eventually the large wooden door slid shut and darkness settled over the inside of the coach. Slits in the side let small rays of sunlight and cold air waft through the car. "Going to be a tough trip," an American grumbled to Robert. "No telling how long they'll have us in here."

Robert nodded. He looked at the shorter man. The soldier's steel helmet was pulled down over his eyes, giving him a somewhat sinister look. He'd shaved sometime in the last several hours, and he looked like he was maybe nineteen or twenty years old. "Where you from?"

"Detroit."

"Detroit? Interesting."

"Yeah. Where you from?"

"Oklahoma. Fort Towson."

"Where?" the man grimaced.

"Never heard of Fort Towson?"

"You got to be kidding. Nobody's ever heard of Fort Towson."

Robert laughed. "That's my hometown."

The man shook his head. "Nope. Never heard of the place. Long way from Detroit to Oklahoma."

Robert nodded. "Long way. Where do you think we're going?"

"Got no idea."

Robert rolled his shoulders and moved his arms up and down. “Think we’ll be in here more than a day?”

The man from Detroit shrugged. “Got no idea.” He rubbed his chin. “I’m afraid this could be a very long trip. They say most of ’em are.”

~

Freezing cold wind made the night unbearable, and by the time the sun rose the next day, most of the men were sick. Virtually no one had slept. The soldiers were so tightly packed in the forty-et-eight car that the men couldn’t sit down. Eventually they devised a system for taking turns sitting down. The system worked during the day, but not for sleeping at night. To survive the freezing weather, they eventually concluded that they must protect their feet at all costs. Frozen toes meant sure death, so at night the prisoners paired off, shoving their stocking feet beneath the field jacket and armpits of a partner. The only advantage of the overcrowding was that it provided more body heat than would have been possible in an open-air car. To pass the time, the men told jokes and stories and played round-robin games they had learned at church or in the Boy Scouts. The hours dragged by. Eventually it became difficult to stand for a very long time. By the morning of the next day, diarrhea and stomach cramps attacked the vast majority of the prisoners. The conditions remained intolerable through the third day and night.

“Listen!” a man sitting next to Robert suddenly demanded.

"Sounds like airplanes. Up there." He pointed to the ceiling of the boxcar.

The train started to slow down, and Robert strained to hear.

"Yeah. Sounds like they might be getting ready to dive."

"Think they're German?"

Robert listened carefully. "Hard to tell, but if I was going to make a guess, I'd say they sound like P-38s or something close."

The sudden roar of an aircraft sounded over the top of the train. In the distance the fire of machine guns seemed to be strafing the front of the train.

"Sounds like our boys," Robert said. "I think the Allies are going to hit this train hard."

"What do we do?" The soldier looked frightened.

"Stay down," Robert said. "Keep as low to the floor as you can."

The roar of machine gun fire cut across the top of the car. Splinters of wood flew in every direction. An airplane shot across the train and disappeared.

"They'll be back," Robert warned. "Stay down."

Soldiers began falling in every direction. Men bounced against the walls of the boxcar, falling on top of each other. Several men piled on top of Robert and the man next to him.

"Watch out," the soldier groaned. "This thing is going to get real serious before it's over."

"They'll be back. Keep down! Cover your heads!" Robert yelled at the top of his voice.

An airplane flew across and fired into the car. What sounded like a P-38 seemed to be flying up the length of the train, hitting one car after another. The train began to slow.

Maybe I could get out, Robert thought. *If I could get to the door and drop out of this car, I'd be able to work my way through the countryside. Wouldn't be many soldiers around here.*

Machine gun fire again exploded into the boxcar at a much lower level than before. The sound of bullets whizzing past terrified Robert. He knew that one lead bullet could literally cut through every man in the car and come out the other side. The train slowed to a halt. Far off in the sky he could hear what sounded like a dogfight. Apparently the *Luftwaffe* had shown up and joined the scrape.

No way out, he reasoned. *There's simply no route out of here unless they let every one of us loose.*

No one moved for more than five minutes. Eventually they could hear Germans running alongside the train yelling. Robert got back on his feet. Even though the sides of the train had been well shot up, the boxcar remained a solid prison cell.

"Let us out!" the prisoners cried through the walls of the train.

"We've got wounded men in here! Shot and killed!"

"Help us with the injured!"

"Open the door!"

Robert looked around the car. At least twenty men had been hit. They were dead or dying fast. Unless the wounded received immediate attention, they'd bleed to death, but no one unlocked the massive side door. The Germans periodically stopped and checked the lock to make sure it was secure but said nothing to the pleading prisoners. In about an hour, the train started moving again.

Although he tried to move closer to the wounded, Robert found that it was impossible to move far. Most of the wounded were dead by the time the train reached full speed. The few survivors wouldn't make it through the night. Eventually the system of standing and sitting began again. Freezing night air whistled through the boxcar of prisoners. The terrified prisoners huddled together, fighting to stay alive. Far too many weren't.

Eventually the men piled the bodies of the dead against the front wall of the boxcar, where rigor mortis stiffened them into a ghastly mound. The train pulled to a halt on a side track. If the temperatures warmed above freezing, the smell in the train would quickly become unbearable.

For two whole days the entire train stayed detoured on a side track before the journey started again. Because prison trains had the lowest priority on the travel schedule, they were forced to wait for everything else to pass.

Walker remained in the boxcar for five days and nights. Not once did the Germans allow them out of the car or remove the dead. Eventually Robert began to think that he would surely die before he walked in the light of day again.

During the entire week of travel, the prisoners received one bowl of soup and one cup of water.

Thirty-Three ~

MARYLAND, APRIL 2000

The hospital door swung open and an orderly backed into the room. "Suppertime."

Robert stopped telling his story, turned, and smiled at the man bringing in the tray of food. "Put it here," he said, indicating the table next to his bed.

"You bet. I think you'll like what we've fixed for tonight." He removed the cover from the entrée and steam curled up. "How about a little roast beef and mashed potatoes? Have some cooked carrots too. Even got a good dessert for you."

Robert smiled. "Looks good, but I'm not sure that I'm hungry enough to eat all of this."

"Once you get into it, your appetite will take over." The orderly winked at Mary. "Sorry. We only get one of these per customer. Afraid you'll have to eat down in the cafeteria."

Mary smiled. "No problem."

"Enjoy yourself." The orderly shut the door behind him.

Mary stood up. "I think that I'll take a little walk, Robert. You eat your supper, and I'll get some exercise. Stretching is what I need."

"You need to eat."

"Afraid not." Mary laughed. "I've already had too much too many times. But I do need to move my legs. You eat and I'll walk a bit." She opened the door. "Don't be in a hurry. Just let yourself relax."

Mary walked to the elevator and went down to the first floor. For a while she walked along the sidewalk, looking at the flowers and watching the sunset. Lights began to come on along the streets, and cars started turning on their headlights. Before long, night would fall over the city. She knew it would be important to find a place to sleep again, but those matters would take care of themselves in due course. After thirty minutes, Mary went back up the elevator to the second floor.

Mary pushed open the door to Robert's room. She could see the empty dishes pushed to one side on his tray. Leaning back against the pillow, Robert's eyes were shut. Mary quietly opened the door and slipped in.

"Ah, you're back," Robert said, opening one eye.

Mary looked up, surprised at his voice. "Oh, I'm sorry that I woke you."

"Just resting," he said. "Catching my breath. Always helps after a big supper."

Mary sat down. "Had a lovely walk outside."

"Good. Good." Robert turned slightly. "Actually I've been thinking about my story I've been telling you. Funny, but I haven't thought about some of these things for a long time."

"We've got plenty of time, Robert. You don't have to tell me everything tonight."

"I was just thinking about what happened after Christmas that year." He scratched his head. "You know, that proved to be as hard a time as any of it did." He flopped back and looked at the ceiling. "Hard, hard time it was."

"I'm listening."

"I remember leaving that place," Robert said. "Unforgettable experience."

"How did it happen?" Mary asked.

Robert closed his eyes. "Wasn't easy," he said slowly.

"Proved to be demanding in a different sort of way," his voice trailed off. "Nothing was easy . . . "

STALAG IV-B, GERMANY, JANUARY 1945

On New Year's Day the trainload of prisoners pulled into Stalag IV-B. No one knew what German town they were near. The puffing locomotive sent spiraling waves of smoke into the morning air. Snow covered the ground around the tracks, and German officers stood outside in woolen and leather jackets. Most of the soldiers looked more like young boys than the hardened SS troops the men of Canon Company had seen along the way. Robert stood with his face pressed against the side of the cattle car gulping fresh air as the train came to a halt before a barbed-wire enclosed compound.

"Out!" a Kraut kept wailing at the train cars. The men began standing and shuffling toward the door.

The men moved as quickly as possible, but many found it difficult. Robert glanced at the front of the car where the stack of dead men lay. Most of the bodies had been turned toward the front of the car so their faces couldn't be seen.

"Stehen," guards yelled into the boxcars. *"Schnell!"*

The door to Walker's car slid open, and cold winter air blasted in. The contrast in air made Robert realize how awful the coach had come to smell.

"Stehen!" the guard at the door yelled and motioned for the men to move quickly. The SS trooper pointed his rifle menacingly.

Robert hobbled toward the exit. His stomach hurt and ached from having eaten only once in five days. He was weak and feared that he might fall.

"Out!" a Nazi cried in English.

Outside, Walker walked down a gravel corridor leading into the camp. He saw American soldiers walking in the open yard and looking out the windows of wooden barracks. They shouted and waved, and he returned their salutes.

"What do you think they're going to do with us?" a familiar voice said from behind him.

Al King was walking only a few feet away.

"Al! How you feeling?" Robert slowed down to stand alongside his friend.

"Rotten. You?"

"About as bad. Been a tough trip."

King shook his head. "I thought maybe I'd die." He looked straight ahead without blinking. "Wasn't sure I'd get here. Thought they might shoot me. Had terrible diarrhea."

Robert shrugged. "Yeah. Didn't we all."

"You still going by the name of Jones?"

"I guess so." Robert shrugged. "They're the only tags I've got. For better or worse, I'm stuck being Jones until we get out of here."

"Out of here? Ha!"

Robert shot a hard look at King. "Don't talk like that. Nobody knows what tomorrow will bring."

"I was near the front of that car where the dead men were. Another day on the track and I'd probably have done something stupid to get myself killed. I'm near the end of my rope."

Robert took hold of King's wrist firmly. "No, you're not. Shake it off. Nobody knows what tomorrow will bring."

Private First Class King looked straight ahead.

"I mean it," Robert growled. "I don't want to hear that kind of talk again."

King said nothing but marched on, as if strangely detached from the group.

"Line up!" Loudspeakers in the center of the camp demanded that the Allies form lines in front of open doors. "Line up in rows." The microphones kept broadcasting the same instructions over and over again.

Walker ended up in a slow-moving group of men working their way into a large administration building. Once inside, Walker felt like he'd stumbled into a zoo. Hundreds of men were milling around, and no one appeared to know what they were supposed to be doing. Eventually it became clear they were to form lines. During the next several hours the prisoners were inspected and checked by doctors and camp personnel. They were stripped, and their military clothes were taken away. The men were issued old clothes provided by the prison. All money was confiscated. By midafternoon, Walker and the remainder of Canon Company had been shuffled off into a compound of English prisoners of war with a few Americans.

Any comparison with America had disappeared. The building looked to be more than a hundred years old with ancient shingles high overhead. The brick floor was worn; obviously the place had been used for many purposes over the decades. He could only see two small cooking stoves on the side, but the place seemed much warmer than the train car. The stoves were old wood burners.

"I say, old man," a Brit extended his hand as he spoke, "welcome to our little castle on the hillside."

Robert shook his hand. "It has a great deal more heat than where I've been for the last five days. My name is Robert Jones."

"Sounds British enough. Me name is Archibald Kent." He pointed toward the stoves. "They only let us burn the stoves for three hours a day, but we get by."

"Mostly Brits in here?"

"Mostly." The Englishman smiled. "You'll learn to like us."

Walker smiled. "No question about it."

"Actually they treat us better than I expected. If you really get sick, they've got doctors. It doesn't seem to be too big a problem should you run out of clothes. They'll give you more old ones."

Robert rubbed his stomach. "Do they feed you?"

"On a daily basis."

"That's a vast improvement."

"Not much." Kent pursed his lips and looked pained. "They'll only give a cup of soup a day. Put in about six or eight small boiled potatoes and pass out about a sixth of a loaf of bread. Now and then the Nazis throw in a spoonful of sugar and a bit of margarine. 'Tisn't much to survive on."

Robert winced at the Englishman's sunken cheeks. "How long you been here?"

"Little over a month."

"You look weak," Robert said.

"The truth?" Kent shook his head. "I feel like I could fall on my face."

Robert patted him on the shoulder and walked away. He found a place by the back window and looked out. His legs hurt, and he felt the need to lean against the window. Maybe that cup of soup would come before long.

For the first time in several days, he suddenly thought about Mary McCoy. How long had he been a prisoner? Much more than a week? Was it two weeks? Time seemed fuzzy and unattainable. Maybe it had been a month.

Would Mary even know he was gone? Who would tell

her that he'd been shot from the sky and captured? Maybe the Germans had marched all the way to the sea by now. The thought pained him. Could the war effort have spun out of control?

Mary must be sleeping every night in a nice warm bed with a hot stove pumping out warm air. She'd ride to school in a car with a heater blasting out hot air. Three meals a day would have kept her stomach full. Mary McCoy wouldn't have known anything of the pain he'd felt marching through the freezing air. For a moment he resented the ease that surrounded her day and night.

His stomach hurt and his legs ached. Probably a lack of calcium. His system seemed to be missing an important ingredient, and Robert couldn't understand what had happened to him. The airplane attack on the train and the days of riding with dead men had done something indefinable to him. More than anything in the world, he wanted to eat.

"Hurry!" someone yelled from the front of the barracks. "They are getting ready to serve. Hurry up, and we'll get in the front group." Men immediately rushed from their bunks, pushing each other aside.

Robert turned on his heels and tried to race out of the building. He walked as fast as he could, not hesitating to push his way through the men in front of him.

Thirty-four ~

MARYLAND, APRIL 2000

Robert awoke with a start. Something was kicking about inside him. A dream, a wandering thought, an inner premonition. Robert rolled restlessly in the hospital bed and looked out the dark window. The sun would be up in a short while. He could still see the faint shape of the moon settling into the distant horizon. Mary would be there shortly, and they'd spend another day talking about the war, what had happened . . . maybe about them.

Them? Robert shook his head. *Could I really be having such thoughts? Us?* He took a deep breath. *What in the world had really brought this woman all these miles? Why had she come? Could Mary truly care so much that she'd travel halfway across the country simply to talk to me?*

He reached for his pack of cigarettes and took one. The doctors would be irate if they knew he hadn't slowed down smoking one iota. Sure, they'd warned him, but he probably didn't have much time left to live anyway, and he wasn't going to stop enjoying every last one of them, regardless of the hospital rules. Robert flicked his Zippo lighter and took a deep drag off the cigarette. He held it for a minute and then blew out a long trail of smoke.

Mary truly seems to care, to worry about me, he thought. *She has kept a sort of distance, the distance one maintains when one wants to come much closer but isn't sure how the other person will receive the encroachment. I can almost feel her wanting to reach out and touch me.* He took another puff off his cigarette. *Yes, to touch me.*

A sudden surge of guilt flashed across his reverie. Robert thought about his deceased wife and how she might feel about his wanting to hold Mary's hand. *Make her right mad, it would! But that's the way everyone would feel. You don't let yourself think about such things. They're far too human and personal. But after all, I've known Mary the longest. I held her hands and kissed her lips first. That's got to count for something.* Robert looked up at the ceiling. *Lord, help me! I've got myself in a real old-fashioned bind here.*

Robert closed his eyes, just for a moment. Before he realized what had happened, sleep overwhelmed him, and he drifted away. The earlier dream came back, but it felt much warmer this time. He dozed in an easy sense of peace.

Bump! The noise jarred Robert awake. *Thump.* He opened one eye and looked to the side. Mary was standing there at the edge of the bed, looking down at him.

"I'm so sorry, Robert. My cane caught on the rack holding your intravenous bags, and I hit the end of your bed."

Robert reached for his glasses. "Shucks. I should have been awake an hour ago."

Mary looked distressed.

Without thinking about it, Robert reached out and took her hand. "Just having you here when I wake up is worth everything."

A slight touch of red filled her cheeks and went down the side of Mary's neck, but she kept her hand in his. Robert smiled.

"Are you up for another day of long-winded tales?" Robert asked.

"I can't begin to tell you how much I enjoy everything you've been telling me." Mary pulled up a chair but didn't let go of Robert's hand. "I'm ready for more."

Good, Robert thought. *She's holding on to my hand. What an excellent sign. Who knows where this may go?*

"Please continue from where you were last night, Robert. I want to know every last detail of what the Germans did to you."

Robert smiled broadly. "Let's see. As I remember, I was telling you about how the Nazis forced us through the snow. Talking about those endless night walks." He shook his head. "Man, those jaunts like to have killed me."

~

STALAG IV-B, JANUARY 1945

January slipped into a predictable mode of little food, little work, little entertainment, little else. The men in

Stalag IV-B spent most of their time locked indoors with nothing to do. Robert no longer groaned for food, but boredom hung heavily like a rock.

Shortly after the middle of the month, he awoke one morning to the usual whistles of the SS guards, struggled out of his wooden bunk, and walked to the window. The German standing on the other side of the window couldn't have been much more than sixteen years of age, probably younger. Boy soldiers guarded every exit. American soldiers in captivity to a bunch of Boy Scouts!

He hadn't thought about his mother for a long time and wondered if she knew he was gone. Maybe the military didn't even know where she lived. Robert remembered the first time he saw her name on an envelope. "Mrs. Stanley Mills," the return address read. The letter began simply, "Dear Son." She didn't mention his name, and she didn't even sign it.

She had just walked out. No hints. No clues. No warnings. No nothing.

The letter that she sent read like it was part of the bewitchment that had changed his world from a happy home into an empty crate in that small, backwoods Oklahoma town. Ma had said she cared for him and loved him. But she lived over a thousand miles away, in the land of Hollywood and swimming pools. Her words didn't sound right. Possibly somebody else wrote the letter. A friend? The jerk she ran off with?

Then again, maybe this is the way of life. People you love and trust just vanish one day. They say that they care, but then they simply leave you lying in a ditch. *Boom*. Like a rabbit an illusionist makes disappear.

As the weeks went by, Robert couldn't get his mother off his mind.

Each January day seemed to lengthen and become even lonelier. The men in Stalag IV-B had no idea where they were being held in Germany. Security remained tight, and no information was exchanged with the guards. Contact with the other barracks didn't happen. Day after day the SS, with their guns poised, kept their distance. Robert struggled to keep from falling into complete depression.

The initial strangeness of the detention center began to feel more familiar. Old brick floors looked less dirty. Stark wooden walls took on a more comfortable feel. He accepted wooden, primitive eating bowls and utensils carved out of wood without a thought. His tastes adjusted downward as he made the necessary adaptations to enduring the prison. Even the camp guards felt less threatening than when he had first come. He no longer thought of the boy soldiers as being able to kill him.

But Walker also felt his meager strength gradually slipping away. The inadequate diet, along with the lack of forceful exercise, took its toll. Robert knew he had lost too much weight. He found it harder to think of trying to escape. Settling into the daily routine seemed normal and acceptable. Whether it was part of some German master plan or not, mentally he was turning into a prisoner.

By the middle of the month, the Germans changed how the internal affairs of the camp were run, turning much of the administration of the prisoners over to captured English personnel. The Brits immediately hopped to the challenge and set up long teaching sessions, lecturing the Americans on everything from their poor appearance to the Anglican religion.

Robert thought about Mary McCoy frequently but found it harder to remember her voice. He could still vividly see the details of her face, but she, too, seemed to be sliding away from him. Sometimes he'd fantasize about her, but at other times, he found it hard to visualize her. The warmth and love he'd felt before arriving in England appeared to be evaporating.

During the month in Stalag IV-B, Robert discovered how much he'd given up in switching dogtags and rejecting his officer status. Although the conditions of officers' retention were clearly part of a prison, they stayed separate from the other men and reflected the respect Germans had for officers in general. Allied officers were better fed and kept much warmer, and they had more stoves in their quarters. Walker recognized that he had given up a great deal of comfort and warmth in order to protect the war secrets he carried with him.

Near the end of January, the Brits really got themselves into high gear, preparing to regulate the camp as if it were downtown London. The Germans liked the thoughts and plans of the English, and soon the prisoners were being photographed, fingerprinted, and pushed into a top-drawer operation. The Americans were generally the targets for the futile exercises, and they found themselves pushed, shoved, cursed at, and moved like a herd of dogs into second-class status. What had been jovial exchanges turned into nasty confrontations. Old animosities between the Americans and the British were rekindled.

Robert felt that he lived under several degrees of persecution: The Germans were clearly in charge of the camp; the British became the instruments of torturous lectures; and the Allied officers enjoyed a privileged category.

One evening following the usual soup, potatoes, and bread, Robert sat down against the cold wall of the barracks and watched what he saw happening around the prison yard. The vastness of the world was shrinking to nothing more than the inside perimeter of this barbed-wire hole. Men were no longer playing a game to keep the Krauts off their backs. Men were losing any sense of who they were and why they'd gone to war.

Robert's ribs rubbed against the side of his shirt. A strange docility had crept into his bones and eaten away at his sense of anger and protests. The men ought to be organizing for resistance to the Nazis, not succumbing to the commands and orders of their captors parlayed by the Brits.

For a few moments he felt as if he might be going crazy. His ideas shifted around in his head like a subject being brought into focus by a photographer. He had to quit being a pawn; he had to stop the prison camp system from devouring him.

Walker stood up and walked toward a group of Englishmen. No one looked up or seemed to pay any attention as he approached.

"Do you realize what's happening to us?" Robert said.

"Huh?" Archibald Kent looked at him. "I say, I don't think I get your drift."

"Do you people understand what's going on in this place?"

The three Brits exchanged a mystified look. Kent frowned.

"All this nonsense about fingerprints, pictures, the crap that your leadership is pushing is nothing more than a game to keep us under control while the Germans do whatever they wish with us."

Archibald pursed his lips and frowned. "I don't think I'm following you."

"Look. The SS has turned your officers into our persecutors. All of this lecture business is nonsense to force us into a more compliant mold. Get it?"

"Still don't think I'm following you."

Walker leaned into the group of men. "Watch the men around us. They're turning into automatons, robots, mechanical people. We don't need to be doing this daily nonsense that your officers are coming up with. We need to be planning how to escape."

"Escape?" The eyes of the Brit widened.

"Exactly!" Robert's voice rose. "We've got to keep our wits about us, or we'll do nothing more than sit here and die."

"I think you've taken this process all wrong," Archibald protested. "Our officers are simply trying to take us through various exercises to put each of us in touch with what counts."

"Counts!" Robert growled. "What counts is getting ourselves out of here."

"Listen, mate." The third Brit sounded harder and tougher.

"You try something funny out there and 'em Germans will fill you with so many holes, you'll leak like a broken faucet. I suggest you keep 'em crazy ideas to yourself and join in our little party. At least we eat once a day. 'At's better than you done before gettin' 'ere."

"Yeah? And just how tough and strong are you on that cup of hot water you got tonight?" Robert pushed his point.

The three men looked at each other again and turned away. Robert found himself looking at the backs of the Brits as they talked to each other.

I can't let myself settle into this maze, he thought. *I've got to find some way to stay mentally tough. Resistant. I've got to keep my mind strong, my spine straight.*

Walker turned away from the three men and went back to the window, where he watched a British officer going from barracks to barracks with a swagger stick under his arm as if he were running the entire camp.

"The idiot!" he mumbled under his breath. "I will not succumb to this nonsense. I've got to find a better way. I can't let these Jerries turn me into nothing more than a wrung-out dishrag!"

Thirty-Five

STALAG IV-B, GERMANY, FEBRUARY 1945

As February began, Walker became increasingly obstinate, refusing to listen to the British lecture and pushing the leadership to the point of revolt. Even though the officers chastised him with promised discipline, Walker refused to cooperate, and he found himself marginalized in the sleeping barracks. In some ways, the struggle worked. He stopped thinking about his personal struggle and concentrated on the group problem in the stalag. He soon had a few Americans listening to him and also refusing to cooperate with the British officers. He found himself caught between Germans, who would kill him, and Brits, who threatened him.

On February 10, Walker stopped two of the American soldiers he'd come to know in the dining hall. The men stood as far away from the men going through the food line as possible.

"Listen to me," Robert told the American soldiers gathered around him. "No matter what the Brits attempt to make you do today, don't respond. Don't do it."

"Stop it," the American private hissed under his breath. "The Germans will kill us if we cause any trouble."

"The Germans aren't running this scene," Robert argued. "The Brits are the whole show in their heads. When the chips are down, the English aren't going to hurt us."

The sergeant standing next to the private shook his head. "I don't know. Nobody wants to get thrown in detention or a hole of some sort."

"Look around you." Robert pointed in all directions. "We're guarded by nothing more than a bunch of kids. You think these little boys want to come in here and fight with us?"

"They've got the guns," the sergeant countered, "and there's older men working around this place. Walker, you've got to be careful or they'll get your number."

Walker smiled. "Kinda nice to think that no one has to guess which side I'm on in this fray. Anybody want to argue that these Brits look like pseudo-Nazis?"

The sergeant rubbed his mouth nervously. "You got a point. Let me think about it." He shook his head. "Give me a little time."

"I'm with you, Walker," the private declared. "Count me in. We'll give Winston's boys a little something to think about."

Walker smiled again and squeezed the man's hand. "Good. At least nobody can doubt where we stand."

The sergeant ducked and hurried away.

Walker finished eating the minimal rations and started back to the barracks. He'd barely gotten out the door when two older SS guards stopped him.

"Come with us," the guard demanded in broken English.

Both men looked tough and hard. One man carried a small machine gun. *These aren't the boys to play with,* Robert thought. He nodded his compliance.

"Follow," the guard pointed to a third officer standing about ten feet away.

Robert shrugged, and the SS guard beckoned him to follow. The three men walked along the edge of the assembly yard and toward the train tracks. In a few minutes, Robert recognized that the other Americans in his barracks were standing by the tracks. Off in the distance he could hear a train approaching. By the time Walker reached the platform, the train had pulled into the area.

"Get in!" the SS officer behind him demanded again.

Walker turned and looked at the men. "What?"

"Get in *now!*"

Robert turned back to the train and watched his friends climbing aboard. "I'm afraid—"

The SS officer with the machine gun leveled it at his stomach. "*Now!*"

Without another word, Robert slipped onto the train coach with the other Americans. To his surprise, he and the other thirty prisoners sat like regular passengers in the train coach. He looked toward the back and discovered that German Army—not SS—officers were stationed at the front and the back of the car. The guards looked more like kids than grown men, but the rifles were real, and it wouldn't take much to get shot.

"What's going on?" Robert asked the man next to him. "I feel like they're getting ready to take me on a little fun ride."

"I understand they're shipping us to another camp."

Robert blinked several times. "Another camp?"

"That's what I got from a young guard I developed an acquaintance with back in the camp. He told me yesterday evening that they were sending some of us on work assignments."

Robert studied the thin-faced soldier next to him. The man needed a haircut and probably wasn't much past twenty. He looked tired.

"Name's Jones." Robert offered his hand. "Private Jones, but everybody calls me Robert."

"Davis. Warren Davis." He shook hands.

"So you got to be buddies with one of the Jerries?"

"The man wanted to learn English. Studied language in school and looked for opportunities to talk with us. I learned quite a bit from him. He worked at being Mr. Nice Guy."

"How come they're sending us on? I mean, look at where we are. This isn't the usual cattle car. We're sitting here like German tourists."

"I'm not sure. They may have decided that the Americans were more difficult to corral than the British. Maybe some other reason."

Robert suddenly laughed. "Haven't heard a joke like that

in a month." He spoke into Davis's ear. "You can bet I gave these stupid Brits a hard time."

Davis nodded. "Yeah, several of the guys in here were bad boys. It fits. The German told me we are going to Werdau, the center of the German textile industry. They need some workers over there."

"Werdau! That's means we're very deep inside Germany."

"That's what I got from the Kraut."

Robert settled back against the backrest. The seat material felt soft and comfortable, like home. At least he was going to have a good time riding over the hill to Werdau, regardless of how long or short the trip proved to be.

WERDAU, GERMANY, FEBRUARY 1945

Three hours later the train arrived in Werdau, and more youthful soldiers met them on the train's platform. The harsh conditions Walker had seen in the other stalags were gone. The town hadn't been bombed, and life looked normal. People looked like they were going about their business in a normal way. The trains pulled into the station as if they had arrived for a social visit. A few German citizens stood around the platform and watched the prisoners marching into the train station, but most paid little attention.

One guard locked the station doors, and other Krauts stood outside the windows with their rifles and machine guns poised, but they seemed to look through the windows more from curiosity than anything else.

"They look like boys, mere boys," Robert whispered to Warren Davis.

"They are!" Davis snorted. "Probably not more than fourteen or fifteen years old."

"What do you make of it?"

Davis scratched his head. "I think the Germans are sinking fast. They've sent the hard-nosed capable troops to the front for a last-ditch fight. Little boys are all that's left to guard the likes of us."

Robert looked again at their faces. Woolen caps were pulled down over their ears. Most wouldn't need to shave more than once a month. Their bravado seemed to mask their fear.

"You don't want to push a scared soldier," Davis added. "Weakness can lead to desperate actions."

Robert agreed. Wouldn't take much to cause these tense boys to start firing. Now wasn't the time to provoke anyone. He'd wait.

The door opened at the front of the station house, and the guards motioned for the American men to start marching out. Most of the townspeople only stared as the prisoners walked by.

Robert thought that Werdau looked like a quaint town, the sort of place tourists came to see before the war. Far from the world of war that he'd been in for weeks, the German countryside seemed quiet and pleasant. The freezing temperatures were gone. Robert felt more like he was walking down the street with a group of college students, stopping for a nice, short visit during a college seminar on Germany.

Fifteen minutes later, the Americans turned into a large

holding area with a ten-foot, barbed-wire fence surrounding it. At the far end he could see factories, and in front of him barracks awaiting their arrival. The prisoners marched into the barracks and searched for places to sleep. From the number of bunks, they quickly calculated that one hundred and fifty Americans must already work in the woolen mills and that most were housed there. The thirty new men were taking the places of others who had died, escaped, or whatever. Empty bunks meant somebody was being replaced, and they were it.

Robert sat down on the edge of an empty bed. At least he had his own place. The bedroll even felt bearable. For a moment, Walker stretched out on the bed and relaxed, but soon became aware of the gnawing in his stomach. Much of the time the painful emptiness could be displaced; at other times the hunger seemed unbearable.

"Hey! They feed us twice a day," a soldier yelled from the doorway. "You're going to love the new schedule."

Walker swung his feet off the bed and found Warren Davis standing in front of him.

"You got that from a guard?"

"Speaking a little German helps." Davis raised an eyebrow.

"What do you mean?" Robert asked more cautiously. "What kind of meals?"

"You get to eat at noon and suppertime," Davis answered. "Unfortunately, lunch is nothing more than watery turnip soup, and supper is a sixth of a loaf of bread. What can I say?" Smith shrugged and walked on.

We've missed lunch, Robert realized. *What a lousy break.*

Nothing tonight but bread crust. His stomach seemed to answer with an increased longing for food.

He stood up to shake away the lingering churning and saw Al King at the other end of the room. During the month at Stalag IV-B, he had not seen his old friend. King was sitting on the end of a bed staring at the floor. Robert hurried toward him.

"Al, it's me!"

King looked up. He shook his head a bit. "You're uh . . . uh . . . Walker. Right?"

Robert studied the man's watery eyes. His face and hands seemed unusually thin. Bravado had disappeared.

"How you feeling, Al?"

King blinked several times. "I don't know," he said. "I can't tell anymore."

"Imprisonment's got to you. Right?"

King shook his head.

Robert dropped down on one knee beside Al's bed. "We can beat this thing, King. We've got to be tough and fight these Krauts. You can do it."

King looked at him blankly but said nothing.

"Do you understand me? We're not going to give up on this fight. We've got to resist them."

King looked up as if he couldn't quite grasp Robert's words.

"I'm telling you that we're far from through fighting these Jerries, and I need your help. You must pull yourself together. We've got to break out of this place. Understand?"

King blinked, but his eyes conveyed nothing.

Thirty-Six ~

WERDAU, GERMANY, FEBRUARY 1945

During the days that followed the beginning of their confinement in Werdau, Robert carefully watched Al King. The painful experiences had done something to the private's mind. King was disconnected and confused much of the time, as if lost in a fog and wandering lost through a forest. In the factory, Al would sit slumped in a chair, staring straight ahead. If Robert didn't encourage Al, the man would soon be in deep trouble.

After the first week, the textile manufacturing job Walker and several of the men had been performing suddenly stopped. Something unknown had changed what the factory was doing. Robert found himself mostly confined to the barracks again, facing prolonged periods of boredom. The food proved to be better, but doing nothing for days was hard and long. He felt increasing hostility toward the boy soldiers who guarded the building, and often antagonized the guards by refusing to respond to a call to attention. The young soldiers waved their guns at him and barked commands, but he knew they would do nothing. The increasing tension around the housing unit kept him from succumbing to their subtle attempts to make Robert tick like an ordinary servant of the Third Reich.

As the fourth week at Werdau began, a trainload of Russian prisoners arrived heavily guarded by older, more seasoned German troops. The Russians were marched to another section of the prison camp, but from the window of his barracks Robert could watch the forlorn stragglers. Gaunt faces hung beneath uncombed hair sticking out in disarray. Their cheekbones protruded and shrunken eyes appeared hollow and empty, and the Germans kept striking the Russians brutally. The guards often kicked them down, as if wanting to provoke a response so the Germans could shoot them.

On Wednesday evening Robert watched five SS officers rush a dozen Russians out of the barracks. The terrified men stumbled and fell on the ground, got up, rushed onward like drunken boys. The disheveled and barefoot Russians staggered. The SS forcefully herded the frightened Russians into the center of the large courtyard, forcing them to kneel on the ground with their hands over their heads.

One of the Nazi officers began slowly circling the six men, screaming obscenities at them. The Nazi suddenly snapped and cracked a large black bullwhip in the air. As he walked around the group of Russians, he popped the whip at increasingly lower and lower levels. After several turns, he cracked the whip inches above the Russians' heads. The prisoners tried to protect their faces, but the Nazi caught the first man on the ear and then the next on the side of his face. He then systematically beat each Russian, carefully and methodically alternating between the men, who writhed on the ground. The more he hit the prisoners, the more the Nazi seemed to enjoy himself.

The whipping continued for more than thirty minutes until beads of perspiration dotted the SS trooper's forehead and he rubbed his arm. When he finally stepped back, the rest of the officers immediately began striking the Russians with their rifle butts. At first the prisoners screamed, and then as the attack continued they became increasingly silent. After five minutes of kicking and beating, the Germans walked away, leaving the dying Russians battered and broken on the ground.

Robert watched until the bodies were motionless. The men had to have died, but dead or not they would be carted away during the night.

Walker finally turned away from the window. Before this moment, he had not quite hated the Germans as he now did. They were his enemy. War was war. But after watching the SS soldiers savagely beat the life out of the helpless Russians, Robert began to see the Germans in a different light. The SS were nothing less than barbarian savages. *Evil.* Robert cursed what he saw in the blackness of night. He hated the Germans.

No matter what it took, Robert knew he was going to get away. They fed him better than at the last two camps and some of his strength had come back, yet eating better and being warmer wasn't enough to hold him. Even if they beat him to death, Lieutenant Robert Walker would find a way out.

~

The next day, Warren Davis from Detroit came back to the barracks after working two of the shifts in the textile factory. He looked worn and more than slightly exhausted. Davis sat down on the bunk next to Robert and rubbed his eyes.

Robert looked around to make sure no one was looking. "I watched the SS beat a dozen Russians to death last night," Robert said factually. "Did it with a bullwhip. Systematically. Like a game."

Smith nodded. "Yep. The Germans treat them like pigs. I hear they're not feeding the Russians half the meager amount we get."

"Are the Russians working in the factory?"

Davis shook his head. "I hear that they're routinely shooting, gassing, whatever—annihilating every one of the Russians. The best picture I can get is that they want to get rid of all of them."

Walker's jaw flinched, and his eyes set hard.

"You see, the Russians did not sign the Geneva convention affecting how war is to be executed, so the Germans see the Russians as existing outside the rules and regulations. Sorta like killing runaway dogs they've picked up. The SS seem particularly intent on enjoying destruction of Russians and Jews."

Robert ground his fist in his palm. "I've got to get out of here."

"Look. No matter how badly they treat us, the Geneva convention is still in place for us. We've got some protection. Sure, there's problems, but you try to run for it and they'll butcher you."

Robert stared straight ahead.

"I don't think this stinking war can go on much longer. Sit tight and we'll all survive this thing."

"Would you try to make a break for it with me?"

Davis laughed. "You have to be kidding."

"I'm very serious."

Davis stood up. "I appreciate what you're saying, but I don't want to get into something that has all the earmarks of killing me. If you make plans, don't tell me about what you're doing. They'll question me if you actually get out of here, and we'll both be better off if I know nothing." Davis patted Robert on the back and walked away.

For five minutes Robert sat on the end of the bed, trying to make sense out of what he'd just heard. A soldier should do everything in his power to escape. Warren Davis was a good man but was avoiding a responsibility, Robert thought. Someone had to do it. And Walker was the man to try.

Al King sat at the other end of the room, staring straight

ahead. Time had done him no good. If nothing else, getting out of this place would jolt him back into touch with reality. He'd get his mind back and become alert again. A hard run through the forest was all he needed to become a man of action again.

Robert walked up to the private. "Al, how are you?"

King looked up.

"You okay?"

King didn't say anything.

Robert dropped down on one knee. "Listen. We've got to get out of here, and I think I know how to do it. Will you try?"

King only looked at him.

"Those Russians in the other barracks won't last a week. By the time we get to next Monday, they and the SS troops will be gone out of here. When the lights go out, we can run for the front gate. These boy soldiers hanging around here don't pay good attention. We'll be out of here before anyone notices we're gone. What do you say?"

King frowned. "I don't know," he muttered. "Someone could get hurt."

"Not us! It'll be them."

Al's eyebrows furled, and he scratched his head. "Hmm. I don't know," he mumbled again.

"Unless you tell me no, I'm going to count you in. Got it?"

King looked blank.

"Okay. You're my buddy for a break next Monday." Robert turned and walked away.

We'll do it, he thought. *I've got to watch the gate and make sure that I've got my timing down, but I'm not afraid of anything. We'll run over those little runts guarding the gate like chasing Boy Scouts home on Halloween.*

Thirty-Seven ~

MARYLAND, APRIL 2000

Robert stopped talking and closed his eyes for a moment. He took a deep breath and fell back on the hospital's pillow. "Need to catch my breath," he mumbled apologetically.

Mary waited, saying nothing. After about a minute Robert opened his eyes again and looked up at the ceiling. "Did you think about me during those hard days?" she asked before he could start the story again. "About how much you cared for me?"

"Of course I did!" he said, raising partially up from the pillow, then dropping down again. "In the beginning I thought about you all the time." He nodded his head and looked up at the ceiling. "But, Mary, I'll have to admit that the longer I stayed in that camp, the harder it was to keep in touch with what was happening in the United States. In fact, I tended to lose what was going on anywhere but right in front of my face. Things got warped and changed around in my head as the days went by."

"I think I can understand that." Mary frowned.

Robert rolled over and looked at her. "No," he said firmly, "I don't think you can. When your most basic need is to keep from starving to death, hunger pushes everything out of your mind."

"Really?" Mary raised her eyebrows.

"You think about food, worry about food, look for food, dream about food. After all, the only thing on your mind is food. Understand?"

"Yes." Mary shook her head.

Robert turned back over and looked at the ceiling. "The Germans seemed to have made an art form of starving us. They knew how to keep us barely alive and weak enough that we didn't do much more than function. Even remembering people you once loved was hard under those circumstances."

Mary suddenly smiled. "I'm sure," she finally said softly.

Robert looked back up at the ceiling. "There are days that I can still feel the aching and gnawing in my stomach, almost like it was last week . . ."

~

WERDAU, GERMANY, FEBRUARY 1945

February proved to be warmer than expected. Some snow still piled up around the barracks, but the piles were gradually diminishing. The nights were cold, but the days were much warmer. Robert reasoned that it was a good time to be running through the farm fields of Germany. He spent his days and nights glued to the windows, observing the details of their incarceration and trying to recall everything he'd learned in basic training about escaping. By the time Monday arrived, Robert was ready to act. He had the gate schedule down pat. At midnight he would drag Al King out with him and they'd make the break. They would go over the fence next to the gate at exactly the time of the changing of guards in the turrets several hundred feet away. The climb would be easier at that point and allow them a clear shot to disappear into the farmland at the edge of Werdau before anyone missed them.

Just before their supper of nothing but bread, Robert cornered Al. "You ready for tonight?"

King looked blank.

"Remember, we're going to break out at midnight? That's when the guards change. The best time to run for it. You ready to make the big break?"

King stared at Robert out of the corner of his eye. "Tonight?"

"Yep. We'll dash for the gate just about the time the midnight guard change begins."

Al scratched his head. "When the guards change?"

"You got it. Be ready." Robert moved away quickly, leaving King standing there. Al had been Robert's friend, and he liked him. In his present condition Al would be easy to maneuver. When he passed Warren Davis, the soldier looked away. Robert kept walking.

During the evening Robert stayed mostly by himself, periodically watching out the back windows to see what the guards were doing. The senior SS troops had left the camp on Saturday. Apparently all the Russians were gone, victims of cruelty and oppression. Each time Robert thought about their dead, mangled bodies, he became angry. No matter what happened, he would at least try to get out of Werdau concentration camp.

Lights went out in the barracks at around 2100 hours. Some of the men were already asleep. Most of the rest would quickly succumb to the fatigue of working at least two straight shifts.

At 2330 hours Robert glanced around the room. His heart leaped, and he took a deep breath. Everything seemed to be okay. In thirty minutes he'd be out of this godforsaken place. Without making a sound, he swung out of bed and put his shoes on, carefully tying the strings on his boots so that nothing would come loose.

He crept across the floor and found Al King awake, staring at the ceiling. The man was completely naked.

"What are you doing?" Robert implored. "Get your clothes on."

King looked at him for a moment but then slowly began to dress.

"Don't make a sound. We've got to get out of here without being caught. Hurry up," Robert prodded.

King stood up, pulling his frayed sweater down over his chest. He looked around the room mechanically, standing on the floor in his bare feet.

"Get your socks and shoes on," Robert whispered in his ear with irritation. "Come on. Time is running out!"

King bent over and pulled his socks over his bare feet. He dropped one of his shoes. The sound reverberated across the room.

Robert froze and grabbed King's arm. "Careful!"

King sat down and languorously pushed his shoes on. He put on the fragment of a sweater that the Germans had given him as a coat. He followed Robert out the front door.

Robert crouched against the dark wall of the barracks and watched around the corner. He glanced at his watch. Five minutes left before the guards changed. Robert beckoned to Al and hurried on to the side of the next barracks.

In three minutes, they had come to the last barracks. The gate stood only forty or fifty feet away. When the spotlight shifted to the far side of the camp, they'd run for it. Even getting a few scratches, they should be over the fence before the searchlight came back around. Robert looked at his watch. It was 2400 hours.

"Now!" he whispered to Al. "Run!"

Robert broke from the side of the building the second after the searchlight went past. He ran like a college boy in a track meet and slid to a stop at the foot of the fence. Catching his breath, he turned and looked for Al.

Private First Class Al King was walking across the open corridor like an aristocrat strolling through a park. Without any sense of where he was going, Al leisurely walked on toward Robert as if he had all day to get there.

In the moment that he should have gone over the fence,

Robert stared at Al, trudging toward him like a man in a trance. Suddenly Al stopped and stood rigidly as if looking toward something far off in the distance.

"Al!" Robert gasped. "Run!"

Al didn't move. The large beacon had already started its inevitable sweep across the yard. Time had run out. Al stood like a statue, waiting to be exhibited to some watching crowd.

"Run!" Robert suddenly shouted.

The spotlight swept over Al like a wave hitting the beach. One second he stood in darkness; in the next Al King hovered in the light. Instantly machine guns opened up from the towers. For a few seconds Al quivered as the gunners riddled his body, and then he slumped to the ground in a motionless heap. Men began running in every direction.

For some reason he couldn't ever explain, Robert ran toward his friend, grabbing his lifeless body. He had barely reached Al when the Nazis descended on him. Intense pain wracked his body as rifle butts pounded him to the ground.

When Robert came to, a cold brick floor pressed against his cheek. He hurt so badly that it was difficult to move. Trying to get up, Robert discovered that his arms and his feet were chained. His ribs were either bruised or broken. His mouth hurt, and his tongue told him several teeth were gone. He blinked several times and then looked around the room. They had imprisoned him in a small room with a single lightbulb hanging from the center of his cell.

Robert huddled on the harsh floor. Consciousness came and went; he had no idea how long he'd been in the place. Every inch of his body was wracked with pain. Finally the cell door opened, and an SS officer entered.

"*Stehen!*" the officer demanded.

Robert tried to understand. His mind felt like a mangled mess.

"*Stehen!*"

Robert forced his eyes open and realized the side of his face was swollen. He tried to see the man. A heavyset, fat-faced German guard came into view. The man looked to be around forty to forty-five years old.

"You are paying attention?" The officer kicked Robert on the leg.

Walker groaned.

"You tried to escape?"

Robert blinked, trying to remember exactly what happened. He could only stare at the SS guard.

The officer suddenly struck him with a small, leather riding crop. The blow stung and Robert groaned, gasping for air.

"I want to know what happened tonight." The officer pulled a small stool over with his foot. "We've never had one of your people try to escape before."

Robert tried to think, and an idea slowly came into focus. Maybe, maybe, an explanation would work. "Al," he muttered. "Al's sick in his mind. He wandered off. I tried to help him."

The SS trooper suddenly struck him across the face with the riding crop. Robert screamed in pain.

"Let me have the truth!" The officer kicked Robert in the stomach.

Walker gasped for air and couldn't speak. He coiled up in a knot on the ground. The whip had cut across his forehead and nose with excruciating pain.

"The truth!" the Nazi screamed at him.

"That's all I've got. I tried to help my friend." Robert felt pain rising up from his stomach and dizziness dropping over him like a shroud. The officer's face seemed farther and farther away. "I can't tell you . . . any . . . more." A trickle of blood ran down his forehead. The room faded into blackness.

Robert had no idea what time it was when he awoke. Blood had dried on his face, but his jaw still had seepage where the three teeth had been. He found it difficult to breathe and tried not to move. The pain felt worse than anything he'd ever known.

Some time later, he heard the jail door being unlocked. Out of the corner of his eye he could see two SS soldiers standing over him. They hoisted him to his feet and forced him forward. Barely able to keep his balance, Robert shuffled down a dark corridor.

At the end of the hall, a wooden door opened and the SS officer who had interrogated him sat behind a desk. Boy soldiers stood around him with rifles on their shoulders. Robert thought he would collapse on the floor.

"I understand that you have been the source of some difficulty," the officer began. He stopped and took a long draw off his cigarette. "My guards tell me that you seem to have trouble responding to their commands. The normal course of events is to shoot you." He leaned over the table and stared at Robert.

The officer's words rang through his mind, echoing off the walls of his skull. Death had to be better than he felt. Maybe this was to be the best escape he'd find.

"However, we would not like your fellow soldiers to think you were so easily disposed of so they might try some similar action. We have other plans for you, Private Jones."

The SS officer snapped his fingers, and the guards dragged Robert away.

Thirty-Eight ~

MARYLAND, APRIL 2000

The gentle sunbeams danced across the hospital window for a long time before Robert spoke again. He lay quietly, staring out over the treetops, preoccupied, swallowed by his thoughts. After several minutes he turned to Mary. "I thought the Nazis would kill me. I truly did."

Mary nodded her head mechanically.

"They beat the Russians to death. Why not me? I couldn't do anything to stop them."

She nodded again.

"Took me a long time to find out what actually happened." Robert stopped and lit his cigarette again. "Probably would never have known, but five years later I was eating supper in Munich—you know, during the time when I flew airplanes into Russia."

Mary smiled but looked blank.

"I looked across the restaurant and saw a man dining

with a woman. I took another look. How could I ever forget *that* face! Sure enough. He was the SS officer." Robert took a deep breath. "Martin Schoenberg was the ole boy's name."

"Schoenberg? Really!"

"Yeah. By that time I had learned that most Germans were much more approachable than it felt like when I was lying on that cold rock floor with my teeth knocked out. I got up and went over to his table and introduced myself."

Mary's eyes sparkled. "You didn't!"

"Yep!" Robert nodded his head. "I sure did."

Mary shuffled her chair forward. "What did he say?" She leaned over the edge of the bed. "What did the man do?"

Robert laughed. "You understand that none of those Krauts ever actually served in the army. They all said their family just got them in to ease things at home. Never had one admit to even holding a gun." He chuckled. "The man turned out to be a polite local hometown boy out for the evening with his wife. He invited me to sit down for a glass of wine, just like I was an old friend." Robert snorted. "She looked terrified. You *bet* he remembered who I was."

"I'm amazed." Mary slipped her hand over her mouth. "Totally amazed."

Robert tapped his cigarette over the trash basket again. "Something like this probably wouldn't happen again in a million years, but this night the man wasn't the least bit hesitant to talk."

"What did he tell you, Robert?"

"It was a story." Robert looked out the window again. "A strange, unexpected story."

"Yes?" Mary beckoned for him to continue.

"It seems this former SS officer was something of a friend with the camp's commandant. My little attempt to escape produced an interesting conversation between the two of them. I caused some interesting discussion around that little camp on that afternoon." He leaned back and looked up at the ceiling again. "Rather revealing."

Mary waited patiently. Finally she said, "For heaven's sake, don't stop now! Tell me what you learned."

Robert kept staring at the ceiling. "It seems that two days after my escape attempt, the boys had one of their regularly scheduled meetings with the concentration camp staff, reviewing the general situation at both the prison and the textile mill. SS Officer Martin Schoenberg told the officials about what he learned during my interrogation."

"Must have been fascinating to listen to his story."

Robert nodded his head. "He was quite straightforward. Lying here at this very moment, I can hear him talking just like it was yesterday." He looked over at Mary. "Now, I want you to pretend that you're in the room with Schoenberg and the commandment and that you overheard everything that happened."

"Okay," Mary said slowly. "I'll simply close my eyes and pretend that I'm there, listening."

Robert smiled. "Now imagine yourself in the commandant's rather plain office. Typical army desk. A few decorations on the wall. A map or two pinned here and there. Several officers are sitting around the room, and Martin Schoenberg is finishing his report."

"I'm there," Mary said with her eyes closed. "I can see the place in my imagination."

Robert looked up at the ceiling again. "Like yesterday morning," he repeated himself. "I can hear that German's tenor voice. He was saying . . ."

~

WERDAU, GERMANY, MARCH 1945

"In conclusion," Schoenberg finished his report, "since the American shot at the gate seems to have been mentally deranged, and no one else in the barracks appears to have known about any planned escape, we conclude that this man named Jones, now held in solitary detention, was probably trying to return King to his barracks. Therefore, we sentenced Jones to two weeks in solitary confinement." The officer looked around the room with a harsh, disciplined stare, daring any negative response. "Should Jones live, the man will be returned to the unit to serve as an example to the rest of the Allied prisoners of what discipline awaits any infraction of rules." He nodded to the commandant and sat down.

"Do we have any other reports?" Commandant Albert Karthaus looked around the room. No one responded. He rapped on the desk. "Then the meeting is dismissed."

The staff saluted and stood, and officers started out the door.

"Oberst Schoenberg," Karthaus called to the SS officer. "Please, if you have a moment."

Schoenberg stopped in the doorway and turned around,

walking through the exiting group of soldiers. *"Ja, mein commandant."* He saluted.

"Sit down, please." The commandant smiled and pointed at the chair in front of his desk. "Perhaps a cup of coffee?"

Schoenberg stiffened, as if not sure of what to do about the unusually friendly and informal gesture. "Of course." He finally snapped his heels together.

Karthaus nodded to his aide. "Two coffees, at once." He sat across from the SS officer as the assistant immediately left the room. "I was interested in this attempted escape. We've never had one before."

"Our conclusion remains that it was not an escape," Schoenberg said stiffly.

"Yes, yes." Karthaus smiled. "I got that message in your report. But are you convinced?"

Schoenberg's back stiffened. The line of questioning was totally unexpected and made him feel uneasy. "I have reviewed the reports of the men at the scene of the shooting. There is unanimity in their report, and I find that the prisoner named King seemed to be walking like a zombie across the open yard when the yard lights came around. The only error in judgment may be that he shouldn't have been shot in the first place. I think some of our . . . the younger soldiers overreacted to the situation at hand."

"They shot out of panic?" Karthaus kept smiling.

For a moment, Schoenberg hesitated, trying to read the smile. Nothing seemed to be threatening in the commandant's eyes. He had never known Albert Karthaus to be politically suspicious, and, as an SS officer, Schoenberg didn't have to answer to the man. Yet the question seemed more than an innocent inquiry. "Yes," the SS trooper finally said. "That would be my conclusion."

The aide hurried in with two small cups of black coffee, giving one to each officer. He turned on his heels and was gone.

"Think this man you picked up with the dead private will survive isolation?"

"Difficult to say. Probably."

Karthaus shook his head and shrugged. "We shall see." He took a drink of coffee. "I would like to speak with you on a more personal basis." The commandant leaned over his desk and began talking in a lower voice. "You happened to be here the night of this escape, but I noticed in your records that you've recently come back from the western front." Karthaus's eyes narrowed, and he looked unusually concerned. "It would be helpful to have some sense of how the war is going."

Schoenberg relaxed. For the first time he realized what the entire conversation was about. Schoenberg took a big drink of coffee and smiled to himself. The commandant wanted gossip from the front lines. Nothing more.

"I recognize that we are only talking, shall we say, privately," Karthaus continued. "As two, uh, friends, discussing about what is happening in the war effort."

Schoenberg sat back in his chair. What could he lose by being candid with the commandant? Most of what people heard these days was ill informed anyway. Why not tell the truth?

"Maybe a little insight would help us to know how to

more effectively run this operation." Karthaus smiled again. "Feel free to call me Albert."

"The news is not good," the SS trooper began slowly. "During the month of December we expected to take Saint-Vith and Bastogne. The fight proved to be vicious and costly." Schoenberg stopped and reached for his coat pocket. "Do you mind if I smoke?"

"Of course not." Karthaus kept smiling. "By all means."

The SS trooper returned the smile and pulled out a pack of cigarettes. "May I speak frankly?"

"Of course. Absolutely."

Schoenberg suddenly felt as if he wanted to describe everything he'd seen. For days he'd been holding back the pain of the losses he witnessed. He hadn't talked with anyone because the SS troopers maintained an attitude of superiority and victory at all costs, but that invisible spirit had broken in Schoenberg. On one of the worst days, the carnage and destruction had nearly overwhelmed the hardened officer. He took a deep puff of his cigarette.

"I'd like to have an accurate picture of where we are in this war effort," the commandant encouraged Schoenberg. "Your thoughts will remain my secrets."

"I don't know where this army of General Patton's came from, but the Allies proved to be like sand on the seashore. Their airplanes came at us from every angle, diving out of the sky like screaming hawks. This Patton marched his men over an impossible terrain and hit us hard in the Ardennes. The Americans wouldn't give up at Bastogne, and our best effort resulted in massive losses."

The commandant's face sagged. "I heard something of this unfortunate effort." He sipped his coffee. "I understand that massive numbers of men and machinery were destroyed."

Schoenberg took a long drag off his cigarette. "I came back through Vianden, where our soldiers were in retreat, and saw what I'm about to describe to you." Schoenberg raised one eyebrow and looked out the window as he talked. "On January 22, massive numbers of troops were in retreat near Vianden and Dasburg. Our amassed vehicles ranged from horse-drawn equipment to motorcars and armored vehicles. The entire retreat became congested when Allied aircraft dropped rockets, incendiaries, and everything else they had on our soldiers moving east. Their medium-size bombers made runs at our columns, strafing them from one end to the other. By the time the attack was over, the Allies had destroyed 1,177 vehicles and damaged nearly 550 others." Schoenberg took a deep breath. "Does that give you something of a picture of where we are?"

The commandant only shook his head slightly. "In retreat?" he concluded.

"Yes."

"Losing large amounts of equipment?"

The SS trooper nodded his head yes. "We have lost thousands and thousands of motor transport—tanks, trains, railroad cars, gun positions. Our soldiers lay everywhere, scattered like pieces of splintered wood."

Karthaus rubbed his chin for a moment. He sat back in his chair and looked straight into the eyes of the SS officer. "We are losing the war?"

Schoenberg took a deep breath. "That is not for me to say." He sounded suddenly professional.

"I am only asking for an opinion."

The SS officer shook his head. "I hear that the Russians are coming very quickly on the eastern front. I would be circumspect in everything that I did in this camp in the days ahead." He cleared his throat. "That's the reason we did not shoot the prisoner who's lying down there in the cell."

"Thank you for your candor." The commandant stood up. "I understand you will be leaving us shortly. Tomorrow."

Schoenberg finished his coffee, put the cup and saucer on Karthaus's desk, and stood. "Yes, I will be leaving tomorrow."

The commandant nodded his head. "I am glad you were here when this incident happened last night." He smiled. "Certainly makes my job, shall we say, easier. Be careful out there. Don't get yourself shot."

Oberst Schoenberg smiled for the first time. "Yes, that is the objective, isn't it? We must keep ourselves from getting killed." He saluted and turned to leave.

"Not getting killed is also one of my goals," the commandant said dryly.

Robert stopped telling the story and looked at Mary. "Get the picture?"

She opened her eyes. "Like I was sitting in the room! What an account."

"If their war effort had been going better, they probably would have killed me." Robert took a deep breath. "But they didn't, and my life went on in that camp."

"Don't stop now," Mary insisted. "I want to know how you survived under those terrible conditions."

Robert lit another cigarette. "Yeah, I know they'll scream at me if they find out that I'm smoking these things." He took a big puff. "I guess I'm simply too far along in this heart disease game for it to make much difference to me now." He tapped the cigarette over the edge again. "Okay, I'll tell you what followed their conversation."

Thirty-Nine

Werdau, Germany, March 1945

During the first week of solitary confinement, Robert moved very little in the dark cell beneath the basement of the administration building. Most of the time he lay on the floor and shivered in the cold, hearing nothing but the dripping of water somewhere in the room. The odors from the sewage pipe made it difficult for him to breathe in the six-foot-square room. When Robert moved his body, pain from multiple broken ribs surged through his chest. For several days his jaw remained swollen, and it was difficult to open his mouth. Seven days passed before a guard appeared with a plate on which someone had placed a half-dozen small potatoes and a slice of bread. The German set the dirty plate on the moldy floor and hurried back up the steps.

For a few moments the light from the top was blinding, and Robert tried to cover his eyes. As soon as blackness returned, he turned his face toward the smell of the food. Robert dragged himself over the wet rocks of the floor and devoured the bread and potatoes. Chewing was difficult, and as soon as he was through, Robert fell back into a restless sleep.

By the middle of the second week, Robert was more aware of his circumstances and insatiably hungry. He spent time leaning against the brick wall but agonized if he moved quickly. The aching of his ribs hadn't improved much, but he knew he needed to sit up lest his condition turn into pneumonia. Fortunately, the weather had improved and he no longer feared freezing to death, but the dampness of the cell remained dangerous. And everything about the place stank. Robert knew he had to walk around and exercise.

For the first time in weeks, fear returned, like a ravaging animal, waiting to devour him in a dark corner of his cell. Because he could die at any time, the fear of death clutched at his throat and made him shake. Yet anxiety became strangely more comfortable than he would have thought possible. Robert realized that fear had actually been his friend. Contempt for the Nazis seriously undercut his awareness of how dangerous they were. Even the boy soldiers only had to squeeze a finger once and it was all over. The dread he felt when parachuting down through the sky had kept him sharp and alert initially, but the loss of fear had made his thinking sloppy and his actions impulsive.

He should never have taken Al King with him. If he'd left Al alone, at least the man would still be alive. Robert felt guilt every time Al's face came to mind. He'd been responsible for his friend's demise. In the cold solitary cell, Robert wept time and again over his friend's death.

Robert didn't have a clear sense of time. Had he been in this hellhole a week? Five weeks? Three days? He was no longer sure of anything. Although the SS hadn't taken his wristwatch, days and nights blurred together in the constantly night-black room, erasing any sense of whether the sun was up.

His body didn't hurt as badly as it had earlier, but he still ached enough that he took small short breaths. Lack of food had turned everything inside him into dull emptiness, leaving him weak. He wouldn't be able to resist anyone now.

Only in the midst of brokenness did Robert begin trying to remember where he'd come from. At first he found it difficult to concentrate and make his mind fasten on the past. Events slowly came into focus. For the first time in days, he thought about Mary McCoy. By now she must surely know that he was missing in action. Undoubtedly she would worry, but probably Robert was now no more than a fading memory for her. Maybe some other guy had come along. Yet he remembered those important words she'd quoted to him that last night in Sterling. *"It is I; be not afraid."* She had written that on a special piece of paper that he kept with his things in England. And what about those things? Were they still there? Probably not. Some officer would have packed up his gear and stashed it some place that by now had disappeared. Maybe the name Robert Walker had vanished from the face of the earth.

Each phrase of the Bible passage ran through his mind, turning over and over endlessly in his head. The solemn promise that Jesus the Christ would be with him as his consolation seemed like a life preserver thrown to a drowning man. The call to not be afraid consoled him. The truth was that anger, not faith, had prompted him to take Al with him in the escape.

Robert began to weep again. He'd gotten back in touch with the most important truth that he'd lost in the grimness of watching Germans killing Russians. He had to keep in touch with this one promise that could keep him from making other foolish decisions. His consolation was in God, not Robert Walker.

~

Several hours later the door opened. Robert looked up into the face of one of the boy soldiers. He motioned with the barrel of his rifle for Robert to stand up. Slowly, but with some less pain, Robert got to his feet.

"Marsch!"

Robert hobbled past the young man and lumbered down a long hallway. Near the end of the corridor, another soldier opened a door and Robert stepped outside for the first time in two weeks. The fresh air hit him in the face with a suddenness that invigorated everything in his body. The horrible smell of the solitary confinement had become so common that he had no longer realized how bad it was until the fresh wind struck him in the face. He took a deep breath and felt more alive than he had in days.

"Marsch!" the guard demanded.

Robert tried to stand taller and walked down the path between the barracks. In a few minutes, he was back in front of the long wooden building he'd escaped from. He was so weak that it was difficult to step up into the barracks, but he forced himself through the door.

Silence fell over the room. Fellow prisoners stared in amazement as he straggled in. He looked around at their surprised faces. "I'm still alive," he muttered. "I'm back."

Instantly men gathered around him, offering him help and assisting him to sit down on the edge of the nearest bed.

"I must look pretty bad." Robert looked around at the group of prisoners and smiled. "Huh?"

"I've seen better." Warren Davis put his hand on Robert's shoulder. "Looks like you've lost a lot of weight. They came in here after you made a break for it and interrogated us for hours. Fortunately, no one had anything to tell them."

Robert nodded his head. "Haven't eaten much in two weeks, I guess. I'm a little weak."

"Anybody got anything?" Davis looked around at the men. "They don't exactly leave us with the leftovers, you know."

"I got a crust," a man said reluctantly. "Had it hidden."

"Give it to him," Davis ordered.

Moments later someone thrust a piece of stale bread into Robert's hand. He immediately began eating.

"How'd you survive?" someone else asked.

"By the grace of God," Robert said. "That's literally all that kept me alive."

"It's been tough while you were gone," Davis added. "We had a couple of men die. Probably from diarrhea and lack of food. The Nazis simply came in and carried them off. No funeral ceremony, nothing."

Robert nodded his head. "Any news on how the war is going?"

"Not much," Warren said, "but I think our troops are moving forward and might be closer than we think. The Krauts got to be dying like flies out there."

"We've seen our airplanes go over," a new man added. "I think that strikes are happening someplace not far away."

"Would you mind if I tried to lie down on my bed?" Robert asked the soldiers around him. "I'm feeling a little poorly."

Immediately the men helped him stand and supported him as they walked across the barracks to his bed. He collapsed in a heap. Warren Davis sat down on the edge of the bed.

"I guess—" Warren stopped and ran his hands nervously through his hair. "I guess that I'm sorry I didn't try to go with you, but I admire what you tried."

"I shouldn't have taken Al with me."

"Hindsight's always twenty-twenty. You made the effort. That's what counts."

Robert fought back the tears welling up in his eyes. "Thanks. I appreciate your good thoughts."

"We've got to get some food in you. You look really bad, Robert."

"Lost a couple of teeth. That's what it is. My smile's a little depleted."

Davis smiled. "Get some sleep and let's see what tomorrow brings."

In the middle of night, the roar of airplanes woke Robert. He listened with an inner awareness that they must be American. The roar intensified as they came closer. He pushed himself up in bed and tried to see out the window. Suddenly light broke across the dark night as bright bursts of illumination drifted toward the ground.

"Flares!" Robert exclaimed. "The first wave of airplanes is dropping flares!" He could hear men around him getting out of bed and rushing past him toward the windows.

"They're going to bomb the plant," someone gasped in the darkness. "God help us if they hit the barracks!"

Flares dropped not far from Robert's barracks. The bright incendiary devices lit up their housing area, marking their barracks for a possible hit.

"Oh God!" Warren Davis exclaimed. "The lead planes have mistaken us for the factory. We're going to get bombed!"

The Nazi camp warning signals began whining through the night. Robert could see German soldiers running out across the grassy area, trying to put out the flares. Moments later a bomb exploded behind their barracks, and the men hit the floor. Robert rolled under his bed.

The explosions shook everything in the barracks. Glass exploded in all directions. Men huddled together and held their heads with their hands, trying to cover their ears. The sound of the bombs erupted with a deafening roar. The blasts rocked the grounds and shook the barracks. Robert kept his ears covered and repeated aloud over and over, "Be not afraid, be not afraid, be not afraid . . . "

And then the excruciating bomb blasts stopped and the pounding ceased. The sound of airplane motors disappeared, drifting off in the distance. Robert struggled to his feet and looked out the windows. The barracks fifty feet away had been hit and was burning. Prisoners would be dying. On the far side of the compound, he could see that part of the factory was also on fire. Out on the edges of the camp, German soldiers ran up and down, yelling at each other. Fire trucks swung down the center of the assembly area. Cold wind blew through the broken windows.

"We're still alive!" Robert rolled over to find Warren Davis but couldn't see him. "Warren!" he yelled. "Davis! Where are you?"

Men shouted back and forth across the barracks, but no one answered Robert. He started trying to walk through the pitch-black room. "Davis! Where are you?" He shouted again. Robert abruptly stumbled over something at his feet and fell forward on top of a man.

Realizing he had tripped over a body, Robert tried to get up. His hands were covered with a warm sticky substance. Robert took hold of the man's shirt and lifted him up so that the moonlight revealed the man's face. He was holding Warren Davis. Warren's eyes stared upward, not blinking or moving. A piece of glass had severed his throat.

Forty ~

WERDAU, GERMANY, MARCH 1945

For two days after the bombing, Walker and the other survivors were locked down in their barracks as smoke rolled from the ruins of the textile factory. German soldiers worked around the yard, trying to put the plant back into working order. At suppertime, only the single group from the barracks marched through the mess hall, but they were fed enough that Robert felt some of his strength returning. During the day, the men did nothing but talk to each other and wait for something to happen. The Nazis seemed bent on preventing any sharing of facts. The men in Walker's barracks went to sleep at night without any idea of how many of their men survived the air attack or how badly the factory had been damaged.

On the third day, the prisoners in Robert's barracks were marched as a unit out of their quarters and to the back of the factory's shipping area. A train, puffing and roaring steam as if it were ready to leave, stood at the shipping docks. Within minutes, the prisoners were in the cars and moving out of town.

"Any idea what's going on?" Robert asked the man sitting next to him.

The man shook his head and shrugged. "Don't know."

"Hope we're going to another camp," Robert said. "Always scares me when we get on one of these trains."

"Yeah." The soldier shook his head. "The factory must have been hit hard is all I can guess."

Robert nodded and watched the German countryside start to go past. He could see a few buildings that looked like they had been bombed. Robert settled into the padded seat, enjoying the comfort. Within a few minutes the train was flying across the rails at an unusually fast speed.

"I think they want to make us as hard a target as possible," the soldier said to Robert. "Probably intend to use us as a bargaining chip as our boys close in. They're sure movin'."

"It's be hard to jump off this thing and survive," Robert observed. "I guess they're covering all the angles."

The two men sank into their own thoughts as the hours wore on. The train stopped periodically, but their coach doors stayed locked shut. And each time the train would start up again. Guards came and went. Sometimes the German soldiers sat in the car watching the prisoners; at other times, the men journeyed alone. After several hours of travel, the sun began to set and they had no choice but to sleep sitting up. Robert quickly acquiesced and had little trouble drifting off. The pace continued for four days.

Around noon the train stopped and a new load of guards got on the coach. The prisoners' clothes were stiff and the men smelled terrible, but the German soldiers sat down without appearing to be particularly offended. Robert watched the young Krauts filter into their car and decided to test the situation. Possibly he could ferret information out of the Jerries. He walked to the back of the car where a couple of guards were now sitting. "Speak English?" he asked.

"Ja!" the young guard answered with a friendly sound in his voice. "I do."

"Where have we gone?" Robert sat down opposite the two German men.

"Gone?" The guard smiled. "You have had quite a trip on dis ride. You touched Czechoslovakia and Poland."

"You're kidding."

The guard pursed his lips and shook his head. "Nah. Isn't true."

"Got a cigarette?" Robert asked audaciously.

"Ja." The German reached in his pocket and pulled out a pack. "Have one." He flipped a cigarette out of the opening.

"Danke schön!" Robert took the long white cigarette and smelled it for a moment before putting it between his lips. It had been months since he had smoked one. The German flipped a match and lit it for him. He took a long drag and let the smoke gently drift out of his nose and started coughing. The warmth still felt good and soothing.

"You smoke?" the German asked.

Robert shook his head. "Not really."

"Not ve-a-lly?" the officer puzzled.

"Yeah." Robert smiled. "Just a hobby. Do you know where we're going?"

The German nodded his head. "In another hour you vill arrive in de city of Crimmitschau."

Robert frowned. The name meant nothing.

"A good place. You like it."

"Thank you." Robert smiled, took the cigarette with him, and moved back to his seat. The train pulled out again and was on the way to their destination.

"What'd you find out?" the soldier next to Robert asked.

"We're going to some place called Crimmitschau."

The man raised his eyebrows. "Never heard of anything with such a weird name."

"Looks like we will be there fairly quickly."

Robert stared out the window, trying to remember what month it had to be. He added and subtracted, finally coming to a conclusion. It must be about March or maybe April. He turned to the prisoner next to him again. "Know what day it is?"

~

CRIMMITSCHAU, GERMANY, MARCH 1945

By evening, Robert and the men in the railway coach had marched through Crimmitschau to a new barracks in the quaint little town that again looked like something from a travel brochure. Even though the camp was surrounded by a ten-foot-high fence topped with rolls of barbed wire, the place felt much more relaxed than any prison Robert had been in. The German guards seemed human and more concerned than those he'd experienced previously. Like the welcome of spring's arrival after a long winter, the environment had a crisp freshness. He still felt weak, but maybe things would prove to be better in this place.

The next morning an overweight German man in plain clothes showed up in the barracks. His blue striped shirt hung leisurely from the back of his pants, which were held up with broad black suspenders. The German boy guards stood around him leisurely. For a moment the man smiled at the prisoners, bouncing his fat fingers together in front of his large belly. He pulled at his large gray mustache, as if in thought and trying to make sure he began with the right English words.

"*Wilkommen!*" the heavyset German shouted. "We are glad to have you here as our guests." He walked down the center of the barracks as if he were an old friend. "I run a stove factory in de lovely city, and you have de good fortune of being with us."

The prisoners stood at attention, saying nothing.

"I am sure you are not aware of what is happening, but please be assured that I will do what I can to make the experience in Crimmitschau good." He stopped and looked at the men, then broke into a broad smile. "I see dat some of you have not been to de cleaners in some time.

Ve vill try to improve on this situation by tomorrow." He winked. "Good day."

Robert looked down at his dirt-smeared uniform. The stiff pants had stains and ragged edges. He looked like something that had crawled out of a sewer and didn't smell much better.

"Tomorrow!" the large man bellowed as he left the barracks. "Ve vill fix this problem!" The fat German smiled, bowed, and disappeared down the path alongside the barracks, with the officers tramping after him.

"Who's the wacko?" the prisoner next to him asked Robert.

"Beats me." He shook his head. "Must run the place, but he sure looks better than anything I've seen so far!"

~

The next morning, a small group of prisoners appeared in the doorway as the men got up. They moved through the barracks gathering up dirty clothes and leaving behind a pile of fresh pants, underwear, and shirts. The Americans rummaged through the new clothing. Robert's group was shocked to smell the fresh clothes. The men broke into shouting and clapping. By the time they were dressed, several doctors appeared with nurses and began systematically examining each man.

Robert stepped before the doctor and tried to stand at attention. He felt weak and hungry. He slumped and was afraid his legs would give out.

The doctor frowned and spoke to the man behind him.

The male nurse nodded and motioned for Robert to follow him. Within minutes he found himself in the back of a truck, rumbling through the village to a small local hospital. A guard at the door motioned for him to follow him into an examination room.

Fifteen minutes later a businesslike doctor appeared and began a thorough head-to-toe examination of Robert. He sat on the edge of an examination table in his clean, baggy underwear, accepting whatever the silent doctor indicated he should do. After about twenty minutes, the doctor bowed graciously and left the room. Minutes later a German officer came in.

"Herr Jones," the officer began politely in excellent English. "Your condition is not good. De doctor recommends dat you be fed vell and given at least a veek of nothing but rest. You vill do no vork until your condition improves. Do you understand me?"

Robert shook his head in amazement. "Yes . . . yes . . . I understand your words. Food and rest?"

"Dat ist correct." The soldier nodded his head. "Ve vill take you back to the barracks after you are dressed again." The man nodded politely and left the room.

Robert looked at his hands. They shook slightly, and he had to rest them against the examination table to make the trembling stop. He couldn't believe what he had just heard. Perhaps this was only a setup before the Krauts put him and the others in a pit and shot the whole bunch. Yet the guards had been kind enough. He took a deep breath and slipped off the table to begin dressing again.

As he reached for his shirt, Robert abruptly realized that a large, full-length mirror stood bolted to the wall behind him. He turned and looked again. Robert had not seen a mirror since being captured. His ribs seemed to almost press through his skin, and his legs looked like wobbly, skinny pieces of bone with emaciated arms dangling beside them. His worn face carried a guantness beyond anything he'd seen before. Robert looked more like a skeleton than a human being. He must have lost more than fifty pounds in the last four months.

Forty-One

Crimmitschau, Germany, April 1945

A week had passed since Walker first arrived in Crimmitschau. The sound of Allied bombers flying far overhead each day filled him with hope, but nothing happened in the town. In addition to resting in the barracks, Robert had been fed German food in normal quantities. By the time the second week began, he felt like a new human being. The hospital doctor had sent pills that he took three times a day, and his entire system improved dramatically.

On the following Monday morning, the heavyset man with the black bushy mustache returned. "*Willkommen!*" he shouted across the barracks. "I see each of you ist doing much better than when you came. *Willkommen.*" He bounced across the room, shaking hands with the nearest man.

Walker stood up and extended his hand. "Thank you for

the excellent treatment and the good food we've received. The care is deeply appreciated."

The bald-headed man shook hands enthusiastically. "Vonderful! I am glad you are feeling better. Allow me to introduce myself. I am Herr Heinz Stadler, the owner of de stove factory. Ve are glad you are here to vork with us." He shook hands again and started toward the door. "Ve hope you like our town."

"I can tell you that we're mighty glad to be here," one of the men said as Stadler walked by. "Thank you."

"Tomorrow ve vill have a little something for you to do. Yes?" Heinz smiled broadly. "Rest, and ve vill see you in de morning."

The prisoners watched out the windows as Stadler bounced across the yard, shaking hands, saying good things, and seemingly making everyone smile. He looked like a politician making his rounds at a gathering of supporters before an election.

"What do you make of him?" one of the soldiers mumbled.

"I don't know," Robert said. "I just hope that when we go to that factory tomorrow nobody's standing behind the door with a machete in hand. I don't want any more surprises."

"Maybe they're trying to drive us nuts and he's the first act in the show," a soldier quipped.

"I don't know whether to laugh or cry," another man said while keeping his eyes locked on the jovial Stadler, who was walking through the back door of the factory. "The guy acts like Santa Claus."

"Man. This prison life is some kind of an ordeal." The

man who had shaken hands with the manufacturer stared at his palms. "I sure hope this guy is for real."

The sounds of a squadron of airplanes roared overhead. Robert looked out of the window. "Me, too. We're running out of time."

~

The next morning, Walker and the new company of prisoners walked into the factory for the first time. To their surprise, they saw prisoners of war from many backgrounds working at various kinds of jobs. Canadians and Frenchmen made up the majority, but a number of Englishmen worked some of the metal presses. No one could see any Russians, but there were other Americans.

Robert watched the scene. Everyone appeared to be going about his job in a pleasant frame of mind. He couldn't observe anything that appeared to be amiss or out of order. Soldiers stood around the doors with guns on their shoulders, but no one seemed threatening or menacing. The place ran like a regular factory. As he watched, Robert also heard airplanes flying over to somewhere in Germany.

"I don't get it," Robert mumbled to the man next to him. "This factory looks like everything is hunky-dory."

"Yeah. Don't know what to make of it."

"Well, here comes somebody to talk with us. We'll find out in a hurry."

A Frenchman walked up to the new group of twenty men. "Gentleman," he began politely in excellent English with a heavy British accent, "good morning. My name is Pierre, and I'm one of you. We only have simple jobs to do. The work isn't hard. Please, follow me and I will get you started."

The Frenchman passed out minimal jobs to the men. The tasks were mainly carrying parts from one place in the factory to another. Most of the work was marginal, and the plant could have run without the Americans doing anything.

"Don't screw up things. We have a good opportunity to finish out this war here and survive. Just do your jobs." He raised an eyebrow menacingly. "No nonsense, please." Pierre turned and walked away.

"Can't believe my eyes," Robert said. "Let's get after it, boys."

For the rest of the day, the twenty new men did exactly as Pierre had told them to do. There was no pressure, and the pace was almost leisurely. Near the end of the day, Heinz Stadler reappeared and thanked everyone for "excellent production," waved, and disappeared again. The men filed out to a good supper and then back to the barracks.

"Can you believe it?" Robert asked the man sleeping next to him.

"No," Ernest Blauw answered.

Blauw was tall and thin, and his blond hair hung down in his eyes. He had been a farm boy in Iowa before the Army drafted him.

"I don't know." Ernest scratched his scalp. "Never seen anything like this ride. We go from one extreme of torture to the other end of the scale, like we're their special guests of honor. No, I don't get it."

"Looks like we've fallen into a gold mine." Robert stretched out on his bed. "All we have to do is play the game, huh?"

"We're not even working in that factory. Just passing stuff around."

"Ernest, did you work hard on the farm?"

"You kiddin'? Sure. Hauling bales of hay is tough work. Worked hard all my life."

"This is easier?"

"You kiddin'? Of course."

Robert nodded. "That's the way I figure it. Got to be some reason why that good ole Heinz Stadler is treating us so well. What do you think it might be?"

Ernest looked blank for a minute. "I don't know," he finally said.

"Hear any airplanes go over today?"

"Sure. Lots of 'em."

"How far away do you think our troops are?"

"What are you suggesting?"

"Think about it, Ernie. We're getting treated well for some good reason." Robert rolled off and closed his eyes. "Think about it." He turned over and drifted away.

~

Somewhere near dawn, Robert awoke. His physical system was only barely coming around to normal, and his body didn't always function like it should. His intestines rumbled and his stomach growled. He awoke feeling okay and wasn't particularly tired. Robert simply couldn't sleep.

Quietly, he slipped up to the head of his bed and looked around the room at his sleeping comrades. Everyone looked peacefully asleep. Fear of dying had greatly subsided. The prisoners seemed to be resting normally, like a gang of high-school boys on a campout.

But things weren't normal. Robert felt like something had left his body. He still struggled to remember the days of the week and found it more difficult than usual for the calendar in his head to make sense. The world around him wasn't anything like what he'd grown up with or expected. America felt like it was a million miles away and had disappeared in the ocean.

Days had passed since Robert had thought about Mary McCoy. He couldn't remember her voice or see her face anymore. She was a lovely memory from a world to which he might—or might not—ever return. Like his mother, Mary had disappeared. In a matter of hours during the night, she had slipped away into nothingness.

Robert suddenly felt extremely lonely. None of the people sleeping in the room had been with him before they landed in this fruit basket. He knew virtually nothing about any of them, and they knew zero about him.

The emptiness frightened Robert. Maybe all he would ever have in this world was what he could carry with him in his pockets. All the guarantees and certainties offered by American society lay broken and smashed at his feet. Any promise of the future seemed to be sifting through his fingers like grains of sand dropping onto the seashore.

Loneliness grew like a giant black cloud arising from the horizon and covering him with darkness. Robert felt small, insignificant. He had lived through hell, but the odor of death had lingered around him and settled into his soul. Brokenness had crumpled him, and the only thing that he could do now was to survive.

Forty-Two

CRIMMITSCHAU, GERMANY, APRIL 1945

During the month that followed, life in the factory and the camp continued at the easy pace Heinz Stadler seemed to fully approve. Increasing numbers of bombers flew over, but nothing happened to the town of Crimmitschau. Like an enchanted village, the little burg seemed completely exempted from the bombing somewhere across Germany. The prisoners functioned like the local citizens, walking up and down the streets as if no war existed anywhere in the world.

On the other side of the camp in a distant barracks, French POWs kept a hidden radio under the floor and daily predicted that the Allies would soon infiltrate the area, but nothing occurred beyond an increasing number of airplanes flying over each day to other targets far away.

Most of the men in Robert's unit maintained a somewhat philosophical attitude about the speculations that were running rampant through the barracks. Maybe the Allies would come soon. Maybe they wouldn't. Getting caught up in the rumors only left them strung out. Robert said little and took each day as it came. His attitude got shaken slightly when Herr Stadler would appear unexpectedly, always acting as a Mr. Nice Guy offering consolation and then disappearing back into the factory. As the Frenchmen's predictions of liberation increased in intensity, so did Stadler's appearances, slapping men on the back, thanking them, and acting as if he were their best friend.

On a Friday in April, the men in Walker's barracks arose for another day of meaningless work. No one said much, and the prisoners straightened the room in a military manner. They had just finished a decent breakfast when Pierre, the French lackey, appeared in the door of their barracks gesturing frantically.

"Listen to me!" Pierre demanded. "I have an important message for you."

"What's up, Frenchy?" one of the soldiers yelled across the room. "Found any champagne for us yet?"

Pierre's eyes flashed, and he pounded his fist into his palm.

"I heard the report on the radio myself. The American army is going to break through into this area today! We will be liberated immediately!"

Silence fell over the room for several moments.

"General Patton's coming after me?" someone called out. "Tell him thanks but that I'd rather stay here. I enjoy the work too much." Laughter erupted around the room.

"I am not joking with you!" Pierre demanded. "Listen to me! We must be ready for your army to come."

Robert walked over and patted the Frenchman on the back. "Hey! We are, Pierre. We got our flags rolled up under our beds. We're ready to break them out the second our boys come rolling in. We were just planning a welcome ceremony when you came in."

The men in the room laughed again.

Pierre raised one eyebrow and glared. "Fools! Whether you believe it or not, they will be here today." He hurried from the room and went to the next building.

"Pierre's been listening to too much radio," someone called out from the back. "Tell him to tune in to a little music." The men laughed again and left for work.

The plant seemed unusually quiet, and almost no guards were there except for the few men standing at the doors. Heinz Stadler didn't make his usual cheerful appearance, but production started up as usual. Walker began his daily work of passing bolts back and forth. An hour later he noticed that no guards were at the door.

Robert walked up to one of the Canadians. "Do you see any German soldiers around this place?"

The young man stood up and looked around the building. "Strange. Looks like we're running this factory."

Robert walked over to Pierre. "Where are the guards?"

Pierre looked out the window. "I told you that the Allied army is coming. The guards have left to escape capture." He went back to his job, contemptuously ignoring the American.

Robert tossed the bolt he had been carrying over his

shoulder and looked around the room. The place ticked away like a wound-up clock, but he certainly couldn't see anybody in charge. The prisoners could simply walk out if they chose.

Why not? Robert thought. *Let's see what happens if I try going out the back door.* He walked across the building and opened the door where the prisoners usually entered. *No one in the parking lot.* He closed the door. *Are we just going to stand here until American soldiers show up and invite us to lunch?* He walked back across the room.

Suddenly the German guards rushed in the front of the building and began shouting. "*Stoppen! Schlange stehen!*"

The prisoners closed their work and watched the German soldiers hurry around the room with guns pointed at them. One of the Germans grabbed Pierre and began speaking rapidly to him in German. Silence fell over the room.

Pierre stepped up on a workbench. "We are to return to our barracks. Stay calm and follow these men." He looked hard at the prisoners. "Do as they say and there will be no problems. If not, the guards will shoot us. We are to leave this building now." The Frenchman hopped down and followed the German officer to the door. The rest of the prisoners fell in behind them, marching out of the room.

"What do you think?" Walker asked Ernest Blauw, who was walking beside him.

"Maybe Pierre is right," Blauw said in low tones. "The Allies might not be that far away."

"Yes, but I don't hear any trucks or guns. Ought to be a war going on out there."

Blauw shook his head. "Not if the Nazis have collapsed. Our people might be taking a leisurely roll through the farm fields around here."

Robert shrugged. "I'm afraid to believe the reports. So many things haven't turned out right. This empty hole in my gums will give testimony to that story."

"Look at the guards." Blauw nodded to his left. "They look worried at best. Frightened at worst. Might be a tad bit on the dangerous side right now."

"I won't give them any trouble today." Robert shook his head again. "I've had all the rough stuff I want."

"Hast!" one of the Germans snapped. *"Schnell!"*

"I think he wants us to hurry up," Blauw quipped but didn't look at the man. "Certainly don't want him to wet his pants."

"Up his nose," Robert answered under his breath.

Minutes later most of the prisoners were back in their barracks. The outside doors were locked and the shutters forced shut. As soon as the building was secured, Robert crept to the window and watched as the German soldiers hurried onto military trucks that sped down the road out of town. Within fifteen minutes the stove factory and the concentration camp were nothing more than a quiet group of buildings sitting by the edge of silent Crimmitschau.

"What's happening?" one of the men huddling around the window asked.

"Looks like Pierre was right this time," Blauw answered. "They're gone."

"Couldn't be."

"Why not? Old Stadler's treated us like his long-lost buddies."

"I think this is nothing but a ruse. We're about to be killed."

"Don't say such a thing."

"Well, the Nazis have done worse."

"Can we break out of this building?"

"Not unless we want to risk being shot up by somebody waiting out there in the bushes with a machine gun."

"Right. Don't try it."

Speculation bounced back and forth like balls in a tennis game, but when everybody stopped and listened, they heard nothing except the wind. Robert eventually walked back to his bed and stretched out. Most of the men stayed around the windows, watching and waiting. An hour went by.

"Look!" one of the prisoners screamed. "Look! Out there, coming up the road. It's one of our tanks!"

Walker leaped off the bed and fought to get a place near the window. He could see three American tanks barreling down the road that ran through the center of Crimmitschau.

"Got to be from the Fourth Armored Division!"

"They're ours!" a soldier cried. "Look! More coming!"

"We're liberated!" another man shouted at the top of his lungs.

The barracks burst into an enormous cheer. Men hugged each other and danced around the room. Robert screamed and beat on the walls of the building. From the buildings around them they heard the roar of men applauding, screaming, laughing.

"We've survived!" Robert yelled at the top of his lungs. "They didn't kill us! We've made it!"

"Hurrah!" the man next to him sounded over and over again.

Robert pressed his face against the window and watched the tanks disappear into the town. No one came out of the houses, and the streets looked deserted. The Americans would have no trouble securing the little village.

"Thank God!" Robert kept saying over and over as he shook hands with the other prisoners. "We're free! Thank God we're free at last."

Throughout the rest of the day, the prisoners huddled near the windows and listened. Occasionally they heard the roar of a bomb exploding somewhere off in the distance, which shook the plant, but very little happened. Nightfall came, but the prisoners could not see anyone outside the building or in the streets of the town. They waited by the windows for Allied soldiers to appear, but only quiet settled over the compound.

Eventually Robert lay down on his bunk, waiting. He pulled a blanket over him to protect against the cool April air. Perhaps the American soldiers would break the doors open at any minute. Maybe not. Robert slipped into sleep with his shoes on.

The sun came up, and light fell over Robert's face, waking him up. He listened carefully but heard nothing. Pulling the blanket up more closely around his neck, he lay in the bed, praying that this would be the last day in his entire lifetime that he would be a prisoner. The deprivation and emptiness of prison life had opened old wounds that he had hoped would die and disappear. The face of his mother came into view once again, and Robert realized the extent to which he had avoided fully facing the truth that she had simply driven off one day and left him, and the family, and Fort Towson behind forever. Surely by now the same had happened with Mary McCoy too. The emptiness of concentration camp life had clamped onto his mind and left him convinced that no relationship was permanent. *Forever* no longer fit in his vocabulary.

Robert thought about the terrifying experiences that he had survived in the past months. The bomber exploding in the sky filled his mind with the memory of the orange fire, the flames, the black smoke that could have easily swallowed his life. The face of the frozen soldier with the bullet hole gaping in his forehead and yet still kneeling with his gun aimed at the enemy returned with new grotesqueness. Robert felt again the emptiness of his stomach after days of marching with nothing to eat. He knew his thighs must now look like skinny legs on a starving chicken. He thought again about the dead soldiers—some of them his friends—stacked like pieces of broken firewood in the front of the boxcar. The smell of the detention cellar where the Nazis imprisoned him after they killed Al King hit his nose and for a moment filled him with nausea. The experiences of the past months whirled through his mind like a fast-running movie projector spinning out of its sprockets.

His thoughts came to a sudden halt when the sound of large trucks roared up the road and turned into the camp. From every corner of the prison he heard men beating on the walls and shouting. Robert glanced at his watch—2100 hours. The Army had arrived.

Robert leaped out of his bed and rushed to the window. A truckload of American infantrymen rolled through the open metal gate and pulled to a stop in the parking lot. The prisoners kept yelling and beating on the doors and windows. The American soldiers hurried out of the trucks and rushed toward the barracks, ready to break the doors down. The men around Robert turned delirious with anticipation. For a moment he stepped back from the other prisoners and looked around the meager quarters where they had lived in this quaint town of Crimmitschau. On so little, the prisoners had managed only by the grace of God to survive. A knot formed deep in his throat. The emotion pushed up, and he couldn't keep the inner pressure down. Robert began to cry.

The Allied soldiers beat on their door and hammered away to break the locks off. Robert's tears flowed down his thin face, and he wiped his nose with his hand. He didn't want to cry, but he couldn't stop. It was over. They were free. He would live.

The door exploded open and the Americans pushed through.

"You're free!" the GI shouted and raised his gun in the air like a spear. "Welcome back, boys."

The tears ran down the sides of his face, and Robert shouted at the top of his lungs, "Oh my Lord! Free! Truly free!" He bent forward with his face in his hands. "I'm going to live."

Forty-Three

MARYLAND, APRIL 2000

Robert looked out the second-story window of the hospital across the expanse of gray-colored housetops. Beneath him the tree-covered town stretched out into residential areas and then spread off into the horizon. The elms stood like gawking skeletons, their branches empty and their trunks twisted. Some of the first green leaves had begun to sprout on the Bradford pears. Spring wasn't too far away. The loneliness of having such a serious operation without anyone to hold his hand when he awoke had broken open wounds he'd hoped wouldn't return. He couldn't help but be afraid that he might die in his sleep or maybe during recovery. Such a demise didn't seem right to Robert, at least not yet.

Robert glanced at Mary out of the corner of his eye. He still couldn't believe that she'd shown up, seemingly out of nowhere, like a figure emerging from a dream. There she sat as if she were a local gray lady, a hospital helper, an old friend . . . but Mary wasn't. She'd been the woman that he believed he was in love with once upon a time. Although the two hadn't spent that long together, they had passed the hours at a crucial time in his life, and she'd become larger than life at a terribly important moment.

"Don't stop now," Mary urged. "You've only just begun."

Robert scratched his head and thought for a moment. "The Battle of the Bulge later turned out to be one of the worst engagements of the entire war," he said thoughtfully. "America lost over seventy-seven thousand soldiers." Robert shook his head. "At least that's the number that are commemorated near Bastogne. Hitler had to bleed his men away from the Russian front to find the reserves to keep his attack going. It's amazing that the man was able to roll a hundred supply trains a day up to the combat zone even while the Allies pounded him with airpower." He looked over at Mary. "You know they were able to separate the American First Army from Patton's Third Army?"

Mary nodded her head. "Frightened us back home. The people of Sterling were terrified. We prayed at the church constantly."

"The times were bad," Robert concluded. "I guess that I was much luckier than I thought. We found out later that the fanatical Nazis executed over seven hundred American soldiers that they caught as prisoners. Bad scene." He stopped and cleared his throat. The story still bothered him.

"But can you tell me anything about why you didn't ever return to Sterling?" Mary interrupted.

A throbbing ache shot through his chest. Robert gritted his teeth and took a deep breath. His mother's face came before him again. With the passing of the decades, he'd only seen Ma two times, and both occasions were a failure. When he came back after the war, Robert took a trip to Los Angeles for no other reason than to see Mrs. Samuel Mills. She met him at a restaurant and didn't even invite him to her home. They ate lunch; she asked a few questions; and in an hour the visit was all over. Just like she'd done years before in Fort Towson, his mother roared off again to some other place, some other person.

The last time Robert saw Ma was at her own funeral. Dried up and old, she lay there with as much emotion as she had displayed years earlier in the restaurant. A lonely, empty service was shared by a hired preacher and maybe ten other people. No, he really didn't want to go back over that territory again.

"How do you know that I didn't come back?" Robert asked, trying to sound casual. "Back to Sterling?"

Mary's face flushed and she looked embarrassed. "I guess that I don't. At least," she stopped and cleared her throat, "you didn't come back to see *me*."

She looked embarrassed, Robert thought. When she had first come in, he hadn't considered that she didn't reveal much about what she actually thought. Mary seemed to be a towering fortress who had moved into his room when he was asleep and didn't leave much hint of what she really had on her mind. He couldn't decide if Mary was there for much more than a long look at his deteriorating condition, but her last comment cut through any lingering doubts. She still cared . . . and maybe . . . loved him.

"Well," Robert said slowly, "sometimes things just don't work out like we think they *might*."

"I don't understand your meaning, Robert."

Maybe he should tell her; maybe he shouldn't. Then, again, what did he have to lose? Mary might simply pack up and go plodding out of his room and never come back. Honesty was about all that was left.

"I *did* go back," he said without much show of emotion. "I went back after I left Europe the first time." He took a deep breath and then exhaled forcefully. "I went back to Sterling."

Mary's face suddenly changed. She no longer looked like a judge interrogating a culprit but more like a young girl hovering on the edge of a precipice of fear and exposure as if in the next moment she could be swept over the edge.

Robert nodded his head. "It took me a good while to get fully back into a healthy condition. I rested a bit . . . actually for many weeks . . . and needed to gain about eighty pounds. After I started recovering weight, I also realized that I wasn't in good emotional condition. Took me a number of months to get myself together again."

"And then you came back?"

Robert thought for a minute, attempting to carefully choose his words. He hadn't thought about what had happened for a very long time, and he didn't like how the memory made him feel. An old empty, sickening feeling returned. He'd fought constantly for years to keep his sense of loss from ever coming back. Just thinking about the time was difficult.

"In 1946 I flew back." He tried to sound factual. "Flew back to Kansas City. A friend loaned me a car. I drove straight to Sterling." He forced a smile. "Thought maybe you were still teaching at the college."

Mary's mouth dropped slightly, and she raised her eyebrows. Slowly her hand came up to her mouth.

"Of course, you weren't. I talked to the switchboard, and they told me that no one by the name of Mary McCoy had taught there in art, physical education, or anything else for a number of months." Robert shrugged. "I thought maybe you'd moved off, gone to another place. I didn't know, so I drove downtown."

"Downtown," Mary said so softly that he could hardly hear her.

Robert nodded his head. "Yes," he said. "I parked on Main Street to see what had changed in the little town."

"And I came walking down the street?"

Robert nodded his head again. "Yes," he said, as if seeing the whole scene before his eyes again. "Wearing a long blue coat."

"And pregnant?"

"Yeah." Robert tried to smile. "I figured that you'd gotten married and at that instant the best thing I could do was to leave town as quickly as possible. I drove off."

"I saw you," Mary gasped. "I saw you. I *knew* it was you, but you didn't come back. You suddenly disappeared again."

"Guess so."

"Did you find out that I was married? What my new last name was?"

"No." Robert looked back out the window. "I figured time had swallowed everything. Seemed like that had been my entire life story, so I went back to Kansas City and left."

Mary's body sagged; her face fell. She folded her hands resolutely in front of her and stared at the floor. Robert studied her face but couldn't tell what she was thinking. She might be feeling disappointment, and then again Mary could be grieving for what might have been. Her face carried an emptiness that surprised Robert.

"I was pregnant," Mary repeated. "I'd gotten married to a fellow who pursued me vigorously. A man named George Oliver." She looked up. "That's my name now. Oliver. Mary Oliver." She raised her right eyebrow. "George has been gone now for about three years. Died in the fall."

Robert nodded.

"And you've taken care of everything." Robert motioned nervously. "I mean to say you've adjusted to the fact that he's gone."

"Wasn't easy, and it took me longer than I thought it might, but George is in the past now. Yes, he's gone."

"Wasn't easy, was it?" Robert asked.

"I suppose it never is, don't you know." Mary rubbed her mouth nervously. "But then again we don't have much choice in these matters."

"Deaths are like that." Robert stretched out on the bed. "After I saw that you were pregnant, I sort of made up my mind that I didn't have any future in America. That's when I decided to go back to Europe."

"I always thought that you were a more sensitive person than you probably realized, Robert. Sounds to me like your terrible experiences proved to be so brutal that you lost your moorings to the past, to our country."

Robert shook his head. "I was like a lost dog wandering around without any idea of where to go. The only place I felt at home was sitting in the cockpit of an airplane. At least up there in the sky no one had much of a chance to get their hands on me." He shrugged. "It was the best place for me."

The hospital door abruptly swung open. "Colonel Walker?" the young man in a white lab coat asked. "Oh!" He stopped halfway into the room. "I didn't know that anyone was here."

"An old friend," Robert answered.

The doctor looked at Mary for a moment. "I believe you're the first guest that Mr. Walker has had in days. In fact, since he's been in here."

Forty-Four ~

Dr. Lewis smiled charmingly at Mary. "I need to talk with Mr. Walker about a confidential matter." He looked pleasantly but firmly at her, hinting that she should leave.

"I understand." Mary reached down to pick up her purse. "I can wait outside."

"Doc," Robert interrupted. "Mary's an old, dear friend. Doesn't bother me to have her hear anything that you've got to tell me. She's probably heard it all anyway."

Lewis looked at Mary and then Robert. "I have some difficult information to share with you, Bob. You sure that a public discussion is what you want?"

Robert frowned. "I thought the heart surgery was the worst that we were going through on this go-round in the hospital."

"Your cardiac surgeon did too," Lewis explained. "Turns out that we were all wrong."

"I'm not following you," Robert answered.

Dr. Lewis looked at Mary again and then shrugged. "Perhaps I'd better have some more light." He walked to the wall and switched on the overhead lights. Shadows instantly disappeared. "Okay. I'll try to be as honest with you as I can be." The doctor scratched his head and sat down on the end of the bed. "We're not exactly sure why the tests didn't catch this problem before your heart surgery, but apparently they didn't. However, during the surgery we saw some tissues that bothered us, so we've been running tests for the last couple of days so I could give you the straight information tonight."

Robert pushed himself up farther in bed. "Sounds like we're talking a serious situation here."

Lewis nodded his head. "Yes, Bob. Yes, we are. Let me be slightly more exact. I'm an oncologist, and my area of specialty is cancer, cancer of the liver in particular. That's what I take care of around here. Your cardiac surgeon called me in to take a look."

Robert pulled at his chin and rubbed his neck. "The message that I'm getting is that you're telling me I've got a cancer problem of some sort. Right?"

Dr. Lewis nodded. "Cancer of the liver, to be exact."

"So you guys sewed me up on one end only to discover that I'm falling apart on the other."

"A little oversimplified, but that's about it."

Robert rubbed his chest and looked out the window. Lights were starting to go on in the houses around the hospital. Night had come. Streetlights illuminated the streets.

The day was ending. After several moments, he turned back to Mary. Her face looked white, as if the setting sun had washed out the color. "You getting a picture of what this man is telling me?"

Mary nodded her head solemnly. "He's saying that you've got a big, serious problem this time, Robert." She turned to the doctor. "Can you treat the type of cancer you're describing, Doctor?"

Lewis turned back to Robert. "You also have lesions on your lungs, Bob." Dr. Lewis shook his head and looked at the floor. "Somehow this situation has been missed in all your checkups." He tilted his head and glanced at Bob out of the corner of his eye. "Which haven't been many until you were seriously ill, I might add."

Robert shrugged. "Always figured that if I didn't bother you guys, you wouldn't bother me."

"You should have *bothered* us," Lewis said dryly. "Months ago."

"Okay," Robert said. "What are we talking here? Can you make me well?"

Dr. Lewis shook his head again. "We can give you chemotherapy and try drugs that are purely experimental. If you're willing, we can attempt to give you every new drug that we can put our hands on."

"Don't kid me, Dr. Lewis. I've lived through some appalling experiences in my lifetime. Mary and I were just talking about World War II and the time I was a prisoner of war. I don't like to speculate. I'd rather cut to the chase and get to the bottom line." Robert cleared his throat. "Am I going to survive?"

"I've seen many people make it, Bob." He took another deep breath. "The truth is, you may need a miracle."

"A miracle?" Robert laughed. "Never had many of those in my life, but a few popped up along the way."

Dr. Lewis nodded.

"Thanks for playing it straight with me, Dr. Lewis. I appreciate your candor."

"We're going to consider how to approach these problems during the next couple of days, Bob, and we need some sense of your wishes. We'll do whatever you want us to."

Walker settled back against the soft pillow supporting his back. "That's why I feel so weak, isn't it?"

"Open-heart surgery is no snap," the doctor noted, "but yes, your energy isn't going to come back like it once was."

"And if I remember right, I'll sleep quite a lot as time goes by."

"That is correct."

"He'll need constant care?" Mary interjected.

"Sure," the doctor continued, "but we can get Robert into a regional hospital to make sure that he has the best of care. After all, his entire career has been with the military."

"Got any other good news for me, Doctor?"

"I'm sorry, Bob. I wish I had another story to tell you."

Walker shook his head. "Your job is to lay the facts on me. My job is to figure out how to live in the time that I've got left. That's the way we play this game."

Dr. Lewis forced a smile. "Why don't you spend the evening thinking about what we've said, and then we'll talk again in the morning?" He slipped off the bed and stood up.

Walker nodded. "We'll do our best. I guess it's customary to say thanks for coming by."

Dr. Lewis kept a smile glued tightly to his lips. He shook hands with Mary and hurried out of the room. "See you tomorrow," he said over his shoulder.

Robert buried his face in his hands and stared at the blanket. "Looks like you certainly came on the right day," he said and looked straight into Mary's eyes. "They're sending me back to one of those World War II concentration camps."

"*That's not at all* what I heard that doctor say," Mary retorted with the sound of matronly indignation. "Seems to me that you're going to be taken care of quite well, regardless of what occurs!"

Robert slid down on the bed so that his feet touched the foot of the bed; he stared at the ceiling as if he hadn't heard anything that she said. "If this doesn't beat anything I've ever known in my whole life. Mary, he just gave me a life sentence. Who knows how much time I've got left?"

Mary looked at the floor for a minute and then stood up resolutely. "Robert, you look awfully tired. I suggest that you take a nap right now. Why don't you go back to sleep, and I'll wait right here? We will talk more when you wake up."

"But—" he started to object.

"No," Mary said firmly, "you need some rest. I'll be right here when you wake up."

Robert opened his mouth wider as if to argue but closed it again. Within thirty seconds, he was asleep.

Mary stood at the edge of his bed, looking down at the long skinny body under the white sheets. She'd remembered him being tall and strong. Today, he didn't even look tall. The illness must have taken a great deal of his strength. Robert's muscular arms were now thin, and the extra skin hung heavy against the sheets. His fingers were slight, and the skin on the tops of Robert's hands had sunken in around the bones. The tips of his gaunt fingers turned slightly in. He had clearly maneuvered through a long life crammed full of demanding experiences.

Mary looked down into his thin face. The youthful handsomeness was gone, and his cheeks protruded. The doctor must have recognized that his loss of weight was an important factor in why Robert probably wouldn't live very long. Life had simply worn too much of his fleshly substance away.

She started to touch him and then didn't. This was the first man Mary had ever loved. Was it possible that she still did? Good heavens, more than fifty years had passed! Whatever she once felt couldn't be any more than adolescent puppy love! Then, again, she remembered the emptiness of believing Robert was dead and the pain of grieving for him only a few weeks earlier. No, she had loved George Oliver. Yes, that was true, and Mary had been a faithful wife. No question about her faithfulness through hard days, and she'd grieved for George when he died. But there wasn't a question in the world that she also loved Robert.

Somewhere down there under all of the years of conflict and a normal life, that love still seemed to be alive. Mary pulled her hand back and walked around the bed again.

The small chair offered her the only place in the room to sit down. Not much comfort there. If she had to spend the night in this room, that worthless chair wouldn't offer any encouragement. On the other hand, Mary couldn't leave the man without anybody watching. He would need a drink of water, the light adjusted, maybe the television turned on, the nurse called during the night, whatever. Someone should have already been there during these past few days. Good heavens! Hospitals weren't what they once were. Without a friend to run interference, they simply left you to wallow in your own unattended bed. No point in even considering an alternative. Mary would simply have to stay there that night with him.

At that moment, Mary realized that she hadn't made any arrangements to stay anywhere that night either. She'd forgotten it! But during the last two nights she'd slept well and caught up on lost sleep.

Oh my, my. She slapped the side of her face. *I guess this hospital room will be fine for this evening!*

But Mary had things to think about, important matters to consider. She needed the time that night to sit and ponder what lay in front of her. Mary had come only to find out if Robert was alive, and now she had discovered that he probably was dying. Like his parachuting down into the field in Europe decades ago, she had landed smack-dab in the midst of the final moments of Robert's life. Decisions had to be made, and sitting there by his bed was the best place to figure out what needed to be done. Wouldn't be easy, but she'd simply sleep in this room . . . with him.

Forty-Five ~

Several times during the night, nurses came in and out of Robert Walker's room, but they didn't turn the light on. Each time either their footsteps or the clanking and banging awoke Mary Oliver. Around 2:00 A.M. she decided that regardless of the hospital's policy, she simply had to stretch out on the floor, no matter how hard the tiles proved to be. She found several blankets in the closets and made herself a pallet near the outside wall. While the coverings only took the edge off the hardness of the floor, at least she could stretch out. Mary closed her eyes and slept fitfully until the next morning when the orderly brought in Robert's breakfast tray.

"Sorry to wake you," the young man said loud enough to wake a horse. "I've got a breakfast tray for Colonel Walker." He placed the plastic tray on the long narrow cart that fit over the top of the hospital bed.

Robert stirred and looked up. "What is it?" he asked slowly.

"Breakfast, sir," the orderly answered. "Nice scrambled eggs and toast. A little hot coffee. Enjoy." The man walked out the door and was gone.

Mary sat up slowly and rubbed her neck. Her back and her legs hurt. She felt painfully stiff. Getting up on her feet again would be a considerable task. "Good morning," she said from the floor.

"Mary? Mary McCoy?" Robert strained to look over the edge of the bed. "You're down there?"

"I'm down here." Mary rolled over on her side and began the arduous task of getting up on her feet. "Not an easy night, Robert."

"You slept on the floor *all* night?"

"Let's just say that I was here *most* of the night. Sleeping is another question."

"I can't believe my eyes." He looked over the side of the bed and stared.

Mary got hold of the end of the bed and pulled herself up. "Ahhh," she groaned. "I need to stand straight up for a while."

"Are you sure that you're okay?"

Mary nodded her head and wiped her eyes. She picked up her glasses from the nightstand and put them on, glancing in the mirror. "Good heavens! Look at my hair." She grabbed her purse and started searching for her comb. "I look like I've been hit by a train."

"You stayed there the whole night?"

"You did well last night, Robert. You didn't even wake up when those noisy nurses came barging in like a herd of elephants. That's progress."

"Mary, I didn't expect you to stay here."

Mary smiled. "A small thing. I just needed to make sure you weren't overlooked last night."

Robert ran his hand nervously through his hair. "I certainly can't ask you to go to such lengths for me. I mean, after all . . . "

"You didn't," Mary answered. "The decision was mine, and the matter's that simple. I wanted to make sure that you didn't have any problems."

Robert shook his head and rubbed the side of his face in bewilderment. "I don't know what to say."

" 'Thank you' is quite sufficient." Mary put her comb back in her purse. "I'm going downstairs to the cafeteria to eat a little something. Get a bowl of cereal and orange juice, I would imagine. You do what you need to do, and I'll be back in a bit."

"Mary . . . " Robert held out his hand. "Why don't you go over to my house? Take a shower, lie down a few moments. Do whatever will make you feel refreshed."

"I couldn't do that."

"Sure you could. I'd be pleased. My house keys are in my pants pocket in the closet. My home isn't far from here."

Mary pursed her lips and thought for a moment. "I guess I could. Probably would make me feel much better. I really haven't been out of this room since I got here yesterday."

"Please," Robert begged. "You'd feel better."

"Okay," Mary said resolutely. "I think that might be a good thing for me to do. I'll get fixed up a bit and come back later."

"Good. Excellent. I'd feel better knowing your needs are taken care of."

Mary opened the narrow closet door and saw a pair of Army fatigues hanging on a hook. She reached in the pocket, feeling the warmth of the cotton fabric. It felt strange to be getting into the pockets of a man's pants that didn't belong to George Oliver. Mary closed the door and dropped Robert's keys into her purse. "I'll be back later." She waved and shut the hospital door behind her.

It took longer than Mary thought it would to find Robert's house. She went back to the downtown square in Chaptico and eventually found the right side street. The two-bedroom brick house was about the size of her own. Everything in the front yard looked clean and orderly. The lawn appeared neat and well cared for, and the front porch looked swept.

Mary unlocked the door, pushed her small overnight bag in, and peered around the room. The well-organized living room looked so fit that it could march in a parade. Even the magazines lay ordered on the coffee table. Robert must have cleaned, dusted, and vacuumed the place well before going to the hospital.

Mary walked around the living room. The furniture seemed to be about what she would have expected. A little worn but nice. Had a man's quality to the chairs and couch, but things felt warm, comfortable. The room seemed friendly, welcoming. She noticed on the front wall over a small brown desk a memory box with his medals, stripes, notice of retirement, the sorts of things that a retired pilot would like to have around for remembrance. And on the bookshelf stood a woman's picture.

Mary looked closely. The woman probably was around forty-five to fifty when the picture was taken. Nice looking. Hair styled like they did back in 1975. Had to be Donna, the woman from England. She picked up the photo and looked at it closely. Donna was probably a medium-weight person with beautiful eyes. Her hair was lighter than Mary's, but the picture gave her a definite red tint. This was the woman Robert had married? Had to be. Mary put the picture back exactly where she picked it up.

"Humph!" Mary said to herself. "I looked that good myself when I was forty-five." She tossed her head and started looking for the bedroom. "Absolutely."

A short hall opened up into a guest room on one side and Robert's bedroom on the other. Mary again peeked around the corner. Robert's room didn't have any pictures on the wall and looked plain, like an army barracks. Everything about the room felt and looked spartan. His bedspread stayed tucked in around the edges as tightly as if a sergeant had made it that evening, not a week ago.

Mary stepped back out and looked across the hall. The guest room didn't have much more of a touch of class except that at least one picture hung opposite the bed. An old Robert Woods painting of a fall scene of trees by a creek bed must have been in every attic in America at sometime or the other. Mary tossed her small suitcase on the bed and sat down. She might not be overwhelmed by the decorations in the house, but the soft bed felt like heaven.

At that moment, Mary realized how extremely tired she felt. Maybe a quick nap after a hot shower would surely pep up her tired body. She opened her bag, took out her toothbrush and robe, and hurried to the bathroom. She brushed her teeth quickly and hopped in the shower stall. The steaming water felt so good that she stayed much longer than normal and came out feeling overwhelmingly relaxed. Mary wrapped her robe around her and went back to the guest room. She stretched out on the bed, sinking into its softness. Several things popped into her mind that she should think about, but she slipped into a heavy sleep.

Mary heard the sound of chirping or ringing in the distance. The noise didn't stop but kept increasing in her ears. Ever so slowly she began to realize that a phone was ringing close to her. And then the full realization struck her. She was asleep and must wake up to answer the phone. Mary opened her eyes.

The ringing came from Robert's room across the hall. She staggered to the door and limped as fast as she could to the nightstand next to the bed.

"Hello."

"Mary?"

"Who is this?"

"It's Robert."

"Robert? Oh yes. My goodness. Robert, are you all right?"

"The question is, are you okay?"

"Yes, quite fine. Why did you ask?"

"I thought maybe something had happened to you. After all, you left here six hours ago."

"What?" Mary gasped. "You don't mean it!"

"Sure do. You left my room before eight o'clock, and it's after two right now."

"Good heavens! I lay down to take a nap and went fast asleep." Mary rubbed her eyes. "I've been lying here on your guest bed all this time."

Robert laughed slightly. "No problem! I just wanted to make sure you weren't hurt or that nothing bad had happened."

"I'll get my shoes on and get right back up there."

"No, no," Robert objected. "We've got all day. I was simply checking to make sure that you weren't in some kind of jam."

Mary bit the side of her mouth. "I'm on my way!"

"Take your time. You have all day and all night as well."

"Okay, Robert. I'll drive carefully. Good-bye." Mary hung up the phone and started back across the hall, shaking her head. "Oh dear," she said to herself. "I've slept for six hours!"

By three o'clock Mary shuffled off the elevator and realized that she had left her cane in Robert's room, leaning against the wall. "Well, I haven't needed it *that* much," she observed indignantly.

"I'm sorry, I didn't get that," a nurse walking by stopped and spoke to her.

"Nothing." Mary smiled. "Just talking to myself."

The nurse frowned and hurried off.

Don't these people know that sometimes people talk to themselves? she thought. *Ought to mind their own business.* Mary shuffled on down the hall. *Robert will think I'm a total idiot. Sleeping half the afternoon like that and all.*

The room door was closed. Probably didn't mean anything, but she pushed the door open only a hair and peeked through the crack. No one seemed to be in there with him, but Robert's legs stuck straight out in the bed, and she could see the bumps in the sheets where his kneecaps were. She pushed the door open farther.

"Robert? I'm here."

"Come in," he answered.

"I must apologize," Mary began before she was through the door. "I simply didn't have any idea that I would sleep like that. Why if I'd known . . . "

"Mary," Robert interrupted her. "Sit down. Up here close to my bed. It doesn't make any difference. Having you here to talk with me is more than enough."

Forty-Six

For most of the rest of the afternoon, Robert snoozed. He started out talking about the past but soon felt overpowered by fatigue and drifted off into a nap. Mary sat in the chair and thought. Mary studied Robert, trying to fill in the blanks that five decades had left in her memory. Was he truly what she'd thought so long ago, or had time changed him into a different man? In some ways, Robert looked the same; in other ways, he didn't. Possibly time had reduced him to no more than a tired old man. Hopefully not.

Shortly after five o'clock the hospital door opened, and two men walked briskly into the room. Mary immediately recognized Dr. Lewis.

"Colonel!" Dr. Lewis called out loud enough to awaken Robert. The doctor smiled an acknowledgment at Mary. "Colonel Walker, we're here to talk with you."

Robert blinked his eyes several times and looked at the

two men as if they weren't in focus. He rubbed his eyes and squinted. "Yes?"

"I'm here with my associate, Dr. Mark Henshaw." Lewis picked up the chart attached to the end of the bed and made a quick reading. "We dropped by to see if there was anything you needed."

"No," Robert said sleepily, "just want to get out of this place." He put on his glasses.

The two doctors glanced at each other.

"Can you tell me when I can go?"

Lewis nodded his head sympathetically. "I can understand your wanting to get on your way home. Certainly." He smiled thinly. "Unfortunately, you've got a few more days of recovery to go here, and we need to run a few more tests."

"A few more days?" Robert sounded irritated. "More tests?"

"Hey, the government is covering your bill," Henshaw added. "Most people get run off quickly, but you've got carte blanche with us."

Robert raised an eyebrow. "I'll pass."

"Can you be more exact about when Robert could expect to go home?" Mary asked.

Lewis turned to her, rolling his tongue around in his mouth. "Well, my best guess is probably day after tomorrow. That is, if everything goes well."

"It will," Robert said resolutely.

"Bob, we need to talk about an issue." Lewis crossed his arms over his chest. "Do you feel up to it?"

"Sure."

Henshaw pulled at his chin and lowered his head as if beginning a serious examination of the patient. Lewis took a deep breath.

"Go right ahead," Robert continued. "As I told you yesterday, Miss McCoy is an old friend. No problem there."

"I was telling you of the seriousness of your cancer problem," Dr. Lewis began slowly as if carefully choosing his words. "Remember? Yesterday?"

"Of course," Robert snapped.

"We've done several more tests in the last twenty-four hours." He turned to Henshaw. "My associate's been assisting me, and I believe that the liver tumor is progressing faster than I originally thought."

"What's that mean?" Walker asked.

Lewis shook his head. "You understand that being honest with my patients is important to me?" Lewis kept shaking his head. "I try to make sure that there are no glitches. Therefore, I need to make an update. I hate to tell you, but I believe the report I gave you yesterday was optimistic. Your problem is progressing quicker than I thought."

Walker nodded. "Is that the point?"

Lewis looked surprised. "Yes. Yes, it is."

"Thank you," Robert concluded. "Keep us up on any other insights that you get, but I'm ready to leave today." He turned and looked out the window. "I think that I want to take a little trip before we start treatments. When I get back, I'll call you."

The two doctors looked at each other in consternation and shrugged.

"Thank you, Mr. Walker." Dr. Lewis sounded surprised. "We'll be back in touch tomorrow."

Walker didn't answer. Mary looked resolutely straight ahead.

"Well, okay!" Lewis tilted his head and rubbed his hands together. "See you tomorrow."

The two men turned on their heels and walked out of the room. Walker kept looking out the window until the sound of the door shutting signaled that the medical corps had left.

"Those doctor boys certainly have a sense of humor, don't they?"

Mary smiled. "Oh, Robert. They're just trying to do their job."

"Suppose so. Unfortunately, *I'm* the job. Dr. Lewis sorta gives me the willies. It's like he's buttering me for a big autopsy or something."

Mary frowned. "Robert, don't you think that's pushing your situation a might far? He's just wanting to be honest and up front with you."

"I wonder if he's cutting me down to a couple of days before I kick in."

"I hardly think so. The doctor's simply telling you that the problem is serious."

"Think I didn't get that message yesterday?"

Mary walked over to the bed and took his hand. The thin fingers and the sunken hand were far from what she remembered back in Sterling, but the warmth was the same. He suddenly clutched her palm tightly.

"Sounds terribly bad," Robert insisted, "now doesn't it?"

Mary smiled slightly. "Of course, it does. Cancer on top of an open heart surgery is a heavy load. Yes, you've got a serious problem."

"What do you think I should do?" Robert peered up into her eyes with a probing, questioning look. The sound in his voice made his question sound deeply sincere, with a tinge of fear hidden in the folds.

"You should do what you want to do," Mary said instantly. "It's your life. Don't let anybody try to take it away."

A broad smile broke across Robert's face. "That's why I always loved you, Mary. You didn't put up with any nonsense. Always straightforward and honest. I like that answer."

"Listen, Robert. If the last fifty years have taught me anything, it's that you better do today what needs to be done and not wait for tomorrow. What you put off only comes back to haunt you."

"You believe that, Mary?"

"I suppose that I ought to tell you about my garage. The first thing that I learned is—" She stopped. "No, you don't need to hear about that mess out there in Oklahoma. My point is that we need to do today, right now, what we want to do. I don't care, Robert, if you live another week or another ten years. You're the person in the driver's seat of your own life. Don't live for what somebody else thinks. Ya hear?"

"My, my, you've become quite a speech maker, Mary." Robert laughed. "Sound significantly more forceful than you did in that downtown Sterling square a long time ago."

"We learn from our mistakes." Mary was determined. "Or we make them again. That's what I've learned."

"For sure!" Robert fell back on the pillow. "I think I need to figure out what I want out of life, regardless of how long or short it is."

"Definitely! We don't have time left for nonsense."

Robert gripped her hand more tightly. "You know . . ." He stared up at the ceiling. "I always wanted to go up there and see Newfoundland. Up there on the edge of Canada. They say it's fascinating."

"Newfoundland?" Mary smiled. "What a wonderful idea for a trip!"

"Yeah, I've thought about it off and on but simply never made the decision to go." He looked back at Mary. "Doesn't that sound like fun to you?"

"Couldn't think of anything more enjoyable." She scratched her head. "A trip to Newfoundland? Wouldn't that be fun, don't you know." She stared out the window.

"How'd you like to go with me, Mary?" Robert reached over and took her hand in his. "Just the two of us?"

Mary looked down in his worn, lean face. For the first time since they'd been there, Robert's eyes sparkled. A hint of color had returned to his face. He looked better than he had in the last four days.

"Robert," Mary laughed, "I think that I'd love to see Newfoundland. I'm ready to go whenever you say the word."

"You mean it?"

"I absolutely do! I'm not going back to cleaning up old garages. Whatever amount of time either of us has got left, we need to live it to the fullest. If you want to fly up to Saint John's, I'm ready to take off with you anywhere you want to go."

"You really, truly mean what you're saying, Mary?" His eyes snapped, and color came back to his blue lips. "You'd go with me?"

"We're not in Kansas anymore." Mary shook her head. "And we don't live in the forties. We might as well kick off our shoes and join the parade. Yes, Robert, I'll certainly go with you."

"Okay!" He let go of her hand and shook his fist at the ceiling. "You're on. I got to get out of here. You can stay in my guest room, and as soon as I can walk, we'll be on our way north."

"Should I check out places we might like to see?"

"And find out about rental cars. You know, I've got several books on Newfoundland at home. We'll need to map out exactly what we want to see."

"I can find them, and we'll read them together up here in the hospital for the next couple of days or so until they let you out."

"Actually!" Robert shook his fist again. "When old hard-nosed Lewis comes back, I'll ask him how quickly I can fly, and that's the day we'll leave."

"Excellent! I'll need to pick up a few clothes . . . maybe a warm coat, heavier shoes, just a couple of items before we go."

"You can find those things at that general store on the square. You won't have any trouble getting everything you need right here in the area."

"You really mean it, Robert?"

"Never meant anything more!"

Mary smiled. "Okay! It's done! We're on our way to Canada!"

Robert jutted his chin out and grinned like a happy child. "Need to rest a minute." His smile got weaker. "Still recovering." He stopped and looked at her with a strange devotion in his eyes. "You know, I always planned to do this back in those days in Sterling, but time ran out on us." He cleared his throat. "I know that we're not like a lot of the kids running the streets these days. If we're going to Canada or anywhere, we need to do things right."

"Yes, " Mary answered cautiously.

"Well, we can't go trotting off together if we're not married. Don't you think we ought to take care of what we never quite finished so long ago?"

Mary squeezed his hand. "Robert, you haven't seen me in more than fifty years, don't you think—"

"Mary, who knows how long I've got. You're the one wandering out on the end of the limb. I can't believe that you've come back here by accident. If you're up to it, then I sure am."

"You truly mean what you're saying?"

"Remember that message you gave me just before I left for the war?" Robert widened his eyes, and a smile crossed his face. "Remember that Bible quote?"

"Oh my goodness. Yes, yes. I always treasured that verse. '*Be not afraid.*'"

"You willing to trust that one again?"

Mary took a deep breath. "I can't believe what you're asking me. You understand that you're talking about us getting married?"

"I sure do."

Mary leaned over the bed near his face and studied his eyes. "Yes, I believe you do." She leaned down and kissed him gently. She straightened up again. "I'd be pleased to be your wife for a day, a week, another hundred years."

Robert's lips quivered. "Thank you," he said. "Thank you so much." Tears welled up in his eyes.

They kissed again, and Robert fell back on the pillow. "What a gift you are, Mary!" He took a deep breath. "All this marriage talk's got me excited. I think I need to close my eyes for a minute and rest."

"Yes, of course," Mary said resolutely. "Why don't you take one of those little naps again? Just rest a tad."

Robert's smile faded. "Yes, just need a few moments of rest." He closed his eyes, and moments later was sound asleep.

Mary watched the bony hand holding hers lose its grip and slip to the side of the sheets like a car running out of gas. Robert's breathing seemed to be more shallow than it had been, and the color drained out of his face. The big question was whether he had enough strength to walk across the room, much less around Canada.

Still, it didn't make any difference anymore. She'd come halfway across the United States to answer a question that had haunted her for more than fifty years and ended up bringing joy and hope to this sick old man. It didn't make any difference whether Robert lived another day. His dreams had been reborn, and hope beat within his breast again. Whenever the hands on the clock stopped moving, Robert would have gone the distance, and she would have been there to make sure that he fought in the last round. Quite enough satisfaction for her.

For a long time Mary looked out the window. Once again the sun was setting and the shadows lengthening. Another day would be spent soon. At the very least, she felt better than she had in years. Zest had returned, returned as it had been back in those first days when she taught in the college in Sterling. How she'd loved those challenges!

Oh yes, her life had certainly been filled with plenty of fear. It had been a battle year after year, and George Oliver hadn't helped any, but she wasn't going to end her days wallowing in consternation. She would stand up, help Robert to his feet, and they would walk as long as he had an ounce of strength left in his bones. If they didn't get to Newfoundland, so what? The most important thing was that they intended to go, and he wasn't afraid.

Mary noticed her cane, still leaning in the corner. She started to reach out for it, then withdrew her hand. In an instant she'd decided the way things would be. She wouldn't be needing her cane anymore. As far as she was concerned, it could stay there forever.

About the Author ~

Robert L. Wise, Ph.D., is the author or coauthor of twenty-four books, including the bestsellers *The Third Millennium, The Fourth Millennium,* and *Beyond the Millennium;* and *The Secret Code.* He is a bishop in the Communion of Evangelical Episcopal Churches and is the founding pastor of Church of the Redeemer in Oklahoma City. Dr. Wise is also the principal lecturer for the Bethel Bible Series, which he has taught in numerous countries. He has planted churches in Canada, England, Hungary, and the United States. Dr. Wise and his wife, Margueritte, live in Oklahoma City, Oklahoma.

Don't Miss These Titles by Robert L. Wise

The Tail of the Dragon

Robert L. Wise and William Louis Wilson, Jr.

Dr. Greg Parker, head of the National Security Agency's geological research department, discovers that the CIA is using technology to manipulate earthquakes. His highly respected journalist daughter, Sharon, finds that these events fit a pattern amazingly parallel to predictions found in Scripture. In this fast-paced techno-thriller, father and daughter quickly learn that they must overcome their estranged relationship and learn to trust God if they are to expose the U.S. government's sinister plans. They race against time to stop the destruction of their country at the hands of CIA operative Alex Majors and his coconspirators—a battle that could put their own lives in jeopardy.

ISBN 0-7852-6983-5 • Trade Paperback • 286 pages

THE SECRET CODE

Paul Meier and Robert Wise

For eight years, Judy, computer whiz Ben Meridor, and Judy's strangely gifted brother, Jimmy, have been unraveling the code embedded in the Torah. Considered subversives by Israeli intelligence because of their warnings of an imminent terrorist attack, they covertly reenter the country. And now, what began as an engaging mathematical puzzle becomes a race against the clock to save Messianic Jews from the impending fulfillment of end-times prophecies.

Paul Meier and Robert Wise create a gripping thriller based on actual historical predictions prophetic dates encoded in Scripture and only recently revealed through computer technology.

ISBN 0-7852-7090-6 • Trade Paperback • 310 pages